2-

HARD
LOVIN' MAN

LORRAINE
HEATH

HARD
LOVIN' MAN

POCKET **STAR** BOOKS

New York   London   Toronto   Sydney   Singapore

An *Original* Publication of POCKET BOOKS

 A Pocket Star Book published by
POCKET BOOKS, a division of Simon & Schuster, Inc.
1230 Avenue of the Americas, New York, NY 10020

ISBN: 0-7394-3905-7

POCKET STAR BOOKS and colophon are registered trademarks of Simon & Schuster, Inc.

Cover design by Min Choi
Front cover illustration by Gerber Studio

Manufactured in the United States of America

For Kathy Baker

For all the miles we've traveled without
turning on the radio,
The wrong turn that took us into Oklahoma,
Searching for excitement in Clayton, New Mexico,
Heading home from Denver at four in the morning,
And stopping at roadside fruit stands along the way.

For your love of reading,
Your joy at the discovery of a good book,
Your unwavering enthusiasm for romance novels
and authors.

For your title suggestions, the cover debates,
and your keen insight,
Your advice, consoling, cajoling,
and encouragement,
The honesty, tears, and laughter.

But most of all,
For the treasured gift of your friendship.

HARD
LOVIN' MAN

Chapter 1

Jack Morgan could spot trouble a mile away. Gazing through the cigarette-smoke-filled haze, he knew beyond a doubt that the girl sitting at the far end of the bar spelled *trouble* with capital letters.

T-R-O-U-B-L-E.

Her black shirt was a little too tight, a little too low, and a little too short, revealing a pierced navel that had winked at every male she passed as she sauntered back from the rest room. Her short-cropped spiked hair was an unnaturally bright orange.

The neon light cast by the sign hanging between the shelves lined with bottles of booze glittered off her earrings. She had a pierced nose, a pierced brow, and a pierced lower lip, and Jack was willing to bet money she'd extended her self-mutilation to include a pierced tongue.

He wondered what possessed any sane person to willingly have a needle poked into her flesh. Taking a swallow of his cold beer, he remembered wondering the same thing when he was in the army and had awoken from a drunken binge to discover a tattoo high on the back of his own left shoulder.

"Hey, Jack, ready for another one?"

The dew-coated mug wasn't quite empty, but the owner-bartender made his living based on how much people drank, not how long they sat. Still, Jack enjoyed simply sitting and studying people. Especially at the Sit 'n' Bull. Maybe because in his youth, he'd desperately wanted to be allowed inside the hallowed walls, to experience the mysteries that drew so many farmers, ranchers, and blue-collar workers to the place that those who arrived late had to park their trucks and SUVs in the weed-infested vacant lot behind the building.

"Not tonight, Morty. Did you happen to card that girl?"

Whether to improve his eyesight or his memory, Morty lifted his white brows, brows bushy enough that Jack wondered if the guy's hair had all migrated south. Morty kept his bald pate polished to a sheen that was as glossy as the countertop of his bar.

He glanced around suspiciously. "Which girl?"

"The one Dave's hitting on." Dave Lighten. Insurance salesman. Even a town as small as Hopeful, nestled within Houston's shadow, needed insurance salesmen.

Morty chuckled, a low rumble that caused his stomach to quiver. Every year, the day after Thanksgiving, he wrapped a Santa costume around that belly and collected toys that he delivered on Christmas Eve. No one knew how Morty determined which kids needed his gifts.

Until Jack had gained entry into the Sit 'n' Bull and learned about Morty's generous nature, he'd never known who'd left the bicycle outside his trailer when he was eight. But he'd damn sure known it wasn't Santa Claus. By that age, he'd experienced enough in his young life not to believe in anything that promised to bring happiness.

"Yeah, right," Morty finally said when he stopped chuckling. "No self-respecting mama is gonna let her underage daughter walk out of the house dressed in that getup."

"Maybe her mother isn't the self-respecting type. Card her, Morty."

"Ah, Jack, geez, come on. I *did* card her, okay?"

"What year was she born?"

"I don't remember."

Jack took out his wallet and laid a five on the counter. "Five says she's sixteen."

Morty groaned. He knew the routine. He was diligent about not serving alcohol to kids who were underage. But he was getting older. Every now and then, one slipped past him.

Jack slid off the stool and walked the length of the bar until he reached Dave. The salesman had his head bowed close to the girl's, obviously trying to sell her on something. Probably the benefits of visiting the No Tell Motel, where a guest could drop two quarters into the Magic Fingers box on the nightstand. The payoff was a vibrating bed. Jack had seen Dave's car parked outside the motel so often he figured Dave had a frequent-visitor discount card—for both the motel and the Magic Fingers.

Jack clamped his hand over Dave's shoulder.

Dave jerked his head around, the alarm evident in his eyes quickly turning to relief. "Hey, Jack! How are you, man?"

"Not bad." Jack shifted his attention to the girl. She ran her gaze over him with an appreciation he'd long ago started taking for granted—as though she'd been contemplating tasting an appetizer with Dave, suddenly discovered the dessert was available, and decided that she'd like to sample that first.

Something about her teased at his memory. Something subtle. The dark green shade of her eyes, the slight bow shape of her mouth. Her abundant dark makeup distorted both, but still it was there. A shadowy familiarity that he couldn't quite place in spite of the fact that he was certain he'd never met her. She was either new to town or simply passing through. Either scenario would explain Dave honing in on her like a scent-specific search dog.

Without shifting his attention from her, Jack said, "Dave, why don't you head on home to your wife?"

She wrinkled her nose. "You're married?"

"Well, yeah, sorta," Dave stammered.

"How can you *sorta* be married, you jerk?"

Jack experienced his first spark of admiration for her. She might not have any taste in fashion, but she apparently possessed a hint of morality.

Dave glowered at Jack. "Thanks, Jack."

He patted Dave's shoulder. "Anytime, Dave. I'm always happy to help out. You know that. Say hi to Marsha for me."

Dave slunk away, and Jack dropped onto the vacated stool, hooking the heel of his boot over the bottom metal rung, narrowly avoiding having his knee bump against the girl's lower bare thigh. The handkerchief he carried in his hip pocket would probably cover more territory than her tight black skirt.

Dipping his gaze a fraction, he caught sight of her thick black shoes. In his opinion, they resembled something that might have been worn by Frankenstein's monster. Which possibly explained all the piercing. She was attempting to hold herself together.

"What's your poison?" he asked.

"Sex on the Beach."

She leisurely stroked her tongue around lips coated in dark red, and Jack realized he'd guessed wrong about the tongue piercing. No studs glittered back at him.

"And I'm not just talking about the drink," she added with a suggestive wink.

Oh, yeah, she was big trouble.

Raising his hand, Jack waved his fingers. Morty trotted over like an obedient dog.

"Sex on the Beach for the lady and a beer for me."

She giggled. Morty squirmed.

"I'll need to see your ID."

She giggled again and tapped Jack's chest with a dark red fingernail. "He looks like a big boy to me." She dropped her gaze to his lap. "A very big boy."

"Yeah, but you don't look like a very big girl," Jack said.

She gave the bartender a beguiling smile as she shoved her empty glass toward him. "You've already carded me, *Morty,*" she said with a sexy little shimmer of her shoulders.

Obvious relief washed over Morty's face. "That's what I told Jack."

"You don't remember looking at her license. Lady, show it to him."

Abruptly, she stood. "You're no fun."

She had no idea.

He wrapped his hand around her arm with just enough pressure to give the unmistakable impression of authority with no threat. "Show *me* your ID."

"I don't have to show you jack shit."

"Afraid you do." With his free hand, he reached into the back hip pocket of his jeans and pulled out his badge. He always carried it—even when he was off duty, even when he wasn't in uniform—because he was always on call.

"Fine," she snapped.

She dropped her purse on the counter and scrounged around inside, finally pulling out her license. She flashed it at Morty. "There, see?"

Jack snatched it from her fingers, causing her to release an indignant screech of protest that nearly pierced his eardrums. He gave her license a quick perusal—all it required to detect its nonvalidity. He'd collect his winnings from Morty later.

"Impressive. But fake. Let's go."

"Go where?"

"To the station, where we can call your parents."

"I don't have parents."

"Your guardian, then."

"Fuck you!"

The toe of her heavy shoe made contact with his shin, sending shards of pain bursting in all directions from the point of impact. She screamed a steady stream of obscenities that made him reconsider his liberal views on censorship and freedom of speech.

Oh, yeah. He recognized trouble when he spotted it.

Kelley Spencer groggily slapped at the snooze button, but the alarm continued its shrill ringing. Slowly, her exhausted mind journeyed through the fog of sleep to become clearer, and she realized it wasn't the alarm that was jarring her awake but the telephone. Struggling up to an elbow, she reached for the phone while squinting at the red digital readout on her bedside clock. One A.M. Trepidation sliced through her, while panicked thoughts flashed through her mind.

The police. A drunk driver. An accident.

But that call had come eighteen months ago, and the ramifications had ensured that she'd be receiving no more late-night calls regarding her parents.

Madison is in trouble again.

But Madison was home. Safe. Looking like an angel, asleep in her bedroom on the other side of the apartment. Kelley had checked on her before she'd gone to bed following the ten o'clock news.

This call had to be an irritating wrong number. She snatched up the receiver. "Hello?"

"Ms. Gardner?"

The deep voice resonated with authority.

"That's my sister," she responded automatically.

Kelley's father had died of a heart attack when she was twelve. One of those strange, unbelievable, unexplainable occurrences. He'd been only thirty-eight. He didn't smoke, drink, or eat to excess. He'd been out on his regular morning jog in the nearby park. By the time her mother had become concerned because he hadn't returned and went to look for him, it had been too late.

Two years later, her mother had married Marcus Gardner. Kelley had been fifteen when Madison was born.

"I'm trying to locate Ms. Gardner's guardian," the nameless voice continued.

Kelley's stomach began its ritual knotting as a fissure of raw fear ripped through her. She'd had other calls like this one in the dead of night. But that had been in Dallas. Not here. Not in this small town of nine thousand that greeted visitors with a welcome sign on either end of Main Street boasting about a state football championship earned in 1969. "That would be me. Kelley Spencer."

"We have your sister in custody down at the police station. We need you to come in."

Her heart kicked into overdrive. Cordless phone in hand, she threw back the covers, stood, and began rushing to the other side of the apartment to Madison's room. "That's impossible."

"I'm afraid it's very possible, ma'am. The chief brought her in himself."

She opened the door to Madison's bedroom and switched on the light. The red bulbs cast an eerie glow over a black rumpled bedspread and bloodred furniture. Freakish, Satanic-looking posters were stapled to the walls. She always felt as though she'd dropped into hell when she entered the room.

Kelley tried so hard to be the perfect parent, to balance discipline against freedom, but Madison always pushed the edge of the envelope, tested Kelley's patience.

Kelley was hit with the unexpected memory of Madison as a baby, sweet and innocent, with the wrinkled, scrunched-up face of an old soul and a pitiful wail.

When Kelley had moved home nine years ago, Madison was still sweet, cuddling against Kelley's side at every opportunity. Then, a little more than a year and a half ago, their parents had been killed by a drunk driver. Kelley had assumed responsibility for raising Madison, something she'd thought she was prepared to handle.

Instead, she'd made one ghastly mistake after another, each one serving to spotlight Kelley's ineptitude as a mother. No matter how hard she tried, she always fell short. In the beginning, she'd convinced herself that raising a child from infancy was different—parent and child grew together, adapted, adjusted. Although she and Madison lacked that foundation, she feared the problem was more deeply rooted. Her escalating failures within the past year had forced her to accept the truth: she lacked some sort of motherhood gene.

"Ms. Spencer?" The deep voice cut into her thoughts.

She sighed wearily. "Yeah, I'll be there as soon as I can."

Where had sweet little Madison gone?

"Thank you, ma'am. Just check at the front desk when you get here."

"Unfortunately, I'm familiar with the routine," she told him, resigned to facing the battle ahead.

She clicked the off button on the phone. Being a parent was never easy. Being a single parent was much more difficult. Coming onto the scene during the teenage years was virtually impossible.

With another deep sigh, she shuffled back to her room. She was beginning to doubt her ability to survive living with someone who'd suddenly become rebellious. She'd read all the self-help books, but she had no idea how to reach the most important person in her life.

Chapter 2

꩜

Leaning back in his chair, with his booted feet crossed on the corner of his desk, his hands folded behind his head, Jack studied the girl sitting before him. She had *attitude* written—and pierced—all over her. Probably tattooed as well.

She was also scared to death. Her green gaze kept darting to the closed door of his office, and she'd gnawed all that horrible gunk off her lips. Now she was busily working on her fingernails.

"So, what happened?" he asked. "You were standing too close to a jewelry box when it suddenly exploded?"

"Ha ha. That's pretty fucking funny."

He straightened, his boots hitting the floor with a resounding thud. Her body jerked while her eyes grew big and round. He leaned menacingly toward her. He'd had the menacing look down pat since he was a kid. It was the only way he'd managed to survive.

"If you use the *f* word in my presence again, I'm hauling you down to the bathroom and washing your mouth out with some pretty vile-tasting soap."

Apparently not impressed with his threat, she visibly relaxed and rolled her eyes. *"F word? That is so totally lame."*

F word? Surely he hadn't said *that.* He retraced his thoughts. Shit! He had. How intimidating did that make him? Not intimidating at all.

He'd slipped because she was just a kid. He could only hope he never made the same careless mistake while he was interrogating a hardened criminal. Not that many resided in Hopeful. But still, he had a hard-fought-for reputation to maintain.

"How lame is it that you have a sewer mouth?" he asked.

She curled her upper lip. "You wouldn't wash my mouth out with soap. I'd sue your butt for police harassment."

"Darlin', I don't make threats I'm not prepared to carry out." He eased back a little. "Look, I know you're scared—"

"I'm not scared. I just want to go home."

"Your sister should be here any minute."

"She's going to be so totally freaked out."

"Does she ever hit you?" he asked.

She looked at him as though he'd just spoken in Klingon. "Of course not."

"But she freaks out easily?"

"Wouldn't you if the police called you at one o'clock in the morning to tell you that they'd arrested your kid?"

She wasn't technically arrested, but he hadn't informed her of that fact. Better to let her worry about the ramifications of her actions for a while.

"You should have thought of that before you went bar hopping," he admonished.

"Bar *hopping* would imply there was more than one bar in this dump of a town."

Ah, now he was getting somewhere. "So, you're not impressed with Hopeful?"

"That's some remarkable deducing there, Sherlock."

Damn, but she made him want to smile. "How long have you been in our illustrious town?"

"Too long."

"What's your grade classification? Freshman? Sophomore?"

She heaved an exasperated sigh that indicated she wondered why she was even bothering to answer the moron sitting behind the desk. "Junior."

"The Hornets kicked butt tonight," he said, referring to the team's 21-to-7 victory over their long-standing rivals, the neighboring Wildcats. What high school student didn't get excited about football?

She scowled. "Why would I care?"

Okay. He should have guessed she'd be less than enthusiastic or impressed. "You didn't go to the game?"

"Why would I? It's not like I've got friends—"

The sharp rap on his door cut her off and made her flinch.

Mike Warner opened it and stuck his head inside the room. Mike, being the youngster he was, fresh out of the police academy, hadn't been able to disguise his surprise when he'd seen Jack walking in with what looked to be an extraterrestrial in his custody. Even now, he stared at her as though he couldn't quite believe she existed.

"Mike, you knocked for a reason?" Jack prodded.

Mike jerked his attention to Jack. "Right, Chief. Miss Gardner's sister is here."

Although it was difficult to be a hundred percent sure, Jack thought his detainee paled beneath her thick layer of makeup. "Send her in."

"Yes, sir."

Jack came to his feet, while the girl slouched lower in her chair. If not expressing remorse, at least she appeared to be embarrassed. Maybe there was hope for her yet.

He turned to the door as Mike moved back, and a young woman stepped into the room. Blond hair, green eyes, and a body that simply would not quit. Jack felt as though he'd taken a swift, brutal kick to the gut. Of all the police stations in all of Texas, why in the hell did she have to walk into his?

Especially with that just-crawled-out-of-bed look that made him want to tumble her back onto the rumpled sheets. She'd fueled his fantasies when he was nineteen. Hell, if he were honest with himself, she fueled them now.

"Miss Spencer?" he asked, reflexively reverting to the manner in which he'd addressed her for most of the time he'd known her.

She had that deer-in-the-headlights expression, her eyes reflecting confusion and disbelief. All the blood rapidly drained from her face as recognition dawned. She nodded jerkily. "Jack?"

"Oh, great," Miss Attitude muttered. "Another one of her former students."

Oh, yeah, he was a former student, but she'd taught him far more outside the classroom than she ever had inside it. His senior year had been her first year to teach. She'd tried so damned hard to reach her students. With his bad-assed, take-no-prisoners attitude, he hadn't made her job easy.

Maybe that was the reason he'd felt a connection to the girl at the bar. Nine years ago, he'd been exactly like her. With a chip on his shoulder the size of Texas, he'd dared the world to call his bluffs.

Obviously disoriented, Miss Spencer shifted her bewildered gaze between him and the girl, as though she recognized that she needed to deal with both of them but didn't have the physical or emotional strength to deal with either of them.

"Mike?" he called out.

Mike poked his head back inside, his novice-cop gaze darting quickly around, trying to assess the situation. "Yeah, Chief?"

"Why don't you take Miss Gardner for a tour of the facilities, so she'll understand exactly where she'll spend the night if I catch her drinking again before she's twenty-one?"

"Sure thing," Mike said.

"Drinking?" Miss Spencer asked at the same time. "Madison, tell me you weren't drinking."

"Okay. I wasn't drinking."

"Don't lie to me."

"I was just telling you what you told me to tell you."

Miss Spencer shook her head, her expression one of surrender, as though she'd suddenly discovered her entire arsenal had been spirited away.

Jack gave a pointed glare at the little felon. "Go with Officer Mike, and leave your car keys with me."

"Why the fu—" he glowered ominously at her— "fu-fudge do I have to do that?" she demanded.

"The main reason is that I told you to. The other, less important reason, is so I can pick up your car from the Sit 'n' Bull and drive it home for you."

"I can drive it home."

He shook his head. "Not on my watch. I'm releasing you into Miss Spencer's custody, which means she'll drive you home."

"You're such a hard-ass."

"Darlin', you've got no idea. Now, go with Officer Mike while I discuss the terms of your release with your *guardian.*"

Slinging her keys onto his desk, she sashayed toward the door.

As though in a trance, Miss Spencer put her hand on the girl's arm. "Why are you doing this? Why are you making everything so difficult?"

"Why shouldn't I? Not everyone is Miss Goody Two-Shoes like you. Besides, it's what you expect, isn't it? I can't even breathe without asking permission.

You're not my mother. I wish you'd quit trying to act like one, because you're lousy at it."

Miss Spencer looked as though she'd just been the victim of a hit-and-run. He was tempted to grab his detainee and teach her some manners, but family counseling wasn't within his jurisdiction unless the infractions turned criminal. Jerking free of her sister's hold, the girl stomped from the room.

Miss Spencer simply stood there, watching her sister go, as though she'd fought one too many battles with the little hellion and had lost the majority of them. Jack made his way around the edge of his desk and strode to the door.

Apparently dazed, Miss Spencer watched him reach past her to shut the door as though she couldn't quite figure out what he was doing there.

He knew he could have simply asked her to close the door in her sister's wake before taking a chair. But he recognized his actions for what they were: a desperate excuse to get close enough to inhale her fragrance. A sweet, flowery, welcoming perfume that haunted his dreams. Beneath it all was that just-woke-up scent that he loved most. He envisioned her naked, spread across the bed, ready and waiting for him to lower his body over hers.

"What are you doing here, Kelley?" His voice sounded rough, hoarse, even to his own ears.

She lifted her wounded gaze to his and raised her hand as though she were about to explain the diagramming of a sentence that she'd written on a blackboard. "Someone called me."

"I'm not talking about the police station. I'm referring to Hopeful. What are you doing back in Hopeful?"

"Trying to keep Madison safe."

Every protective bone and muscle in his body snapped to immediate attention. "From whom?"

She gave him a wry smile. "From herself. Obviously, I'm not doing a very good job of it."

As though needing to reassure herself that he was real, that his presence wasn't simply a nightmare she'd eventually wake up from, she laid her delicate hand against his beard-shadowed cheek. The warmth of her touch speared him clear down to his boot heels.

It took all his inner strength and resolve not to cover her hand with his and turn his head to press a kiss against her palm.

"I didn't know you'd moved back, either," she said softly, as softly as she'd once whispered endearments near his ear.

And he couldn't help but wonder, if she *had* known, would she have returned, would she have risked facing a past that had scarred them both?

Giving her head a quick shake as though she needed to clear it, she dropped her hand to her side as her eyes lost their dullness and became sharp and clear. "Madison. I'm here to deal with Madison. You wanted to discuss the conditions under which you'd release her?"

"Yeah." He cleared his throat, fighting the need to beg her to touch him again, fighting the urge to take her in his arms, and fighting the impossible yearning to latch his mouth onto hers as though tomorrow had never come to destroy what they might have had. "Have a seat."

He only dared to follow her with his eyes while she walked to the chair in front of his desk, her hips swaying slightly and enticingly. She still had the cutest little ass he'd ever seen. Nice and tight. Firm and heart-shaped. The lady made the cheapest pair of jeans look like a million bucks.

"Coffee?" he asked as he turned to the coffeemaker that he kept near his desk. He'd started brewing a pot as soon as he'd returned to his office with the hellion, figuring he'd need something to help keep him alert. Now he wished he'd grabbed a bottle of Jack Daniel's off the shelf on his way out of the Sit 'n' Bull. Oblivion had never looked so damned inviting.

"Thanks. I could use the caffeine. I feel as though I'm trapped in a fog," she responded.

Feeling the same way, he poured the strong brew into two mugs. He glanced over his shoulder. "Still like it the same way?"

Color jumping into her face, her cheeks burning a bright red, she nodded slightly. He wondered if she was remembering all the moments they'd shared that he could never forget.

He dumped two teaspoons of sugar and one of creamer into a mug, stirring until the coffee turned the light chocolate shade she preferred. He handed her the mug before dropping into his chair behind his desk. Studying her over the rising steam of his black coffee, he took a slow sip from the chipped mug he'd magnanimously taken for himself—the one that proclaimed that he had, over time, donated two gallons of life during the local blood drives.

She brought her mug to her lips, bare of any lip gloss. He'd always preferred them that way. Possessing a natural beauty, she never required makeup in order to appeal to any man still breathing. He wanted to yank off that scrunched-up thing holding her hair in a ponytail, so he could see the heavy strands brush her shoulders, could more easily envision the satiny feel of them gliding over his bare chest.

Her eyes were the green of the clover he'd often fantasized about laying her down on. Although they still reflected softness and kindness, her eyes also held sorrow now. He wondered if he were partly to blame. Or worse, if he were completely responsible. She'd had tears in her eyes the last time he'd seen her, but then, he'd been close to having them in his as well.

Looking at her from a distance, he could see a strong resemblance between her features and those of the hellion. That's what had haunted him back at the bar. Eyes he'd gazed into a thousand times, lips he'd kissed not nearly enough.

She had both hands wrapped around her mug as though she needed something to hold on to, something to offer support. Incredibly tempted to lend her a shoulder, he watched as she swallowed. He'd loved the feel of her silken skin against his mouth, the beat of the pulse at her throat against his lips.

"How long have you been in town?" he asked.

She seemed to snap to attention, as though she'd been wandering through some deep and mystifying thoughts. He wasn't egotistical enough to imagine she'd been reminiscing about him instead of thinking about her sister. Although nine years ago, he would have been. Back then, he'd thought he was the center of her universe. Probably because she'd been the nucleus of his.

"I moved back in July. I'm teaching at the high school again."

How had he managed to miss that little tidbit of news? He wasn't exactly a recluse in this town. But in July, he'd gone camping near Jackson Hole, Wyoming. He'd probably been hiking around Jenny Lind Lake when news of her arrival had been circulating around town.

"When did you move back?" she asked quietly.

"Five years ago."

She ran her tongue around her lips, not in the provocative manner her younger sister had earlier. Still, her action caused his gut to clench and his chest to tighten, and he gripped his own mug as though that insignificant action could keep him shackled on his side of the desk.

"After you married Stephanie and joined the army"—she lifted a delicate shoulder—"knowing how much you hated this town, I didn't think you'd ever return."

That answered his earlier self-asked question. The

hope of running into him had never entered her mind.

"There's something to be said for the familiar," he responded flatly.

"I suppose. How is Stephanie these days?" she asked.

"I wouldn't know. After the kid was born, we got divorced, and she split. Haven't seen her since."

He saw the disappointment in her eyes, just as he had countless times while he'd sat—defiant and rebellious—in her classroom. He resented her judgment now more than he had then. She knew things about him no one else did. And yet he still couldn't measure up.

"I'm really sorry to hear that," she said.

He loosened his grip on the mug and leaned back in his chair, striving to give the impression that he couldn't care less what she was sorry about. "All you told me was that I needed to do my duty by the girl and the kid. I did that. But we're not here to discuss my failings. Tell me what's up with Cruella De Vil."

Her eyes rounded in surprise. "I wouldn't have expected you to know the name of a character from *101 Dalmatians.*"

"Yeah, well, there's apparently a lot about me that you don't know. So, what's her story?" he prodded impatiently.

She set her mug on the edge of his desk and popped her knuckles—a habit that signaled she wasn't comfortable with the situation. She'd exhibited the same action every time she'd made him stay in her classroom after school. He'd given her lots of reasons to punish him. Her punishment had always been his reward.

"Madison is my half sister. Same mother, different fathers." Her cheeks flushing with embarrassment, she laughed self-consciously and avoided his gaze. "You probably figured that out, since we have different last names."

"That was my first assumption. But I've learned you can't build a case based on assumptions. You have to collect facts. Therefore, I try not to *assume* anything."

Concern darted into her eyes as she looked back at him. "Are you trying to build a case against her?"

"I'm trying to determine how best to handle the situation." *How best to help you.*

She nodded. "Okay. Fair enough. The summer you left, I moved back home. About eighteen months ago, my parents died in a car accident. I became Madison's guardian. Since then, she's become almost impossible to control.

"We lived in Dallas. Big city. Easy access to drugs. I think Madison was experimenting with them. One of her friends died of an overdose. I was terrified the same thing would happen to Madison. I thought if I got her out of that environment . . . I thought a small town, with small-town values." She shook her head. "Like you said. There's something to be said for familiarity. I was happy here—"

"Were you?" he cut in. He'd never known for sure.

"For a while," she admitted.

"I wrote you after I went into the army. You never answered."

"Of course, I didn't answer. You were a married man."

Her answer irritated him. Yeah, he'd been married, but he'd needed her. "Let's get back to your sister."

"There's not much more to tell. I just want her to be happy, and I'm not having much luck accomplishing that goal. These middle-of-the-night visits to the police station make me feel like a failure.

"Anyway, I'm not here for analysis. You mentioned something about her car being at the Sit 'n' Bull."

"That's where I ran into her flashing around a fake ID and that very provocatively dressed little body of hers."

"Oh, my God." Kelley buried her face in her hands. "Why is she doing this?"

"She obviously likes to punch your buttons. I can relate to how much fun that is."

Her head came up, fire flashing in those emerald eyes. "Yeah, I'll just bet you can. The difference is that she can get *hurt*—badly—if she keeps up these rebellious stunts."

He'd been hurt as well, more deeply than he cared to admit, more profoundly than he wanted her to know. He needed to keep their meeting focused on the business at hand, not personal matters. Unfortunately, he'd already made the mistake of letting it get far too personal.

Giving his throat a sound clearing, he straightened and planted his elbows on the desk. "Dave Lighten was hitting on her. He has a reputation for wearing out the mattresses at the local motel. Why his wife puts up with him is a mystery to me. But I'll have a talk with him to make sure he understands Madison is jailbait. I've confiscated her false ID, but she can probably get another one easily enough. Morty will kick her out if she shows up at his bar. You might consider grounding her."

"She was already grounded. You see how well that works."

"I can hold her in a cell for the rest of the night. It's cold, lonely, and damned frightening to be locked up. Might give her some time to reflect on the ramifications of her actions."

She shook her head. "No, *I* need to deal with this situation. I simply want to get her home for now."

"All right. Her real driver's license still shows a Dallas address, so write down your address in town, and I'll deliver her car to you in the morning." He passed a pen and a pad of paper to her.

He watched as she wrote in what he knew was beautiful flowing script. He'd spent hours gazing stupidly at her as she graded papers, while he was supposed to be reading classic literature. Little wonder he'd nearly failed her class.

He'd been held back once. Along with cutting as many classes as possible, he'd stopped doing homework his sophomore year. An act of rebelliousness. He hadn't truly believed the teachers would fail him or that the school administration would enforce the state's mandatory attendance law.

It was a hard lesson learned. After that, he'd made more of an effort to pass, but still he'd done only enough to ensure he made it to the next grade. He was a year older than the majority of the students at his level. And when Kelley Spencer had walked into that classroom the first day of his senior year, his hormones had reacted with a savage awakening.

Much as they were doing now, making him acutely aware that he was male and she was female. After everything that had passed between them near the end, he shouldn't want her now with this powerful intensity that was downright irritating.

She placed the pad on his desk. "There. Can I take her home now?"

"Yeah." He took the pad, tore off the top sheet with her address, scribbled a note on the next page, and handed it to her. "Give this to the young kid who brought you to my office."

" 'Mike, let her go home'?" she mused aloud as she stood. "Isn't that a little informal?"

"She was never technically arrested."

"What time will you bring her car by?"

"What time will you be up?"

"Around eight."

"Still an early riser on the weekends?"

"Old habits are hard to break," she said, blushing. "Thank you for handling this situation the way you did."

"Sure."

He found it difficult watching her walk out of his

office, out of his life. Almost as hard as he'd found it nine years ago.

He'd always heard that in every kid's life, there was one special teacher. Kelley Spencer had been his. Unfortunately, she'd been a hell of a lot more than that. She'd been the first woman he'd ever loved. The first he'd ever hated.

Her being back in town was the last thing he wanted.

Chapter 3

Jack Morgan is in town. Jack Morgan is in town. Like an irritating song stuck on replay, the unsettling refrain kept running through Kelley's weary mind. *Jack Morgan is in town.*

As she drove through the quiet, tree-lined streets, Kelley knew she needed to focus her attention and energy on dealing with Madison's disruptive behavior. A confrontation between them hovered on the horizon. With the fine hairs on the back of her neck bristling, she sensed the escalating tension shimmering off Madison as she sulked in the passenger seat and stared out the side window, her arms crossed over her chest, her shoulders curled as though she wanted to draw herself up into an invisible ball.

But Jack Morgan is in town. Kelley had always worried that he'd end up entangled with the law. But she'd envisioned him having the handcuffs slapped on him, not doing the slapping himself. She couldn't quite wrap her mind around the fact that he was the police chief.

How had he managed to transform himself from a rebellious youth into someone holding a respected, authoritative position in the community? A position that caused him to cross paths with Madison?

Madison, who thrived on bucking authority. She was too young to comprehend how quickly and effectively she was slamming shut doors to her future, destroying bridges, cutting off her options. In retrospect, though, Kelley had always assumed Jack was accomplishing the same thing.

From the moment she'd walked into her classroom that first day, she'd been held hostage by his intense blue gaze. He'd been only a year older than the other boys, but he'd *seemed* so much older. His eyes held neither innocence nor dreams. He looked at the world as though he didn't trust it not to hurt him.

Her heart had gone out to him, and yet, at the same time, she'd wanted to smack him. She'd been incredibly nervous facing her students for the first time, striving to put into practice everything she'd learned while earning her degree and certification.

While explaining the syllabus, she'd been unable to shake off the sensation that he was mentally undressing her. Button by button. Strap by strap. Piece by piece. That he'd somehow known she wore a lacy black bra and matching bikini panties beneath the navy blue skirt and blazer she'd worn for the express purpose of appearing older, more in charge.

Only her determination not to fail had prevented her from stammering under his intense scrutiny, even though a flush of heat had caused her skin to prickle, her palms to grow damp.

Jack Morgan had been a test she'd come close to failing. Throughout the year, his bold glances and sensual grins never reflected happiness but still managed to promise joy. The longer he sat in her classroom, the more time she spent with him, the easier it became for him to lure her into giving into temptation. To be with him the way she wanted to be with him. Forbidden. Reckless. Dangerous.

Of all the challenges she'd expected to cope with and overcome in her first year of teaching, resisting the longing of her heart had never been one she'd contemplated. She'd never considered falling in love with one of her students, someone younger, someone with whom she should have had so little in common.

But she'd been young as well, only twenty-two, not much older than Jack's nineteen. Recently graduated from the University of Texas, she'd been traveling unknown territory, living completely on her own, without the shelter of dorm life and the comfort of college roommates. Working full-time. Beginning her adult life.

She'd been excited, thrilled, terrified.

And Jack Morgan had intensified every emotion.

Just as he had done tonight.

She'd walked into that police station bracing herself for a confrontation with Madison, trying to determine exactly what was going on in Madison's mind and how best to handle her. Then she'd stepped into the police chief's office expecting to see a white-haired, paunchy man—the stereotypical Rod Steiger cop she saw in the movies.

Instead, there stood Jack Morgan with his whipcord lean body and that same hungry look in his eyes that promised sensual satisfaction beyond a woman's wildest dreams. His presence had knocked the wind from her sails.

Then she'd caught sight of Madison dressed as though she expected Halloween to arrive early this year . . . and it had all been too much.

Her mind had shut down, because she found it too painful to remember the past, too excruciating to deal with the present. But the present had to be dealt with, and it had to be dealt with here and now.

She pulled her white Camaro into the closest empty parking slot. Before Kelley turned off the engine, Madison was out the door and running up the stairs to the second-floor apartment. Kelley hurried after her.

Fortunately, Madison lost precious time unlocking the door. She slipped into the apartment, and Kelley was hot on her heels, closing the door in her wake, praying they weren't going to get evicted for disturbing the neighbors in the wee hours of a Saturday morning.

Rushing to Madison's door, she threw her body against it before Madison could slam it shut and lock it.

"I hate this town, hate going to school here, hate the kids!" Madison yelled as she threw herself on the bed. She grabbed a pillow, wrapped her arms around it as though to shield herself from the reprimand she knew was coming, and glared mutinously at Kelley.

"Half of them listen to country music, for God's sake."

"Keep your voice down," Kelly scolded, finding it difficult to face the hate she saw in Madison's eyes. How did parents survive their children's teenage years? Leaning against the door frame, she folded her arms across her chest. "Do you know how lucky you are that Jack ran into you—"

"Getting arrested is hardly lucky."

"Then don't place yourself in situations where you can get arrested. What were you thinking, Madison?"

"I was thinking that this town is so totally dull, and I wanted to have some fun."

"Fun? Dressing up like a hooker and traipsing into a bar in the middle of the night? Flashing a false ID? Not to mention you did all this without telling me, so you knew it was wrong to begin with."

Madison curled her lip. "It wasn't *wrong*. I just knew you'd freak."

Seething, Kelley stepped away from the door and whispered harshly, "It damn sure was wrong. It was illegal! You were breaking the law."

"It's a stupid law. Even the president's daughters do it."

Kelley groaned at the idiocy of that statement. "And they weren't immune from getting into trouble, now, were they?"

"It's a rite of passage."

"No, Madison. It's not a rite of passage. It's stupid and dangerous. Jack said some guy was hitting on you."

"I wouldn't have gone to the motel with him," she responded petulantly. "I was just humoring him because he had the corniest pickup lines."

Kelley wanted to screech. "And what if he'd thought you were a tease? What if he'd gotten angry and hurt you?"

She shrugged. "I had my mace in my purse."

"Oh, Madison, you don't intentionally put yourself into a position where you think you might have to use your mace."

"I didn't do anything really bad. It's not like I was doing drugs."

"You were drinking. What if you were involved in a car accident?"

"Like that's going to happen. There's nobody on the streets after dark. It's like they're all afraid of vampires or something."

Kelley had to admit it was a quiet town. That was part of its appeal. But she was certain there were things going on if one knew where to look. She and Madison would simply have to explore the opportunities together.

"I love you, Madison," she said softly, trying to reach this girl who obviously had no desire to have her defenses breeched.

"No, you don't! If you did, you wouldn't have brought me here."

"As I've explained time and again, we moved here because you were getting out of hand."

"You're not my mother!"

Kelley's chest tightened at the cruel, unintentional reminder. As Madison wiped furiously at her eyes, smearing her makeup, Kelly walked farther into the room and sat on the edge of the bed. "I'm not trying to be your mother."

"Yes, you are. I need your permission before I can do anything." She made *permission* sound like *abuse.* "I never had to do that before."

"Things are different now. I have a greater responsibility for you."

"I hate it." Madison stuck her fingers into her hair, the spikes too stiff to allow much more. "We have to write this stupid paper in English about what we admire most about our mothers. And I don't have a mother."

Tears burning her eyes at Madison's anguish, Kelley wrapped her arms around Madison and hugged her. So much of tonight's behavior was beginning to make sense. She'd read several books on grieving. Everyone experienced it differently, but for many the first year was one of numbness. The second year was the hardest.

"Maybe you could write a memory, a special moment when you were just really glad that Mom was your mother."

Madison sniffed. "I guess I could do that. I get mad at her sometimes. I feel like she and Dad just abandoned me. It hurts to feel abandoned."

Kelley felt the painful squeezing on her heart. "They didn't abandon you, Madison. It wasn't their choice to die. They loved you very much."

"It's not fair. You had them longer than I did."

"It doesn't make losing them hurt any less."

Madison worked her way out of Kelley's embrace. "Their dying sucks."

"I know. I'm not trying to replace them, Madison. I'm simply trying to get us back on the right road. Tell me what I can do to make things better."

"Move back to Dallas."

She shook her head. "I've signed a contract with this school district. I have to finish out the school year." Besides, she truly did believe Madison was safer here. They were simply going through a period of adjustment following the move. Things would settle down.

"You should have asked me before you made all these plans with my life," Madison said.

"You're a—" She cut herself off.

"What? Go ahead and say it. You think I'm a child."

"Not a child. Young. You're young, Madison. Too young to make decisions that have such an enormous effect on our lives. You were getting involved with the wrong crowd—"

"Oh, and you don't think Podunk has a wrong crowd?"

She knew it did. Or, at least, nine years ago it had. Jack Morgan had been the ringleader. But she couldn't envision the kids here making suicide pacts or hooking up with drugs.

It was the carefully contracted suicide pact she'd found in Madison's glove compartment when she was replacing her proof of insurance that had scared Kelley so badly. To think Madison would value her life so little . . .

"I truly believe there is less opportunity for you to get hurt here," Kelley admitted. Although Madison was still in contact with her friends, Kelley thought—hoped—phone calls and e-mail provided a buffer against rash behavior.

Madison rolled her eyes.

"Two more years, Madison, and you can do whatever the hell you want. But on my watch, you will *not* go to bars, you will *not* get drunk, and you will *not* end up in police stations. If you continue this rebellious, destructive streak, I'm going to take away your car—"

"You can't!"

"I can, and I will. And I'll paint all this furniture yellow and buy you a bedspread with big daisies on it." Kelley hated coming down so hard on Madison, and she usually tried to lighten her tone at the end—balancing being a mother against being a sister.

A corner of Madison's mouth twitched. "You wouldn't."

"Oh, yes, I would," she insisted, feeling a little bit of the tension leaving the room. "Worse than that, I'll replace all these awful red lightbulbs with"—she grinned evilly—"with white ones."

"Then I'll really hate living in this tiny apartment. I can't even play my music loud. That old goat downstairs complains."

Kelley sensed a crumbling in the wall of resentment. She knew Madison could rebuild it quickly, but maybe, if they could reach some sort of compromise . . .

"Okay. I think we can fix that problem easily enough. I can dissolve the lease with a thirty-day notice. We'll go house hunting, find someplace we'll both be happy with. Together. We'll look together."

"I guess." Madison pushed her lower lip out into a pout. "I just hate this town so much. Promise me that we'll go back to Dallas at the end of the year. Let me have my senior year with my friends."

"I'll promise to think about it." She wrapped her hand around Madison's. "Sweetie, I'm simply trying to get you through high school. Then you can do whatever you want with your life."

"Well, staying in this dump of a town is definitely not what I'm going to do with my life." Madison scrunched up her face. "He said the same thing, by the way."

"Who? What?"

"The sheriff. About not letting me do anything on his watch. Sounds so military. What's with you and him, anyway?"

Alarm bells clanged in Kelley's head, and she focused on the least significant aspect of the question. "He's not the sheriff. He's the police chief."

"Okay. So, what's between you and the police chief?"

"Nothing is between us. As you figured out in his

office, he was one of my students. Shortly after he graduated, he got married and went into the army. I didn't know he was back in town, so I was surprised. That's all."

"He's hot."

Oh, yeah, Kelley thought as the warmth swirled through her, making her flush. Jack Morgan was definitely hot. More so now than he'd been at nineteen, when she'd thought she'd fallen in love with him.

Tonight, he'd been wearing a black shirt that revealed the breadth of his chest, the narrowness of his waist. His faded jeans had hugged his ass and thighs. He'd filled out in the past nine years, but he didn't have an ounce of fat on him. He was a solid wall of mature muscle.

He wore his black hair shorter, not quite a military cut. It had been longer in high school, curly at the ends. His beard had been heavier than most of the boys' back then. Tonight, he looked as though he'd gone a day or two without shaving.

Although she knew it wasn't possible, she could swear that she still felt the impression of his jaw against her palm. She'd known she shouldn't touch him, but she'd needed to confirm that he was real. And he was. Warm flesh, rough stubble. Mesmerizing blue eyes that were more powerful, more knowledgeable. But they still managed to form an effective barrier to his inner thoughts and emotions. She wondered what he'd seen in the past nine years that had added the furrows in his brow, the creases at the corners of his eyes.

Unsettled by the direction of her thoughts, Kelley got up and started turning down the covers, playfully elbowing Madison in the process. "Now, come on, you need to get to bed."

"I gotta shower first and get all my makeup off before it makes me break out."

Kelley almost commented on the stupidity of putting it all on to begin with but decided against it. She had a feeling that tonight Madison had wanted to hide. She didn't usually go for the garish and outlandish—but when she did, she went all out.

Madison rolled off the bed and snatched her robe off the floor. Kelley headed for the door.

"Kell?"

Kelley stopped and turned back to Madison. "Yeah?"

"Are you a virgin?"

"Madison, you don't ask another woman that question."

"I just don't remember you dating anyone seriously."

"I've dated off and on. There was just never anyone I wanted to introduce to the family."

Madison ambled toward her, a worried frown on her face. "You're not interested in the sheriff, are you?"

"Absolutely not."

Nine years ago, Jack Morgan had carried her to heaven, then deserted her in hell. He was the last person on earth she wanted to get involved with.

Chapter 4

Kelley looked like hell. She felt like it, too, with a headache threatening to erupt at any minute. Through eyelids swollen from lack of sleep, she squinted at her reflection in the bathroom mirror. Her skin was far too pale. Her light application of makeup didn't help, but she certainly had no desire to imitate Madison's guise from last night.

And talk about a bad hair day. Even though she'd shampooed and dried her hair, it possessed no sheen, no shine. It simply hung—limp and dull—to her shoulders. She was halfway tempted to pull it back, but she had this incredible urge to feel feminine, to look feminine. It was in direct response to Jack's ability to look so damned masculine.

Her obsession with her appearance was ridiculous, considering the fact that the only thing he was going to do was drop off Madison's car. No more than that. Any minute now, he'd pull into the apartment complex, park the car in a designated slot, give her the keys, and leave. She'd be in his presence for five seconds, tops.

So why did she care how she looked?

Because he still had the ability to make her heart pound a little faster, considerably harder. But he was trouble with a capital T. Trouble she didn't need right now. She needed to devote her attention to Madison, to ensuring that she was available for Madison.

Therefore, any involvement with a man was definitely out of the question. Men took time, required attention. Jack Morgan required a lot of attention. At least, he had when he was nineteen. And those muscles hinted at beneath the shirt he was wearing last night led her to believe his testosterone level had increased, not diminished, over the years.

Why was she even experiencing any angst over him? Other than that first feral, ravenous look, he hadn't given any indication he'd retained the remotest bit of interest in her. He hadn't pried into her past, asked about her dating status. Although he'd admitted Stephanie had left him, he could have remarried or had another lady waiting in the wings to become Mrs. Morgan.

He'd had numerous girls hanging off him when he was the local bad boy. Now he was the chief of police. Respected. Admired, no doubt. He probably had women draping themselves over that incredibly well-toned body of his.

The doorbell chime nearly made her jump out of her skin. She ran her hands over her hair one more time, over her clothes—which she'd changed three times, finally deciding on jeans and a red off-the-shoulder T—and headed for the door. She swung it open and had the breath knocked out of her for the second time in less than twelve hours.

Jack had obviously showered, shaved, and spruced up—much as he had the last time he'd come to her door. They'd both known it *would be* the final time. And it had hurt. It had hurt so much she'd thought it would destroy her.

Inwardly, she shook herself back to the present. As he had last night, he still wore jeans, but now a blue cambric shirt stretched across his amazing shoulders, the sleeves rolled up to reveal his forearms, which even in repose appeared muscular. He didn't look like a man who had been awake for more than half the night. While she looked like something the cat had discovered behind a Dumpster and decided to leave there.

"Morning," he said with a deep rumble that sent shivers vibrating through her.

She held out her hand for the keys. *Take them. Close the door. Shut out the memories: the good, the bad, and the ugly ones.* She could do that. "I appreciate you bringing the car by."

"Not a problem. But I was hoping you could give me a ride to work. Mike dropped me off at the Sit 'n' Bull to pick up the car last night, so my truck is still at the station."

She hadn't considered the logistics surrounding his offer to bring Madison's car home, hadn't considered that he might still be in the habit of manipulating situations so he could make excuses to be with her. He'd been very good at it when he was nineteen. She didn't want to contemplate how much more skilled he might be now.

Still, to refuse his request after his kind offer was unthinkable. "Sure. Let me just turn off the coffeemaker—"

"You wouldn't happen to have any left, would you?" he asked.

"Coffee?"

"That's what a coffeemaker usually makes."

"Actually, I have a full pot. I haven't sat down for breakfast yet." Her stomach had been a tangle of knots while she'd waited for his arrival. Her lack of morning caffeine was no doubt contributing to her headache.

"I'm dying for a cup," he said.

Against her better judgment, she found herself nodding and saying, "Come on in."

He made his way past her. Suddenly, the apartment seemed smaller, as though he had the power to make everything around him shrink into insignificance. She shut the door and rushed for the kitchen, pointing toward the small dining area beside the front window. "Why don't you sit at the table there? I'll bring you a cup of coffee."

She escaped through a narrow arched doorway into the kitchen. She needed some distance, some time to reestablish her equilibrium. But apparently, Jack had no plans to grant her a reprieve. Ignoring what she'd considered a polite suggestion that he sit in another room, he ambled in behind her and dropped onto a stool at the tiny island.

"Nice place," he said.

She snatched two ceramic mugs off the mug tree, aware of his presence dominating the room, his tangy scent wafting toward her. It had changed somewhat over the years. It was somehow deeper, more masculine. She couldn't explain it. Even in his youth, he'd given off a virile magnetism. Now, he was almost lethal.

"It's a little small, and the walls are too thin. We're contemplating trying to find a house to rent," she babbled inanely, anything to stop herself from focusing on him as she poured the coffee. She inhaled the rich aroma, hoping it would distract her, would block out his scent. It didn't. Not in the least. She handed him a mug.

His mouth curved up into a devastatingly handsome grin that flashed his perfect teeth. "Black. Just the way I like it. After all these years, you remembered."

"Hardly," she lied. "I noticed last night, early this morning—whenever it was—that you didn't put anything except coffee in your mug."

He tapped his mug against hers. "To yesterday."

She skittered around the island and took the stool opposite his. "I'm trying to forget yesterday, thank you very much."

She took a quick sip, refusing to acknowledge that he might have been referring to yesterdays that were nine years old, instead of the one that had caused them to cross paths last night. "Any idea where I might start looking for a house to rent?"

"Try Mrs. Lambert. Sweet, silver-haired lady with the negotiation skills of a barracuda. Her office is on Main Street. You can't miss it. She'll cut you a good deal if you can find a house."

"Thanks." She took a slower sip of her coffee, unable to shake off the feeling that being around him was wrong. She still experienced the little adrenaline rush, the fear of being caught. Was that the reason he'd appealed to her long ago? Because, as Madison had pointed out, Kelley had tried so hard to be so terribly good, and Jack tempted her into being terribly wicked?

"Where is the hellion this morning?" he asked, breaking into her thoughts.

"Still in bed, but we resolved a few issues after we got home last night. I think moving into a house will make a difference."

"You're kidding yourself if you think she's rebelling because of this apartment."

"She's rebelling because she's sixteen. She's rebelling because her parents were killed by a drunk driver—" Releasing a gust of air, she combed her fingers through her hair. "Look, I'm sorry. I'm exhausted right now, and I'm not in the mood to discuss my family situation. How you can look as if you recently had twelve hours of sleep is beyond me. I find it extremely irritating."

"There's a massage parlor in town—"

She held up her hand to cut him off, surprised by the jolt of jealousy that speared her. "I don't want to hear about your decadent lifestyle."

His blue eyes darkened, his nostrils flared. "I remember a time when you wouldn't have objected to a little decadence."

"Jack, the past is the past. We've both traveled a lot of years since then. We're different people now."

He planted his forearms on the counter and leaned toward her. "I think with a little exploration we'd discover we're not so different."

He leaned toward her a little more, and she silently cursed the island for being so narrow, but she wasn't going to give him the satisfaction of seeing her withdraw.

"I remember the way you tasted the first time I kissed you," he said, his voice low and seductive.

"Jack—"

"I remember the way you tasted the *last* time I kissed you."

"Jack, I really don't need this right now."

"Do you remember how I tasted?"

She dropped her gaze to his luscious, wicked, talented mouth. Oh, yes, she remembered how he tasted.

He leaned a little nearer. "Care to see if we taste the same?"

"We'd taste like coffee," she said a little too breathlessly.

"I like coffee."

How did he manage with only a few words, a few heated looks, to draw her in, to make her seriously contemplate pressing her mouth against his? To experience again the seductive nature of his kisses, the sensual stroke of his hands, the firm press of his hardened body—

"What are you afraid of, Kelley? I'm not your student anymore," he reminded her.

And that was what terrified her. That with all the barriers removed, he could hurt her worse than he had before. She'd barely survived. Her humiliation had been private then. No one had known they'd been involved. To even contemplate trying again—

"Oops! Sorry, I didn't know we had company."

Guiltily jerking back, Kelley looked past Jack to where Madison lounged in the doorway, freshly showered, barefoot, wearing black shorts and a black spaghetti-strapped top. Madison had developed an aversion to bright colors, to anything that gave the impression her life might contain an inkling of joy.

"I thought coffee was small payment for him bringing the car by," Kelley hastily explained.

"Whatever." Madison ambled into the kitchen and opened the refrigerator door.

Jack settled back on the stool and glanced over his shoulder at Madison pouring apple juice into a glass at the counter. "What happened to the orange hair?"

Shrugging, she turned and leaned her narrow hips against the counter. "I washed it out."

"What about all the piercing?"

"Fake," she reluctantly admitted, extending her glass toward Kelley. "You think *she'd* let me get anything besides my ears pierced?"

"There may be hope for you yet, kid."

"Yeah, right. So you're not that old. How'd you get to be sheriff?" Madison asked.

"I'm not the sheriff. I'm the police chief."

"Same difference."

"Not really, but I doubt you're interested in a social studies lesson. As for how does a young stud like myself get to be police chief?" He rolled his shoulder into a careless shrug. "A town this small . . . they take what they can get."

"Yeah, but you gotta have some qualifications," Madison insisted.

"While I was in the army, I learned to be very good with a gun." He turned his steel-blue eyes on Kelley. "I need to get to work."

Kelley had been so intent on his conversation with Madison that she was startled by the abrupt change of subject. She nodded. "Right, of course you do. Madison, why don't you put on your shoes? You can go with us." She didn't want to be alone with Jack—not if he was in the mood to reminisce about how they'd both tasted, smelled, felt. "Jack said there's a real estate agent who can help us find a house to rent."

"Awesome."

Madison walked out of the room, and Kelley got to her feet. "I'll get my purse."

"All right." He grabbed her mug and his, walked to the sink, rinsed them out, and set them in the drainer. Then he washed out Madison's juice glass.

"I don't remember you being such a domestic," she said from the doorway where she'd stopped to watch.

He reached for a kitchen towel and started to dry his hands. "Yeah, well, you learn to do for yourself when you don't have a wife."

"I'm sorry things didn't work out for you and Stephanie."

"We all went into it knowing it wasn't going to work."

She'd hoped that maybe Jack would put forth some effort, would try for the child's sake to be a good father.

"What did she have? A boy or a girl?" Sometimes in the early years, after she'd left Hopeful, Kelley had imagined Jack with his child. A child he'd conceived six weeks before graduation, six weeks before he'd shown up on Kelley's doorstep, graduation cap in hand.

"A boy," he finally said.

"Do you ever see him?"

"Every day."

His answer surprised her. "You have custody of your son?"

"That's right." He tossed the towel onto the counter and held her gaze, a challenge in his. "It's like I told you. *She* split. I didn't."

Chapter 5

As Kelley drove him to the station, with Madison in the backseat, Jack didn't know what irritated him more. That Kelley continually expected less of him or that in his youth he'd behaved in a way that had led her to believe that less was all he had to give.

He'd been more honest with her than he'd ever been with anyone in his life. But, for him, more honest still hadn't been totally honest. It was his nature to hide the better part of himself. Life was less painful when he didn't hang his feelings out there for the whole world to see.

Jack was further irritated by the fact that Kelley had chosen to wear a sexy little red top that left one shoulder bare. He wanted to lean across the front seat and trail his mouth along her warm flesh. Probably the reason she'd brought the little felon along—to keep him in line.

"When did Stephanie split?" she suddenly asked, so quietly that he wondered if she was hoping to be discreet enough that she wouldn't arouse her sister's suspicions.

Kelley's brow was deeply puckered, her mouth grim, the way they always were when she graded a paper, concentrating on identifying errors and weaknesses in answers. Only he had no desire for her to determine what sort of mark to give his life.

"She hung around for about a year after the kid was born, but she wasn't any great shakes in the motherhood department. Or the wife department, for that matter."

She jerked her head around.

"Keep your eyes on the road," he ordered.

She shifted her attention back to the street until she came to a red light. Then she angled that pretty little head of hers at him. "She was terribly young, Jack."

"We were all young."

"You never see her at all?"

"Nope."

"What about your son? Does she ever visit him?"

"Nope."

"Not ever?"

"Why do you find that so hard to believe?"

"I just find it difficult to imagine a mother not wanting to see her child. Family is so important. I find it sad."

"Trust me. He'd be a lot sadder if he saw her." Stephanie could have taken lessons in being a mother from his mother. She had been that bad.

"You know, that light's not going to turn any greener," Madison piped up from the back.

Kelley jerked and directed her attention back to driving, but not before the car behind her honked. She twitched, glared in the rearview mirror, and continued on down Main Street.

"What do you tell him about his mother not being around?" she asked softly.

"I told him that I'm too hard to live with." No way was he going to tell Jason the truth, that his mother hadn't wanted him.

Jack pointed toward the police station, glad this conversation was going to come to an end quickly. Kelley still had the ability to irritate and fascinate him at the same time. "Just pull up to the curb."

"I really appreciate your help with finding a Realtor," Kelley said as she brought the car to a halt.

Her thanks irritated him further. It wasn't as though he'd solved any great mystery. A phone book would have revealed the same information. "Go up two lights. You'll see her place on the right. Can't miss it. Rhinestone Realty."

He glanced over his shoulder at Madison. She was really cute when she wasn't made up to look like a misplaced rock musician. She had Kelley's delicate features, but her hair was a golden brown. With the right attitude, she could be Miss Popularity of Hopeful High. "Could be worse, kid. I've been through towns that only had one light on Main Street. We've got six. And one even has a left-turn arrow."

"Big whoop," Madison muttered.

Grinning, he looked back at Kelley, and his smile withered. He was old enough that he shouldn't want her approval. He'd never cared what anyone else thought. Why had her opinion always mattered so damned much? Always.

"Give me a holler when you're ready to move. I'll get some guys together, and we can use my pickup to haul your furniture to the new place."

"You don't have to do that," she said.

Even though she was wearing dark glasses, even though he was, too, he could see that she really didn't want his help. Just like in high school, she had discouraged him from hanging around her. He'd defied her then. Why break old habits now?

"So, what are you going to do? Hire a moving company? Teachers' salaries suddenly skyrocket? Besides, I owe you. If not for you, I never would have read *Beowulf* in high school."

She smiled then, a wistful smile that caused everything inside him to tighten.

"I'm not convinced you *did* read *Beowulf*. But I appreciate your generous offer. I'll give you a call when we're ready to move."

"Good."

He opened the door, climbed out, and moved the front seat forward, just as Mike walked around the corner. Madison edged her way out of the back and slid into the front.

With the door still open, Jack leaned down and looked at the ladies in the car. "Next to the Realtor is

the massage parlor I tried to tell you about earlier.
Mention to Cindy that I sent you. She'll give you a
discount and a full-body massage that'll melt your entire body."

"Are you telling me it's a legitimate massage parlor?" Kelley asked with a hint of sarcasm in her voice.

"Yes, ma'am, I am." He reached into his hip
pocket, pulled out his wallet, retrieved one of his business cards, and extended his card to Kelley. "My cell-
phone number. That's your best chance of getting in
touch with me."

"Thanks, Jack."

With too many things unsaid, he nodded, shut the
door, stepped back onto the curb, and watched Kelley
drive off. Then he strode over to Mike, who was grinning like a fool.

"Hey, she's got another sister. And that one's cute,"
Mike said.

"Only one sister. That's the hellion from last night,
all washed up."

"You're kidding."

"Nope."

"That's interesting." If at all possible, his grin
broadened. "Really interesting."

"She's jailbait, Mike."

Mike's smile disappeared, and his face turned beet
red beneath his tan. "Right, Chief."

Mike wore his blond hair cropped short enough
that he looked almost bald, which should have made
him look older than his twenty-three years. Instead, to

his complete mortification, silver-haired ladies tended to pinch his cheeks in public.

"She cleaned up real nice, though, didn't she?" Mike added.

"Yeah, she did." Jack looked up at the clear blue late-September sky. "Full moon tonight."

"I hate a full moon," Mike grumbled. He fell into step beside Jack as he headed into the police station.

All cops did. It tended to bring out the crazies.

The crazies ended up being a domestic disturbance—an excessive amount of yelling between a husband and a wife, the noise level rising to a crescendo that disturbed the neighbors who called it in. Apparently, the wife wanted to take the kids to Disney World over Christmas. The husband wanted to take them to Disney*land*. After Jack calmed them down, he flipped a coin. Disney World won. He was certain Orlando would never be quite the same after the family's invasion.

Then he handled a drunken brawl at the Sit 'n' Bull. Followed by a guy who got a little too aggressive with a girl at the Broken Wagon, the only honky-tonk in town. The girl was shaken up but not really hurt. Her scream had brought a couple of local guys to her rescue.

Jack took his time hauling the locals off the out-of-towner. Funny thing was, he hadn't gotten a good look at the fellas—even though he'd been standing five feet away—so he couldn't make any arrests, which set the stranger into a cussing spree. Jack advised him to take the closest road out of town. Then he followed him to make sure he did.

He checked on a possible shoplifter at a convenience store. A harried new father had walked out with a box of diapers. Jack returned to the store and paid for the diapers.

Then, to top off his night, Gordy took a fatal shot to the chest.

The owner of the establishment was beside himself with outrage, dangerously close to bringing on a coronary.

"That's the third time, Jack!" Mr. Gunther yelled, punctuating each word with a jab of his arthritic finger in the air. "Third time. I want these felons apprehended."

Jack rubbed the back of his neck. "You know, Mr. Gunther, I'm not sure shooting an inflatable doll with a BB gun is actually a felony."

Lately, it was more like a rite of passage to the kids around here. The twenty-five-foot-tall inflatable gorilla that stood guard outside the gas station was sprawled in an airless heap not far from the pumps it was supposed to draw attention to.

"Well, it should be. Arrest them for firing a weapon in town. I think there's an ordinance against that. If there's not, there should be."

"Yes, sir, you're right about that. Let me make some inquiries, see what I can uncover. What do you think would be a fair punishment for those who shot Gordy?"

Mr. Gunther moved his mouth around as though his false teeth were attempting to escape. "Need my bathrooms painted. Kids have written all kinds of sexual trash on the wall."

"All right, sir."

"And thirty days of cleaning them."

"Sounds fair enough."

By the time he pulled into his driveway at three in the morning, Jack was wound up so tight he couldn't have slept if he tried.

He darted a glance at his neighbor's house. Everything was dark except for the bedroom where her son's night-light glowed. Serena was usually good for a late-night chat. Her husband, Steve, had been his best friend in the army. Their son had been born six weeks before his.

When Steve was killed on a covert operation that was still guarded by the Pentagon, Serena had turned to Jack for emotional support. Which he'd gladly given. Steve's death had devastated him as well. He hadn't reenlisted when the time had come. He'd wanted out.

He'd sold Serena on the idea of moving back here with him. Two single parents with each other to lean on. They'd lucked out when a new housing development was started on the edge of town, providing them with the opportunity to live side by side.

Sometimes, when he stopped to think about it, he found their friendship a little surprising. He'd never simply been friends with a woman. He and Serena had no sexual relationship whatsoever—never had. He doubted they ever would. To him, she was still his best friend's wife.

But he'd driven her to the emergency room the night Riker's fever had spiked and sent him into convulsions. Strep had been the culprit. The kid had never complained of a sore throat.

She'd held Jason on her lap while Jack sped to the hospital the day Jason fell out of the backyard fort and broke his arm.

They were always there for each other. Their sons alternated the weekends spending Friday and Saturday nights together. The arrangement gave him and Serena some time for themselves. In his case, he usually worked so he'd be free to spend the next weekend with the boys.

He owed it to Steve to be there for his son. The bullet that had taken Steve out could have killed Jack just as easily. They'd been standing that close to each other, determined to protect each other's back. Jack had failed at his mission.

With a sigh, he climbed out of the truck and headed into the house. It wasn't fancy, but it was a hell of a lot nicer than the trailer he'd grown up in.

He didn't bother turning on the lights. He simply switched on the television, muted the volume, and dropped into his recliner. Anywhere he looked, he could see evidence that it was a male-dominated environment designed to serve the needs of the hunters, not the nesters. No sign at all of much nesting going on.

No womanly smells. Nothing frilly, pink, or feminine. Pictures on the walls reflected things that Jason liked: race cars and F-14s and dolphins and dogs.

Jack had convinced himself that he preferred the house this way: a reflection of manly tastes. But in his youth, he'd always fantasized about having a house that included the personality of a caring woman. A woman who could make plants grow, furniture shine, hearty meals tasty, and his body ignite with nothing more than a sensual lowering of her eyelids, a slow curving of her lips.

A caring, sexy woman. A woman like Kelley Spencer.

He'd been torn between shame and desire the day she showed up at his trailer . . .

Jack was stuffing his shirt into his jeans, getting ready for his Saturday-afternoon shift at the auto shop, when he heard the car pull in with a thumping that indicated it needed a little maintenance. Looking through the bedroom window, he couldn't believe his eyes.

Miss Spencer.

How many times had he dreamed about her coming to him? Only she was supposed to arrive closer to midnight, when no one would see her. That's the way illicit affairs were handled, and he sure wanted to have an affair with her.

Rooted to the spot, he watched as she climbed out of her car and slowly looked around. He could well imagine what she was thinking. Trailer trash. At that moment, he hated his mother for leaving him here in this dump.

Making her way to the trailer, Miss Spencer carefully stepped over who knew what—the weeds made it impossible to figure out what dangers lurked within. He knew he really needed to mow, but it wasn't as if he actually gave a damn—usually. Right now, he cared more than he thought it was possible to care about anything other than a good romp with a willing woman between the sheets.

She climbed up the steps and knocked. Waited. Knocked again. Cupped her delicate hands around that beautiful face of hers and peered through the screen and the grimy window of the door beyond. He knew she'd realize soon enough that she wouldn't be able to see much of anything.

He considered pretending he wasn't home, ignoring her summons. The inside of the trailer looked worse than the outside. It stank, too. His mom had been a chain smoker. He couldn't get the disgusting stench of cigarette smoke out of the furniture.

"Hello?" Miss Spencer called out in that sweet voice she had. She knocked again.

What the hell. Maybe she was there for the exact reason he wanted her to be. Maybe she just didn't have sense enough to come after dark.

He strode through the trailer, cringing at the dirty dishes he'd left in the sink and the empty pizza box on the table.

He yanked open the door, and Miss Spencer jerked back, nearly tumbling off the steps, her arms doing this little windmill thing until she caught her balance. She wasn't that much older than he was—in years, anyway. In experience, he figured he was three or four times older.

She gave him her shy, nervous smile and began cracking her knuckles. He knew he made her anxious. He was bigger than she was, tougher, unafraid. Her voice had warbled the entire first week of school, while he'd sat there in her classroom and mentally undressed her day after day.

"Hello, Jack," she said. "Is your mother home?"

"Nope." She hadn't been home for more than a year. She'd simply packed up one day and driven away without so much as a fond farewell wave. He pushed on the screen door. "But you can come in."

With her smile faltering, she looked around, unsure, popping her knuckles more quickly. "I really wanted to talk with your mother."

"You can wait inside. I keep thinking she'll be back any minute." And he had thought that. For the first month, anyway. Maybe even the second. Then he'd given up all hope of ever setting eyes on her again. Good riddance, the man side of him that had grown up too fast thought angrily, but the little boy inside him still grieved over the loss.

Miss Spencer gave a quick nod, and he held the screen open. As she edged past him, taking great care not to brush her body against his, he inhaled her scent, holding it deep in his lungs, the way he figured dope fiends did when smoking a joint.

In spite of his reputation for being a troublemaker, he'd never gotten involved with drugs. In addition to being too expensive, they messed up the mind way too much, and he was having a hard enough time surviving as it was. He needed all his wits about him.

He closed the door, and she spun around, backing up a step, waving her hand. "Your mother isn't much of a housekeeper."

"She's not much of a mother, either."

He saw pity touch her eyes and knew letting her come inside had been a big mistake. She was so innocent, so naive, that he had to tamp down his anger. She came from a world of butterflies and rainbows. That fact alone made her totally wrong for him. Add to that little detail the fact that she was not only older but his teacher as well, and he didn't stand a chance in hell of ever being with her the way he dreamed of.

Still, he couldn't get her out of his mind, couldn't stop wondering how it would feel to have her beneath him, couldn't stop hoping that maybe a little of her would rub off on him.

"So what'd you want to talk to her about?" he asked.

She furrowed her brow. "Your grades. You're close to failing, Jack."

"Yeah, but close *isn't* failing." At any given time, he knew exactly what score he needed on an exam or assignment to stay within passing range.

"I don't understand why you refuse to allow your grades to reflect your intelligence. I can see how smart you are, I can see it in some of the answers you give, and it just makes me so angry that you don't apply yourself. I was thinking if your mother would get more involved—"

His harsh laughter echoed between the thin walls of the trailer. "All my mother was involved in was my birth. After that, I was on my own."

The pity in her eyes again. Damn it.

"You didn't come out here to see her," he said in a low rumble. "You came out here to see me."

He took a step toward her. She took a step back.

"Admit it. You like the way I watch you in class."

She shook her head frantically and made a move toward the door. "I'd better come back another time. Will you tell your mother I was here?"

"Yeah, I'll tell her when I see her."

He didn't know what possessed him. Adolescent hormones, probably, but he blocked her way before she reached the door. She pressed her back against the wall, while he effectively moved in to cut off any hope she might have had of escape.

As close as he was, he wasn't touching her. Just staring into those big green eyes of hers. Her breath was coming in short little pants, but she didn't shove him away. If she had, if she'd given any indication at all that she didn't want him this close, he would have stepped back.

Instead, he relished her nearness. He found every

aspect of her beautiful. Her features were flawless. But it was more than that. It was her excitement when she read Shakespeare. Her joy when she asked a thought-provoking question and a student gave an introspective response. The way she walked quickly down the hallway as though she had someplace that she truly *wanted* to be. The only place he truly wanted to be was out of this town that had never done him any favors.

"Why are you really here, Teach?" he asked.

"Because I truly want to help you, Jack. You're throwing your life away, and I desperately don't want you to do that."

He angled his head closer to hers. "Do you know what I think about when I'm in your classroom?" he whispered.

"What I look like naked."

A jolt of surprise rushed through him. Not only because she'd known exactly what was on his mind, but because she'd dared to voice it aloud. Maybe she wasn't the sweet, innocent thing he'd always imagined her to be. Maybe she had a spark of fire within her that could send him up in flames.

"I take it further than that," he told her. "I not only think about what you look like without any clothes on, I think about taking you to my bed."

She shook her head slowly. "That's a fantasy that's not going to happen, Jack. You're my student."

"And if I wasn't your student, would you allow this?" He cupped her cheek with one hand and lowered his mouth to hers.

She was heaven—pure and simple. He'd been imagining this moment for almost five months, and now that it was here, he wasn't disappointed. Desire took a firmer hold as she parted her lips for his questing tongue.

Groaning low, he pressed his body against hers until he could feel her breasts flatten against his chest. She ran her hands through his hair, along his neck, across his shoulders. He wanted that touch with no clothing separating them.

He drew back. "Come to bed with me."

The desperate plea in his voice echoed between them, embarrassed him a little because he sounded so uncool, so not in control. His body was aching with need. He'd never wanted anyone, anything, as much as he wanted her.

"Do you know what would happen to my career if your mother walked in and found me in bed with her son, who happens to be one of my students?"

"She's not going to walk in. She walked out more than a year ago. She's not coming back."

"Are you telling me you live here by yourself?"

He grinned with cocky self-assurance. Bless his mother for taking off. "That's right."

"I should get a social worker out here."

"I'm nineteen. Old enough to be on my own."

"But you're in high school, a student. How do you live?"

"I'm in the work-study program. Classes in the morning, work in the afternoon." He didn't want to get into all that, didn't want to be distracted from his purpose in explaining his mother's absence to begin with. He took her hand. "Come on."

She tugged free. "No."

"There's nothing stopping us."

"Of course there is, Jack. I'm a teacher. There's a measure of trust between the school board and me, a measure of trust between my students and me, their parents and me. I'm not going to violate that trust."

"But you want me," he insisted. "I see it in the way you look at me during class when everyone else is working on an assignment."

"My personal feelings are of no consequence. I'm here as a teacher, not as a potential lover."

"Lover. I like the sound of that. You think I'm hot."

"As long as you're my student—"

"I'll drop out of school tomorrow," he promised her.

"I'd never be interested in a quitter, in someone who didn't bother to finish high school."

He studied her. The determination in her eyes, the defiant angle of her jaw. He felt he'd somehow been manipulated.

"Are you saying the only chance I have of getting you into bed is if I finish school and graduate?"

"I'm saying if you don't, then there's no chance at all."

Chapter 6

&

"Dad, I'm home!"

Jack jerked awake, his neck stiff, his body cramped. He heard the back door slam, the sound of pounding feet moving through the house.

Sitting in his recliner, he looked to the side. Jason rounded the corner and came into the living room wearing a wide grin. He stumbled to an abrupt halt.

"Dad, you look like hell."

"Hey, bud, let's watch the *h* word." Yawning, he scratched his chest. "Do your old man a big favor, would you? Go back to the kitchen, and turn on the coffeemaker."

"Already done." Jason dropped his backpack, which contained his overnight away-from-home survival-gear, hopped onto the couch, grabbed the remote off the small table beside it, unmuted the television, and switched the channel to the Cartoon Network.

"So, how was the sleepover?" Jack asked.

"Awesome. We had a *Star Wars* marathon. I like *The Empire Strikes Back* best. No Jar-Jar."

"*Star Wars,* the way it was meant to be. You had breakfast?"

"Mrs. Hamilton made doughnuts. She lets us put as much icing on them as we want. They're the best."

"You're supposed to eat healthier when you're with her."

"She made us take a Flintstones vitamin."

"I'm talking vegetables, fruits, green stuff."

Jason grinned and cast a sly glance his way. "She said you'd say that. She put green food coloring in the icing so I could tell you that I'd eaten green stuff."

Reaching over, he ruffled his fingers through Jason's hair, hair so blond it was almost white. "My son is involved in a conspiracy to deceive me into believing I can trust the lady next door to take good care of him."

"She does take good care of me."

"I know. Don't know what we'd do without her."

With another yawn, Jack got up, went into the kitchen, and poured himself a cup of coffee. His breakfast. If Jason was hungry, Jack would whip them both up some oatmeal. But when it was just him, cooking seemed like far too much trouble. Good thing he had the kid. He might starve to death otherwise.

He ambled back into the living room. The Cartoon Network had been replaced by a video game. The good guys were splattering the bad guys, or maybe it was the bad guys getting the kills. Jack could never be certain.

"Hey, Dad, guess what?" Jason asked, his eyes never wavering from the television.

"What?"

"Me and Riker—"

"Riker and I," Jack reprimanded gently before taking a sip of his coffee. Kelley had influenced him in more ways than he cared to admit. Jason's teachers were always complimenting Jack on his son's vocabulary, reading level, and writing skills.

Jason scrunched up his face but finally continued. "Riker and I checked the calendar. It'll be our weekend with Mrs. Hamilton when the county fair is going on. Will you switch weekends with her? Please?"

He paused the game and looked at Jack with imploring, hard-to-resist dark eyes. Jack could see a lot of Stephanie in the boy. He couldn't make up his mind if that was good or bad.

"Please," Jason prodded again.

"She likes the county fair. She'll take you."

"Yeah, but she worries too much. She thinks the rides are dangerous because they cart them from town to town and have to take them down and put them up so fast. She only lets us on the kiddie rides, and this year me and Riker"—he grimaced—"I mean, Riker and I want to ride the big roller coaster. We're tall enough. We measured. Please switch with her. 'Cuz she'll never, ever, not in a million years, let us ride the big coaster."

That was a fact. Serena worried more than any woman he'd ever met.

"I'll think about switching weekends."

"Awesome!" He unpaused the game.

"If you keep your room clean until then," Jack added.

"Ah, Dad."

"Hey, all good things come with a price."

"How 'bout if I keep it sorta clean?"

"I don't negotiate with kids, you know that. It's my way or the highway."

Settling into his recliner, he watched the enthusiasm on Jason's face as he fired away, his fingers and thumbs working the controls at amazing speed. If nothing else, video games seemed to improve manual dexterity.

He supposed, considering his line of work, he should dissuade him from playing violent games, but Jack had never adopted the view that watching violence created violence. His approach when it came to raising Jason was to expose him to all things and teach him to deal with them. He wanted Jason prepared to meet obstacles head-on, on his own terms. Much as Jack had done, with more success than Jack had managed.

He'd never expected to love the kid as much as he did. When Stephanie had told him he'd gotten her pregnant, he hadn't believed her. Sure, following the prom, like half the kids who'd gone, they'd headed out to the creek for a little necking session, a session that had eventually gone further than Jack had intended. He and Kelley had fought that night. Jack had been looking for solace with Stephanie. He'd always had the feeling she'd been looking for something, too. He'd always had the uneasy feeling that whatever she'd been searching for, she hadn't found it—at least not with him.

Unfortunately, she'd been sixteen, a month away from seventeen. Her father had threatened Jack with arrest for statutory rape. Jack had been too unfamiliar with the law to realize the charges probably wouldn't hold up in court. Stephanie had been as willing and eager as he had been.

But it hadn't been the threats that finally made him buckle under the pressure and marry the girl. It had been Kelley.

The deep disappointment and immense sorrow he'd seen in Kelley's eyes when he'd told her Stephanie was claiming the kid was his had torn at his gut. He'd used a condom. No way was the kid his.

Kelley couldn't understand what it was to be a nineteen-year-old male with raging hormones. She'd thought something special was developing between them, had expected him to be true to her, even though she'd never committed to him, had never guaranteed there'd be anything between them once he graduated. She'd only promised there wouldn't be anything if he *didn't* get his diploma.

Standing in her living room, he'd known he'd lost her. He'd seen the tears welling in her eyes and knew, no matter what he did, for them it was over.

"You have to marry her, Jack. You have to. You owe it to her and the baby."

"It's not mine, I'm telling you. I'll have some test done—"

"Don't you dare!" she'd yelled. "Don't you dare insult her like that. Don't you dare smear her name or her reputation any more than you already have. I won't stand for it."

He'd stared at her, wondering if he even knew her. He certainly didn't understand her. He'd expected her to be upset about the situation. He hadn't expected her to go ballistic in defending Stephanie.

"You *want* me to marry her?" he asked, dumbfounded.

"I want you to do right by her and the child. She's terrified, Jack. You have no idea what it's like to be a pregnant teenager, to have to tell your parents news that you know will break their hearts. And then to have the father of your child ducking responsibility by shifting the blame . . ." She shook her head as though deeply disappointed in him. "You're better than that, Jack."

"What about us?" he asked.

"Whether you marry her or not, we're over. Because I'd never be involved with a married man, and I'd certainly never care for a man who wouldn't live up to his responsibility."

Now he was the one who was terrified. The thought of losing Kelley almost brought him to his knees. He plowed his hands through his hair, desperate to find an answer. "Okay. Okay. I'll marry her. I'll do right by her. But will you wait for me? I mean, after the kid's born, after I've given him my name, I could get a divorce."

Slowly, she shook her head. "I won't be the reason your marriage doesn't work. For her sake and the child's, you have to make it work. You owe them."

He was nineteen, facing obligations he'd never expected to have—not even when he was old. And if he turned away from that obligation, he knew Kelley's disappointment in him would grow. She'd think *she* was the reason he hadn't done right by Stephanie.

If he did marry Stephanie, Kelley would be hurt— but he'd already hurt her by not keeping his pants zipped. At least, marriage had the advantage of lessening her disappointment in him.

So, he'd chosen the option he wanted least. Because of Stephanie's parents' respected standing in the community, they had a large church wedding, albeit a hastily arranged one. Two days later, he'd enlisted in the army because he needed a way to support his wife, and he couldn't stomach his interfering in-laws.

He'd said good-bye to Kelley, never expecting to see her again. He'd left Hopeful, never expecting to return.

Now, here he was. Back in town with the one woman he'd never been able to forget.

Sitting in bed, glaring at the hodgepodge of empty boxes in her bedroom, Kelley was beginning to wish she'd taken a different tack with Madison. Moving was such a chore.

She'd been unprepared for the number of houses available for rent in a town this small. They'd spent yesterday afternoon inspecting one house after another, with Madison and her disagreeing on the silliest of things: a bathroom that was too small, the absence of a pantry, hideous tile.

They'd finally come to an agreement regarding a one-story, three-bedroom house in an older neighborhood where huge oak and sycamore trees provided shade. The third bedroom was the mother-in-law room on the far side of the house. Madison was thrilled with the prospect of having more privacy, even if she hated the wallpaper in the bathroom. Kelley had some reservations about Madison living in the room on that side of the house instead of the one down the hall from the master bedroom—the room Kelley planned to take—because Madison could sneak out so easily without being heard.

How was Kelley to have known that as a child got older, dealing with her became more difficult? She'd always thought babies required the most time and attention. Somehow, Madison required more.

After they'd taken care of all the paperwork for the house, they'd gone on a scavenger hunt for empty boxes. They'd hit pay dirt at an office supply store that specialized in printing services. Once they'd carted the boxes home, Madison had immediately begun to pack up her things. Kelley couldn't quite work up the enthusiasm to get started.

Leaning back against the headboard, with her coffee mug in hand, she was still putting off the inevitable, dreading the process of boxing everything back up and moving it across town, then unpacking everything. It seemed to take forever to make a place feel lived in, to give it that welcoming sense of home.

That was probably the reason she'd taken Jack up

on his kind offer. She couldn't afford a moving company, and she simply wanted to get this relocation done as quickly as possible.

Mrs. Lambert, true to Jack's word, had not only negotiated to get them a bargain on the house but had taken the matter of Kelley's lease up with the apartment manager. Although the month was half over, with Mrs. Lambert's steely gray gaze honed in on him, he'd agreed to wave the thirty-day notification policy. Kelley and Madison could move out any time before the end of the month.

Unlike Madison, Kelley saw little point in starting the laborious packing process immediately if Jack wasn't available until the end of the month. She didn't relish the thought of living out of boxes. Besides, it never failed. As soon as she decided she didn't need something and packed it away, she'd discover an urgent need for it and have to hunt through the boxes to find it. Even when she tried labeling boxes as she went, she never seemed able to find what she needed. Packing in a rush and not being without anything for any length of time appealed to her greatly.

Still, she had no idea what Jack's schedule was. She set her mug aside, popped her knuckles, picked up the phone, glanced at his business card on her nightstand, and punched in his number.

Jack's phone rang three times before he answered. "Hello?"

Okay, so that youthful voice didn't belong to Jack. Until this moment, his son had been an abstract image in her mind. Still an infant needing to be cuddled and held tightly. She hadn't considered that he'd actually grown over the years, and a part of her wished she'd seen him when he was newly born, wished she'd seen the expression on Jack's face when he'd first gazed at his son.

Had his chest swelled with pride, with love, with hope? What had he felt when he'd held his son, when he'd looked into the eyes of the woman who'd given him a child?

"Hello?" the boy said again. "I can hear you breathing, so I know you're there."

"Yes, I'm here. I got distracted. I'm sorry." She chastised herself for babbling. "Is Jack . . . your dad there?"

"Yes, ma'am. Just a minute."

She smiled at the seriousness in his voice. Jack was raising him to have manners. She hadn't expected that. But then he could have knocked her over with a soft breath when he'd announced that the boy was living with him. How could Stephanie have abandoned her child so completely when she had Jack to lean on?

As Jack had mentioned, no one had expected the marriage to work out, but Kelley had naively expected it to last awhile, at least until the baby no longer needed the stability both parents could offer. As she was coming to learn, though, children always needed stability. Even after they grew up. In a sense, maybe they needed it more then.

For some reason, she'd thought Jack's son would follow in his father's footsteps and be a hell-raiser. She had a difficult time thinking of Jack as a father, but to envision him as a good father . . . a warm sense of contentment settled near her heart. When he'd spoken of his son, she'd definitely heard fatherly devotion reflected in his voice.

With the phone pressed to her ear, she thought she detected the sound of a rushing waterfall in the background.

"Dad?"

"Yeah?"

"Phone."

The cascading water fell into silence, soon replaced by the crackle of plastic and the sliding of metal against metal. Her heart pounded with the realization that Jack was in the shower. Naked. She imagined the water dripping from his hair onto his bare broad shoulders. The drops rolling down his lean torso, along his chest, across the flat planes of his stomach, falling ever lower.

"Morgan," he said brusquely.

She took a deep breath that only served to make her realize she was quivering. "Hi, Jack."

"Kelley?"

"I'm sorry. I didn't mean to disturb you—"

"That's all right. What's wrong?"

Other than the fact that she was talking to a naked man . . . absolutely nothing.

"Nothing's wrong. You were right about Mrs. Lambert. She was a jewel. She found us a house over on Elmwood Lane."

"Great. When did you want to move?"

"That depends on your schedule. I was thinking maybe next Saturday."

"That'll work. What time did you want to get started?"

"I was thinking . . ." She couldn't think. She kept envisioning him standing there, feet spread wide apart, with water glistening on his chest. He hadn't had hair dotting his chest when he was younger. Did he now?

"You were thinking?" he prodded.

"Yes, yes. I was thinking next Saturday might work." *I was thinking how warm your skin was, how it would feel to kiss the droplets away.*

"Right, we already established that. What time next Saturday?"

"What time?"

"When do you want me to get there?"

"Whatever works best for you."

"How about ten? Some of the guys I'm going to bring with me aren't early birds."

"Ten is good."

"Are you all right? You sound kinda funny."

"I'm fine. I just have a lot on my mind." *Like the vision of your perfect body unclothed.* "I assume that was your son who brought you the phone."

"Yeah. We never know when the call might be an emergency, so Jason is good about answering it and not hesitating to disturb me."

Jason. His son's name was Jason. She hadn't known.

The child was becoming more concrete, more real, more a part of Jack's life.

"At this precise moment, I'm standing in the shower," he added, his voice growing gravelly, more seductive, more intimate, as he shared the last bit of information with her.

"I figured." She feared that she was failing miserably at sounding completely nonchalant, as though she often spoke to men when they were taking a shower. "I heard the water running before you turned it off."

"Usually, when I'm naked talking to a woman, she's naked, too. Are you naked, Kelley?"

She didn't like the spark of jealousy that hit her along with the image of a naked woman rubbing her soap-slicked body over Jack's. Nor was she particularly pleased with the unexpected rush of heat that washed through her with the thought of that woman being her.

She was suddenly hot enough to contemplate re-moving her nightgown. She usually didn't get dressed for the day until after her first cup of coffee. She needed the caffeine kick to get started. And right now, she needed a mental kick to get past the slow-motion visions unsettling her.

"No, Jack. I'm fully clothed."

"That's a shame. We could get into some kinky phone sex."

"We tried that once," she reminded him a little testily.

"It worked at my end."

It had worked at hers as well. Since she'd refused to

go out with him, to be seen with him in public, he'd taken to calling her every night. At twenty-two, she'd been flattered and frightened by his attention. She'd had a disastrous relationship in high school, her first encounter with betrayal. She'd been hesitant to get involved with anyone else—until Jack. She'd taken a chance with him. One of his looks could heat her body, steam her senses. She'd been naive to think she could handle him back then. She wasn't even certain she could handle him now. And she certainly wasn't going to put her heart at risk again.

"Jack, I really need to go. I'll see you Saturday."

She hung up, her hands shaking, her body trembling. She tried not to picture him turning the water back on, standing beneath the spray, rubbing soap over his body. Why was it so difficult not to think about him?

What was she doing inviting Jack Morgan back into her life? Other than leaving the way open to having herself labeled as certifiably insane, she was playing with fire. He had the power to stir to life all the ashes of her past, a past that revealed her weaknesses and failings. He could help her move, but she wouldn't open her heart up to him. Not again.

It simply hurt too damned much to be constantly reminded of past mistakes.

Chapter 7

"So, where are they?" Madison asked impatiently as she stared out the dining-room window that overlooked the stairs and parking lot.

"They should be here any minute," Kelley told her.

She'd been distracted all week. Not with the move but with the idea of spending a good portion of the day with Jack. She'd had to grade essay papers two or three times because she kept losing her train of thought. She'd asked a student to read a passage, and then she'd drifted off into thoughts of Jack. Jack in his office. Jack drinking coffee in her kitchen. Jack standing naked in his shower. Jack standing naked in *her* shower.

Dangerous, dangerous thoughts.

"I can't believe you didn't put on makeup," Madison said.

"We're going to work hard, work up a sweat. I didn't see any reason to get dressed up."

Besides, she needed to make certain she didn't do anything to lure Jack into making advances. Her defenses were no match for his offense. She'd gathered her hair back into a ponytail. She'd pulled on a T-shirt over a cotton bra. Over that, she was wearing an unbuttoned cotton shirt, the hem flapping around her hips. If she didn't feel sexy, she wouldn't be sexy, and he wouldn't view her as sexy. That was her mantra. Faded jeans and jogging shoes completed her ensemble.

It was a move-furniture-and-unpack-boxes day. Not a find-out-if-Jack-was-as-good-now-as-he-was-then day. The womanly part of her couldn't see how he could have done anything but improve over the years. What he'd lacked in finesse in his youth, he'd made up for with enthusiasm. If the heated looks he'd given her in the kitchen were any indication, he'd added both finesse and patience to his repertoire. She was probably a fool not to entice him into a firsthand demonstration of what he'd learned in the passing years.

"I can't wait to get out of here," Madison mumbled.

"With Jack's help, we ought to be able to get everything carted over to the rental house today."

"Even if everything isn't moved, I'm sleeping over there tonight," Madison said.

Kelley walked over and tugged on Madison's short hair. "I didn't realize how much you'd hate living in an apartment."

"It just makes me feel all closed in."

Madison stood straighter and stared more intently through the window. "What color's his truck? Two black ones just pulled in."

"That's probably him, then." She peered over

Madison's shoulder. Jack was getting out of his truck. Lord help her.

His black T-shirt, outlining every thick, corded muscle in his chest, back, and upper arms, was tucked into snug jeans. He wore a baseball cap and big grin as he said something to the three very young men clambering out of the truck that had pulled up beside his.

"I thought he'd bring off-duty cops with him," Madison muttered.

Kelley heard the uneasiness in Madison's voice. Kelley had expected off-duty cops as well. She recognized one of the boys. He was in her English class. Chris Farmer. Based on the camaraderie flowing between the boys, she'd bet they were all friends in spite of the fact that Chris wore a cowboy hat and boots while one boy had spiked hair and the other had what she'd call a normal haircut, parted on one side with bangs falling in the front.

"Why did he have to bring them?" Madison mumbled as she moved away from the window.

"Do you know them?"

Madison looked as though she wished she was anywhere but where she was. "No." She grimaced. "I mean, I've seen two of them in the hallway."

"Then this is good," Kelley said, trying to hide her own concerns over the situation. She didn't mind that Madison wasn't dating yet. Although she didn't want her to live like a nun, she wasn't sure she wanted Madison to hang out with boys who were on such good terms with Jack. Bad boys tended to draw bad boys. Still, to get through this day, she had to remain positive. "You'll get a chance to get to know them."

"Why would I want to? They look totally dorky."

"Fine." She wasn't in the mood to deal with an irritable Madison and a hotter-than-sin Jack. "I'll tell Jack we've changed our minds and don't want their help. Moving the furniture will certainly be more difficult—"

"No! Their being here is okay. I mean, I don't have to talk to them or anything."

"I guess if you want to use hand signals to indicate what we need done, that's fine."

Madison stuck out her tongue and ran her hands over her hair. "God, I hate being new here."

She wasn't certain Madison would believe her, but Kelley could relate. She'd been lonely a good deal of the time she'd taught that first year. In the two months since she'd returned, she occasionally had coffee with a couple of the teachers, but she hadn't really developed any friendships. She gazed back out the window.

Jack was walking toward the apartment, the boys in tow. In his youth, he'd swaggered with bravado. Now, he strode with confidence. Where before he'd carried a huge chip on his shoulder and worn anger like a comfortable leather jacket, now he seemed more at ease with himself.

She'd noted the physical changes immediately. The inner changes were more subtle but just as dangerous. She stepped away from the window, mentally shoring up her defenses.

The doorbell chimed. Popping her knuckles, she glanced over at Madison. Why did she get the impression they were both dreading the next few hours, and not for the reasons they should be?

She forced a bright smile and yanked open the door. "Come on in."

Each boy politely greeted her. She always felt incredibly old when they addressed her as Miss Spencer. But she knew she needed to maintain the formality. Adding to the difficulty was the realization that Jack had been only a little older than these boys when she'd first met him. For that matter, she hadn't been much older then, either.

Strange how, in retrospect, she could see how young they'd both truly been.

Jack led the way inside, glancing around as he did so, looking with what Kelley suspected were the sharp eyes of a cop. He settled his attention on Madison. "Hey, kid, you ready to get out of this dump?"

Madison nodded quickly, her gaze darting between Jack and the three boys who flanked him like outlaws ready for a gun duel. Where had smart-mouthed Madison gone?

"Everybody knows Madison, right?" Jack asked.

"No," the boys mumbled.

"No?" Jack repeated. "What? You walk through the hallways with your head up your butt?"

"More like in his books," the boy with brown spiked hair said.

"Right." Jack clapped Chris on his shoulder. "This is Chris Farmer. Avoid him. He's really smart."

"I'm smart," Madison blurted, so obviously offended that it was a little funny.

"Yeah?" Jack grinned. "You could have fooled me the other night."

Madison glowered, her cheeks turning red. Kelley was surprised she didn't have a comeback.

"These other guys are Bryan Jones and Rick Lang," Jack continued. "You and Rick can discuss hair tips."

"Hey, Chief, give me a break, will you, man?" Rick of the spiked hair said. "My dad is, like, terminally bald. I've gotta have fun with my hair while I've still got it."

"Actually," Madison said hesitantly, "the baldness gene is passed from mother to son, so you have to look at your maternal grandfather to know whether or not you'll be bald."

"No shit?" Rick asked.

"Hey!" Jack barked, and everyone—Kelley included—jumped. "Watch your mouth. We've got ladies present."

"Right," Rick mumbled. "Sorry, Chief."

"Yeah, he'll wash out your mouth if he doesn't like what you say," Madison warned.

"That is so old-school," Rick said with an exaggerated roll of his eyes.

Madison actually grinned shyly at him, shifting her stance, tucking her arms beneath her breasts.

"Old-school or not, I'll do it," Jack assured them. "Now, let's get a quick assessment of what we've got here, and we'll figure out the best way to proceed." He turned sharply to Kelley. "All the furniture goes?"

Almost stunned by his sudden switch into action, she nodded.

"Appliances?"

"Refrigerator, washer, and dryer." She pointed. "That's Madison's room. The one on the other side of the living room is mine."

"Madison, show the guys your room," he ordered. "I'll take Miss Spencer's."

He walked across the apartment, a man with a purpose. She heard one of the boys exclaim that Madison's ugly red furniture was totally awesome. He was bemoaning the fact that his parents wouldn't let him do what he wanted with his furniture. Even kids in small towns had secret fantasies.

As for her secret fantasies . . . she followed Jack into her bedroom. He stood in the center of her room, staring at her bed. The mattress was bare. She'd already bundled up the sheets and bedding. She could well imagine what was running through his mind: memories of the one night he'd been in that bed. For the longest time, she wouldn't wash the sheets, crying herself to sleep countless nights surrounded by his scent. Until the fragrance had faded—just like her memories of him.

"I thought you might bring your son," she said, to distract him and herself. She hadn't actually *thought* it, she'd *hoped* it. She really wanted to meet his child. She had such a clear picture of him after hearing his voice on the phone. A younger version of Jack. Untainted.

"Are you kidding? He'd want to help, so it would

take us twice as long. Serena took him and Riker paintballing."

"Serena?"

"My neighbor. Her husband and I served in the army together. He was killed, so she and I sorta lean on each other. Riker is her son."

"Riker?" She was beginning to sound like an echo.

He grinned in a sad sort of way. "Yeah, his dad was a huge *Star Trek* fan. He actually dragged me to a *Star Trek* convention once. Let me tell you, some of those people need a reality check."

"I can't picture you at a *Star Trek* convention."

"My life took some unexpected turns, but for the most part, the roads have led me where I wanted to go."

She was astounded by how content he seemed with his life. She was glad things had worked out so well for him. Even if he'd broken her heart before he'd begun his journey to where he was now.

"Speaking of unexpected turns, it was considerate of you to bring some boys Madison's age to help with the moving," she said as she neared him. "She's had a difficult time making friends."

"Don't kid yourself." He caught her with a gaze that mirrored longing and desire. It heated her to the core. "Being considerate had nothing to do with it. I didn't want any competition."

He took a step closer, and she found herself staring up into his blue eyes, eyes that during the storm of passion turned to the color of midnight. She told herself to move away, to run, to hide, but it was as though his body was a huge magnet and hers nothing more than tiny slivers of desire, drawn against her will toward him.

"I remember the bed," he said. "I wondered if you still had it."

"Jack—"

He grazed the edge of his thumb along her cheek. "Do you know how many times I've thought of you this week?"

She wasn't going to admit it to him, but she'd probably thought of him just as often.

"We didn't work then, we wouldn't work now."

"I think you're afraid we *would* work," he said.

Yes, she was. But for how long? She didn't know if she could survive another failed relationship. So she searched for an excuse that wouldn't reveal her insecurities. "Everything I have to give right now has to go to Madison."

"Devoting yourself completely to one person can destroy you. You need balance in your life."

She scoffed, crossing her arms beneath her breasts in a protective gesture. "You sound like a self-help guru."

"I've taken a few psych courses."

Her mouth dropped open, her eyes widened. "Are you telling me you've taken college classes?"

He skimmed his thumb along her jaw. "Depends. Is a guy with a higher education a turn-on for you?"

"You barely made it through high school," she reminded him.

"Not to mention all the damaging notations they

made on my permanent record. But a smart guy can work his way around a less-than-stellar past. And I'm a very smart guy. You said so yourself that day you came to my trailer."

The day she'd had to admit to herself that Jack was in danger of being more than a student to her. She'd hated seeing where he lived, how he lived. At the same time, she'd felt a burgeoning respect for him. At nineteen, he was working and supporting himself while still going to school.

He lowered his head slightly. "Remember that day, Kelley? Remember how it felt to have my mouth against yours?"

Oh, yes, she remembered. She remembered everything about every moment she'd been in that trailer.

"Hey, Chief?"

She tried to step away, but Jack grabbed her arm as he looked past her. "Yeah, Chris."

She couldn't believe how normal his voice sounded. If she'd been forced to speak, her voice would have echoed breathless anticipation.

"Where do you want us to start?" Chris asked.

"Let's get the furniture out of the front rooms first. It'll make it easier to carry the beds and dressers through."

"Sounds good."

"I've got an ice chest in the bed of my truck filled with drinks. Make sure everyone knows it's there. I don't want anyone getting heatstroke on me. Emergency room is a bitch on the weekends."

"Gotcha."

Chris disappeared, and Kelley wrenched free. "We're through here, Jack."

He hitched up a corner of his mouth into a cocky grin. "Hardly."

He walked out of the room, and she dropped onto the bed. How was it that after all this time, he still had the ability to turn her knees to jelly with nothing more than a touch and a promise?

There was something to be said for watching young men haul furniture. And Jack Morgan was very much still a young man.

While Kelley and Madison carried the lighter boxes downstairs to be placed in the back of one truck, Jack carted the couch down the stairs, holding one end while two of the boys held the other. She silently cursed him for wearing a T-shirt that was snug enough to outline every bunched muscle, resentfully thanked him. Any woman would appreciate his masculine display.

He'd definitely filled out, firmed up, toned up. Not that he'd been a poor male specimen before, but now it was as though he encompassed every female's fantasy. And he took absolute pleasure in knowing that he did.

Every time he caught Kelley childishly gaping at him, he'd give her a slow, sensual smile that implied he knew exactly down which road her fantasies were traveling, and more, he was inviting her to sample again what he had to offer.

And he was right. She feared sampling because she was afraid a sample of Jack Morgan wouldn't be enough. It hadn't been nine years ago. He hadn't committed totally to her then. Was he a man who could commit now?

His marriage to Stephanie hadn't lasted, but, as he'd pointed out, no one had really expected it to. But he had a son to raise, and Kelley had Madison. If she couldn't be an effective mother to Madison, how would she fare as the stepmother for a child whose mother had stolen Jack away from Kelley?

She gave herself a mental shake. She was carrying this scenario way too far.

She watched as he and the boys situated the couch where he wanted it in the bed of his truck, nestled against the love seat. He stood back, studying their efforts, mentally measuring the remaining space.

"We can get all the dining-room chairs in my truck, the table in yours, Rick. Madison, can you reach the cooler in the bed of my truck and toss me a drink?"

Madison started to clamber onto the truck, stopped when Rick put his hand on her arm, and glared at him.

"I was just going to help you," he said, releasing his hold and stepping back.

"I can do it." She managed on her own, but Kelley figured probably not with as much grace as she would have liked.

"She didn't have boyfriends in Dallas," Jack said in a low voice near Kelley's ear.

"No." Then she reluctantly admitted, "I'm not letting her date yet."

"You're kidding?"

The hairs on the nape of her neck bristled at the condemnation and disbelief she heard in his voice. "No, I'm not. Kids are too sexually aware these days."

"You think maybe that's the reason she ended up at Morty's dressed up like a whore? To protest a ruling that's a little old-school?"

"I think it's none of your business."

"It is when she ends up in my police station."

"Look, she's only sixteen. I've let her do some group dating."

"Group dating? That sounds like it has the potential for fun."

She released a sigh of impatience. "It's not what you're thinking."

"How do you know what I'm thinking?"

"Because I know you. You're thinking orgies. Kids today hang out in groups. Boys and girls having *innocent* fun. It gives them a chance to get comfortable with each other in a group setting—without that awful first-date stress. It's not easy being a sixteen-year-old girl."

"You oughtta try being a guy sometime. We're the ones who get all the excuses and rejects when we make our moves."

"I can't see you getting rejected, Jack."

"Since our paths crossed last week, you've told me no at least twice to my face, and that's not even counting all the little subtle hints you're dropping that you're not interested."

Not interested? It was because she was so interested that she was dropping hints like an abducted woman leaving a trail for her rescuers.

"What's everyone want?" Madison called out once she made it to the cooler and lifted the lid.

After the guys got their drinks and headed back to the apartment, Kelley walked to the side of the truck.

"He's got bottled water," Madison said.

"I'll take one of those." Kelley took the bottle, twisted the cap, and looked up to see Madison dangling a plastic bag of sliced lemons in front of her face.

"How did he know you like lemon in your water?" Madison asked.

Kelley lifted her shoulders helplessly. "Lucky guess. Or maybe he likes lemon."

"The sheriff doesn't strike me as a squeezing-lemon-into-his-water type." Madison sat on the closed lid of the cooler and sipped her water. "There's something between you and him."

A past she didn't want to get into. He'd been her student. She never should have gotten involved with him, could lose her reputation as a trusted teacher if anyone found out. Accusations and suspicions—even if never proven true—could be harmful in her profession.

"He had a crush on me," Kelley admitted. "That happens. Students get crushes on their teachers all the time."

"How about teachers getting crushes on their students?"

Kelley shook her head. "Getting involved with a student is morally and ethically wrong, Madison. I would never, ever do that." Although she'd skated up to the edge of the line, she hadn't crossed over it and gotten seriously involved with Jack until after he graduated, until he was no longer her student.

"But he knows you squeeze lemon into your water."

"He probably noticed when I drank water in class. He paid attention. That's all."

She hated not being completely candid with Madison, hated that she didn't feel as though she could trust Madison with her past. But what had happened between her and Jack was the past and was best left there, buried deep, forgotten.

When the furniture and boxes were crammed into every space of both trucks, Jack announced that it was time to take the first haul to the house.

"Madison, do you know where the house is?" he asked.

"Sure."

"Can you find your way there?"

"Not a problem."

Kelley knew what was coming a second too late to cut it off.

"Great. You ride with Rick and the guys in case we get separated. Miss Spencer, you can ride with me and show me the way."

• • •

Jack could fairly see the hairs on the nape of Kelley's slender neck bristling, her nostrils flaring. She was angry at the manipulative tactics he'd used to get her into his truck alone. He hadn't enjoyed himself this much in a long time. She riled so easily. She always wanted to be the one in control. He liked it when she wasn't.

Looking in his rearview mirror, he saw Rick's truck behind him. He could make out Rick and Madison in the front seat. Since both trucks had extended cabs, the other two boys would be sitting behind the couple in the front.

Jack had done a fairly good job of arranging things, if he did say so himself. He didn't really need Kelley to show him the way. All he needed was the address. He had an intimate knowledge of all the streets in this town. Not only had he traveled most of them in his youth, he cruised them at night as part of his job.

"They're talking," he said as he continued driving down the street toward the house Kelley had rented.

Kelley looked over her shoulder through the rear window. "I suppose that's good. I want her to have friends."

"It's easier for youngsters to get to know each other if the old folks aren't hanging around," he said as if he were some sort of expert on raising kids. After taking classes on child development and reading self-help books, he'd decided raising kids was a hit-or-miss adventure. Sometimes, you got it right. Most of the time, you got it wrong.

Kelley turned back around to face the front. "I'm sure it was concern for Madison's social life that prompted your suggestion that she ride with Rick. To loosely quote Madison, 'What are the odds of us getting separated in Podunk?'"

Jack grinned. "Hey, you never know. Could happen."

"Right. By the way, I'd appreciate it if you'd stop dropping hints that we have a past."

His smile vanished. "What are you talking about?"

"The lemon slices?"

"Some women might view my action as considerate. Remembering you like lemon with your water and then providing said lemon. Besides, those guys aren't going to notice—"

"It's not the guys I'm worried about. It's Madison. She's sharp, Jack."

"She doesn't know about us?"

"There is no us."

"There was."

"Jack, what happened between us was so totally wrong. I have a teenager under my care now. How can I guide her into making the right decisions if she learns that in my youth, I didn't always travel the moral high ground?"

He clenched his jaw. It had never occurred to him that she hadn't written back to him because she'd regretted what had happened between them. That in the end he'd disappointed and hurt her he could understand. But still, to have regrets that they'd shared anything at all? He couldn't quite grasp that possibility.

"I wasn't your student that night," he ground out.

"No, but you were every night before that. The phone calls, the notes we passed back and forth, the little gifts you left at my desk. My God, Jack, it was a dangerous game that could have cost me my teacher's certificate." She placed her hand over her mouth as if she thought she could keep herself from talking about the unspeakable. "I was so stupid, risking everything for what in the end turned out to be nothing."

"I never considered it *nothing.*"

"Oh, yeah, Jack. You were so convinced it was *something* that you took another girl to bed."

Having sex with Stephanie hadn't been his plan. He'd given in to anger and hurt and hormones raging out of control.

"I was nineteen and horny. And you sure as hell weren't putting out."

"I was your teacher!"

He slammed on the brakes. She braced her arm against the dashboard, her eyes filled with fury, her breathing hard and heavy. God, he wanted her with a ferocity that was unnerving.

"It hurt, Jack," she rasped. "It hurt so damned much. And it was wrong on so many levels. Can't you understand that I'm ashamed of what happened nine years ago? That I want to forget it?"

Forget the first time in his life when he'd ever felt that he was worth anything to anyone?

Hurting her had never been his intent. He wanted to take her in his arms, comfort her, and reverse her thinking. He glanced in the mirror. The timing for them was always lousy. "We have an audience. We'll discuss it later."

"We have nothing to discuss."

He watched her clamber out of the truck. Oh, they had plenty to discuss. They had too much unfinished business.

Chapter 8

Kelley held her breath as Jack prowled through the house. She was still trembling from their encounter in the truck. How quickly he could prick her temper. How quickly he could make her regret the one night they'd shared that had brought her absolute joy. How quickly he could make her remember how much she'd hurt when she learned that he'd gotten Stephanie pregnant.

None of his excuses warranted a second thought as far as she was concerned. She didn't care that he'd been nineteen or horny. It shouldn't have made any difference at all that she and Jack weren't actively engaged in sex.

In an odd way, they'd been developing a relationship. Clandestine, to be sure. But it was still taking root, growing. She'd expected him to show restraint when it came to his uncontrollable hormones. She'd naively thought that she deserved for him to hold his lust in check for her. Boy, had they possessed differing opinions on that matter.

"We've already signed the lease," she informed him

testily as he checked the windows and doors while she followed him around like a well-trained puppy.

He nodded, as though she hadn't told him anything he didn't already know. Which she realized she hadn't. Still, it grated on her nerves to have him judging her decisions.

"No alarm system," he announced as he returned to the front room where the others were waiting.

"Like we need one in Podunk," Madison said.

"Two beautiful women living alone?" Jack asked. "You bet you need one."

Madison's cheeks turned almost as bright as her hair had been last weekend. The boys were grinning, darting glances at each other as though trying to figure out if one of them had an interest in Madison or who could make the first move.

She was torn between being happy that Madison had their attention and worried that she didn't have enough experience to know when to say no. Or if she'd even want to. She certainly didn't want Madison to end up as a statistic, a teen pregnancy. She knew too well how painful that road was to travel. She probably needed to have a heart-to-heart talk with Madison about the realities that a girl faced when she got pregnant at a young age, the tough decisions that had to be faced.

Tugging on Kelley's ponytail as he walked past her, bringing her back to the present, Jack said, "I'll talk to Mrs. Lambert. Have her tell the owner to get an alarm system in here."

"Jack, we're temporary. Two years at the most."

"One year," Madison reminded her, a challenge in her voice. "You promised—"

"I promised I'd think about it."

"I want to graduate with my friends."

"Look, the alarm system will increase the value of the property regardless of how long you stay. I'll take care of it," Jack said.

Her head was spinning as she tried to carry on two different conversations with two forceful people. She threw up her hands. "Fine, Jack, whatever. Let's just get moved in, okay?"

"The guys and I will haul in; you tell us where to put it."

A miniature regiment, Jack and the boys tromped out to the trucks.

"How was the ride over?" Kelley asked Madison. They hadn't had a second alone since they'd arrived.

"I don't want to be here my senior year," Madison said.

So, they were back to that topic, were they? "I know—"

"Then why not just say that we're leaving at the end of the year?"

"Because I haven't had time to consider all the options and ramifications"—she held up a hand to stifle any further discussion or protests—"and right now is not the best time to get into a heated debate on this subject. Let's get everything moved in, okay? We'll discuss it all later."

Madison did this little roll that made it look as though she were shrugging her entire body. "Okay, but I'm not going to forget what you promised."

A promise to think about it was not a promise to act on it.

"So, how was the ride over?" Kelley asked again, desperate to get Madison's thoughts away from the possibility of moving. Maybe with a little more time, things would fall into place and Madison would be content to stay.

"Kinda cool, I guess. At least, we didn't listen to country music."

"They seem nice."

"They think my red furniture is awesome, but I was thinking about painting it another color."

"Something bright and cheery, hopefully."

"Black."

Kelley cringed. "Black isn't a color. It's the absence of color."

"Rick said he'd help. He even offered to build me some shelves. He said he needed a woodshop project, so I don't think it's anything personal."

Kelley forced herself to tamp down her trepidation and smile. Just because she'd had a bad experience didn't mean that Madison would. "Do you like him?"

"Well, yeah, sorta. I mean, they're not as dorky as they look. Actually, they all know some neat stuff."

She had to admit that she might really owe Jack for having the foresight to hook Madison up with these guys. If Madison could only get a circle of friends going, maybe she wouldn't find life here so unappealing. And maybe trouble would quit knocking at their door.

She also owed Jack for working so diligently to ensure that everything got moved today. She was absolutely amazed by the amount of stuff they'd accumulated. Even though they'd moved a few months earlier, it seemed their belongings had multiplied like rabbits in the wild.

After several more trips to the apartment and back, once every piece of furniture and all the boxes were moved into the house, Jack cut the boys loose. Then he set about putting the beds together. Madison's first, then Kelley's.

She and Madison were lining the shelves in the kitchen when he ambled in. "Think all the macho stuff is done. Only the girly stuff remains."

"You think you're too good to put away pots?" Kelley asked.

"I'm more talented in the bedroom than in the kitchen."

Honestly, why did he have to say things like that when Madison was within hearing distance?

He crossed his arms over his chest and leaned his hips against the counter. "We've worked hard. Why don't you girls call it a day?" Jack asked.

"Because we still have a lot to unpack, things to put away, a need to get settled in," Kelley explained. She hated having a half-done feeling.

He looked over at Madison as though he knew any

argument with Kelley was futile. "There's a dance club in town. The Broken Wagon. One Saturday a month, they put away the booze, have a live band fire up some hip music, and only allow kids under thirty through the doors. Just our luck, tonight's the night." Grinning at Madison, he jerked his head toward Kelley. "Think we can scrounge up a fake ID for your sister?"

Manipulative. Bossy. Domineering. Kelley could think of a hundred unflattering adjectives to throw Jack's way as she sat on a hard wooden chair near the railing that separated the dance floor from the surrounding tables. She could also think of a few flattering adjectives that applied: undeniably handsome, sexy as sin, considerate.

It was the last one that was the most dangerous. With Madison as his ally, he'd managed to wheedle Kelley into agreeing to go to the Broken Wagon. He'd walked out her door with the warning that they had an hour to get ready.

Amid giggles and anticipation, she and Madison had scrambled to prepare themselves for the evening. Kelley had even broken down and applied makeup. Not as much as Madison, of course, and she'd left her hair its natural color, unlike Madison, who had tinted the tips green.

When Jack had returned with punctuality, he was obviously freshly showered and shaven, wearing tight jeans and probably the closest thing he had to a dress shirt—a starched blue cambric shirt.

As far as Kelley was concerned, one of the nicest things about small Texas towns was that getting dressed up still meant going casual.

They'd arrived at the Broken Wagon in high spirits, with everyone anticipating the evening. Even Madison had seemed enthusiastic about spending time at the honky-tonk. She'd laughed with total abandon at Jack's melodramatic attempt to sneak Kelley through the door as though he really believed they wouldn't let her in because she was thirty-one. It was so seldom she heard Madison laugh lately that Kelley had taken great delight in the sound.

Sitting beside Madison and across from Jack, Kelley was becoming increasingly aware, though, that Madison was obviously beginning to wish she were somewhere else. Having grown skilled at recognizing the signs of discontent, Kelley sometimes thought keeping Madison happy was an impossible task.

"I thought you said the music was hip," Madison grumbled.

The band, touting itself as the Outlaws, was a group of youngsters, all dressed in black shirts, black jeans, and black cowboy hats. The older guys were all in need of a shave. They had two lead singers, a male and a female, as though they couldn't quite decide if they wanted to be Tim McGraw or Faith Hill. The lead singers alternated most of the songs between them, occasionally singing a duet. Kelley thought they were really quite talented, but she couldn't imagine many talent scouts passing through Hopeful. Still, she supposed a person needed to start somewhere, and the Broken Wagon certainly drew a large, enthusiastic, appreciative crowd. Kelley understood now why Jack had wanted to get there early. There was barely any room to move.

"That's a Clay Walker song. Very modern," Jack told Madison. "Any other Saturday, you'll be entertained with the great songs of Hank Williams and Waylon Jennings." Grinning, winking at Kelley, he brought his frosty mug of root beer to his lips.

She didn't want to acknowledge the power in his wink or how much fun she was having. She couldn't remember the last time she'd gone out without an agenda in mind. If Jack had an agenda, he wasn't sharing it with her, and she wasn't completely certain she wanted to know what it was, anyway. Where Jack was concerned, ignorance might be bliss, although, in the end, it certainly hadn't been.

She shoved any disconcerting thoughts into the back of her mind, determined not to focus on the past for the next few hours, resolving to enjoy whatever tonight might bring.

"Remind me not to come any other Saturday," Madison said.

"You're too young to get in any other Saturday," Jack reminded her. He shifted his attention to Kelley. "What do you think?"

"I think it's nice that this type of event is made available to the younger set. No smoke, no booze. A lot of young people who really seem to be having a great time."

She'd spotted several of her students. Their eyes had all widened as though they were surprised to see her there, but each took the time to come over and speak. Small-town manners. She'd taken the opportunity to introduce them to Madison. If she could only help Madison find a friend, maybe she wouldn't miss the ones she'd left in Dallas so much.

"We try to have something different available every Saturday for the kids."

Kelley perked up at that admission. "We?"

"The town."

"Not you personally."

"No, not me personally. As police chief, I answer questions about how the events should be managed so my guys aren't called in every five minutes to handle a disturbance, but that's about it as far as my involvement."

His answer had been brusque, carried an impatient tone as though he wanted to explain and move on, which led her to wonder if he were more involved than he let on. Who would have thought the trouble-maker would be the one who now stopped trouble?

"Miss Spencer?"

Kelley looked up to find herself staring at a man with an eager smile. His face had rounded out almost as much as his body, but she knew the smile. "Bobby Lee Fontenot."

"Yes, ma'am. Didn't think you'd remember."

"Teachers never forget their students," she assured him.

"A little surprised to see you in here with Jack, though I did always suspect he was teacher's pet."

She considered protesting, but sometimes not drawing attention to a remark was the best way not to give it any significance. Jack, however, seemed to believe differently.

"Now, Bobby Lee," Jack drawled, a bit of censure in his voice, "a teacher's pet is a student who's spoiled. Miss Spencer forcing me to stay after school was hardly spoiling me."

"That's true enough, I reckon." Bobby Lee waved his finger in the air like a magician balancing a plate. "This here's my place."

She fought not to grimace. His speech had always revealed exactly what he was. A good ole country boy who was the son of a good ole country boy.

"You seem to be doing well for yourself," she said.

If at all possible, he broadened his grin. "Yes, ma'am, I am. I seen in the paper where you was coming back to town."

That was interesting. She hadn't realized there'd been a write-up in the paper, but then, in a town this small, articles tended to be more socially oriented, generally devoted to revealing who was visiting whom and the apparent successes of recent Hopeful High graduates rather than hard-core news.

"Jack seemed to have missed that article," she said, remembering his surprise when she'd first shown up in his office.

"I doubt he ever reads the paper. Most of the articles would be about him, anyway, if he'd take credit for the good he does. Like last week when that fella—"

"Bobby Lee, think you could have Anna bring us another round of root beer?" Jack interjected.

"Sure thing, Jack. Anything you want. You know that. It was good to see you, Miss Spencer."

"You, too, Bobby Lee." Turning her attention to Jack, she rested her elbow on the table, placed her chin on her palm, and studied him.

"What?" he growled.

"What wouldn't you let him tell me?"

"I broke up a brawl. No big deal. Bobby Lee tends to run at the mouth and exaggerate. To hear him tell it, I was up against the Terminator."

"I wouldn't have expected you to be so modest. Are there other good deeds you've done that caused the people of this town to want you to be police chief?"

"This isn't an elected position based on popularity. I'm police chief because when Chief Sawyer retired, no one else wanted the job. I had some army experience under my belt that made me a good candidate. That's all. Don't make me out to be some sort of hero."

"If you say so, Jack, but I always thought you had more potential than you let on."

She could see he had a smart comeback on the tip of his tongue—probably a comment on where his potential really rested: beneath the sheets. He shifted his gaze to Madison and held his tongue. The bad boy suddenly wasn't so bad, and that made him even more of a threat to Kelley.

"Here you go, everyone," Anna said as she plopped mugs of root beer around the table. Another one of Kelley's current students.

Jack dropped a ten-dollar bill onto her tray. "Keep the change."

"Bobby Lee said your drinks were on the house."

Jack winked at her. "I know."

She grinned. "Thanks, Chief." Stuffing the bill into her apron pocket, she walked off.

"So, what are you, rich?" Madison asked.

"Madison," Kelley reprimanded.

"I was just curious, that's all. It was a big tip, so I'm wondering if it was for real or if he's just trying to impress you."

"I don't think your sister is shallow enough to be impressed by the size of the tips I leave," Jack said. He lifted his mug, his eyes never leaving Kelley's as he drank, leaving her to wonder if he thought she was shallow enough to be impressed by the size of other things.

"Hey, Chief."

Jack lowered his mug and stuck out his hand. "Hey, Mike."

Kelley recognized him as the officer who'd been in the station the night she'd gone to retrieve Madison. He looked as if he'd only recently graduated from high school himself.

Jack indicated the empty chair beside his. "Want to join us?"

"No, no. I was just wondering"—he looked at Madison—"if Miss Gardner would like to scoot a boot."

"Scoot a boot?" Madison asked.

He gave her an absolutely adorable grin that caused deep dimples to form on either side of his mouth. "Yeah, you know. Dance."

"Why would I want to dance with a cop?"

Mike looked as if he'd taken an unexpected and brutal kick to the gut, his smile completely disappearing.

"Madison!" Kelley chastised.

"What? It's bad enough that I have to sit at this boring table with the chief of police like I'm some sort of criminal or something."

"Right," Mike said. "Sorry. My mistake."

He walked away as though he were looking for a hole to drop into.

"Madison—" Kelly began.

"You're a piece of work, kid," Jack interrupted. His voice carried a threatening rumble. And if looks could kill, his eyes would have been sharp, lethal weapons. "He's a nice guy who puts his life on the line every time he comes into work."

"*As if.* In this boring town?"

"It only takes one bullet, kid. Some husband pissed at his wife, someone angry at his boss. A gun in his hand. A cop trying to protect. If you didn't want to dance, you could have handled that better."

"You're one to talk. I've been asking around. Seems

you had quite the reputation for being a bad boy when you were my age."

"I was never mean. That's where we differ. The only person I ever hurt was myself. But you've got a mean streak in you and try to hurt everyone around you, thinking it makes you important, when all it does is reveal your pettiness. Now, instead of being in the center of the dance floor with some decent guy, you can sit here and stew all by your lonesome." Grabbing Kelley's hand, he abruptly stood. "Come on. My buckle needs polishing."

Kelley contemplated protesting, sensing that she needed to deal with Madison before this situation escalated out of control. But what more could she add to what Jack had effectively delivered? Besides, he'd wound his hand so tightly around hers that she wasn't certain the jaws of life could pry it free. She skipped along after him as he dragged her through the crowd of youngsters to the middle of the polished wooden dance floor.

He drew her loosely into the circle of his arms. The lights were low, the music soft, the male vocalist crooning.

"I don't think it's a good idea to leave Madison alone."

"Tough," he said in a deceptively mild voice.

"I think you were a little hard on her."

"You're not doing her any favors by spoiling her."

She shook her head. "I'm not spoiling her. She's young, Jack. She wasn't thinking."

"Stop making excuses for her, and just dance."

He was right. She knew he was. Still, it was so difficult to walk that fine line between being a sister and
being a mother. Being a friend, being a guardian. She
felt wholly inadequate. Younger than she was, Jack
had a child, a son he was raising. Although she hadn't
seen him interact with his child, he didn't seem to
question his every action, didn't seem to be wondering if he was up to mischief. Obviously, it was easier
when you'd been with the child from birth. She
sometimes felt as though she'd taken a shuttle to an
alien world, and the mothership had left her to fend
for herself.

He lowered his head. "Remember prom night?"

Her hands were resting lightly on his shoulders; his
were at the small of her back. They shuffled their feet
over the floor, moving very little from the spot where
they'd originally begun. Much as they'd done that
long-ago night. In a stairwell, where no one would see
them, they'd danced to the muted strains of Whitney
Houston's version of "I Will Always Love You." How
was she to have known then that, for them, the song
was hauntingly prophetic?

Holding his gaze, she nodded slightly in response
to his question, confessing at long last what she'd only
ever shared with herself. Even in the stairwell where
no one would see, she'd refused to let her guard down,
refused to allow the intimacy that Jack had so desperately wanted. She'd still maintained a distance. "I
wanted to place my head on your shoulder so badly,

but it would have been entirely inappropriate. You were my student, Jack."

And so she'd danced with him as though her heart weren't fluttering like the wings of a hummingbird trapped in a cage. And she had felt trapped. Confused. Drawn to a student. Dreaming of him every night. Anxiously awaiting his arrival in her classroom each day.

She'd doubted her moral fiber. Determined to stay above reproach, she'd tried to distance her feelings. Instead, she'd found herself doubting her commitment to teaching, doubting the wisdom of her heart.

"I'm not your student now." His voice held a challenge as he cupped the back of her head with his large hand and guided her cheek into the curve of his shoulder.

It felt so right, as though the nook of his shoulder had been created specifically for her. He tightened his hold around her until their bodies were pressed close. He felt incredibly good.

The song ended. Like many of the couples surrounding them, she and Jack continued to move slowly, their feet barely dragging over the floor. They were rewarded with another song, slower than the first.

"The only reason I took Stephanie to the prom was because I knew you'd be there chaperoning," he said, his voice low. "I wanted to see you, dance with you."

He'd looked incredibly handsome in his tuxedo. Renting it had probably set him back a week's salary.

Their gazes must have touched a thousand times that night. Only they'd known they were riding the crest of something so dangerous. And in the end, everything had crashed around them.

"I don't want to talk about the past, Jack. Not here. Not now." She didn't want to talk about the fight they'd had that night, how she'd always feared that the heated words they'd exchanged in the stairway following their dance were what had driven him into Stephanie's arms.

"We have to talk about it sometime, Kelley. We need closure."

"God, I hate that word. It's so overused. Just let me enjoy this moment." She wound her arms more tightly around his neck.

Each moment spent with him weakened her resolve to avoid him. And yet that path would only lead to more heartache.

"I find it difficult to believe you aren't involved with someone," she finally said.

"I'm not."

She lifted her gaze to his. "Were you before you discovered I was in town?"

"I go out from time to time. No one exclusively, no one expecting a commitment. How about you? Are you involved with anyone?"

"Madison. She takes up a considerable amount of my time."

"You know I was referring to any involvement with a man."

She nodded slightly. "No, there's no man in my life at the moment." She'd had an occasional date before her parents died, but after that, she'd been too busy adjusting to motherhood. "And quite honestly, I'm not looking for one."

"That makes it even better."

"I'm not sure how you figure that."

"Sometimes the best things in life happen when we're not expecting them."

And sometimes the worst things happened when she wasn't expecting them. She wasn't certain when she'd become such a pessimist. Sometime between falling for Jack and finding her life turned around. The music drifted into silence.

"I need to get back to Madison," she told him.

"You're using her as an excuse to keep a wall between us."

"So, you're not only the police chief, now you're the town shrink?" she asked.

He grinned. "Admit it. You've still got the hots for me."

"I'll admit you intrigue me," she said as she began walking back toward their table.

He slid his arm around her and drew her against his side.

"But one slow dance doesn't erase all the reservations or reasons I have for not getting involved with you," she assured him.

"Then let's take another slow turn around the dance floor."

She shook her head. "I really need to check on Madison."

He seemed as determined to keep his arm around her as she was to ease away from him. The habit of not revealing that she had feelings for Jack was so ingrained that even now she found herself searching for justifications in their actions—explaining their closeness as a result of the crowds. For a town that boasted a population of nine thousand, it had a lot of teenagers.

They reached their table only to find it empty. Alarm skittered through Kelley. "Where's Madison?"

"Probably dancing," Jack said.

Kelley began scanning the crowds, her trepidation increasing. For a few minutes, in Jack's arms, she'd forgotten her responsibilities. She spun around. "She's not here, Jack."

"Relax, Kelley. She has to be here. I drove. Her only option was to walk, and she doesn't strike me as the walking kind."

"Or she could have hitched a ride with someone." Kelley could envision only too clearly Madison taking that avenue.

"The place is packed. A quick look around isn't going to tell you that she isn't here. You check the bathroom. I'll take a walk through the place. I promise you that she hasn't gone anywhere."

But after thirty minutes of searching every nook and cranny, even Jack had to admit that Kelley was right.

Madison was gone.

Chapter 9

Jack drove his truck slowly through the empty streets. He'd alerted the patrols to keep their eyes peeled for Madison. He and Kelley hadn't been on the dance floor that long. Two songs. Five, six minutes tops. Madison couldn't have traveled far on foot.

Because he knew what it was to be rebellious, he had a soft spot for the little criminal. But that didn't stop him from wanting to grab her by her spiked hair and shake her every which way but loose.

Now Kelley was giving him the silent treatment for handling Madison wrong. As though there were a right way to handle a teenager. Kelley had her crossed arms bunched up beneath her breasts and her worried gaze scanning the dark shadows beneath the trees lining the street.

He wanted to be angry with her for allowing her sister to ruin their evening. But he'd always been drawn to that aspect of her that worried so damn much about others. He'd seen it a thousand times in her classroom. He had been the recipient of it himself.

She wanted the world to treat everyone kindly, and when it didn't, she fought to compensate.

Unfortunately, that attitude resulted in a lot of lost battles and a war that could never be won. Still, he admired her determination to try.

"We'll find her," he said quietly.

Out of the corner of his eye, he saw her nod without any semblance of hope.

"Don't be so hard on yourself, Kelley. All parents make mistakes."

"That's just it, Jack. She doesn't see me as her mother. I'm her sister, her buddy, someone she would pal around with on the weekends. She resents that now I'm the boss. And it certainly doesn't help the situation that I'm so incredibly inept at caring for her."

"I don't think you're inept. I think you're just trying too hard." Or not hard enough. "You need to punish her."

"Punish her?"

"Take away her car, her music. Hell, I don't know. Something she values. We could put her in a community service program."

"Community service? Like in punishing a lawbreaker?"

"It's not that far stretched of an option. Drinking underage is breaking the law. I let it slide. Maybe I shouldn't have."

"I really don't think punishment is the answer."

"Trust me. It is. I did the same thing when I was

her age. I broke all the rules. Dared my mother to put her foot down. Hell, I would have welcomed a slap."

"You're talking abuse now."

How could he explain what it was like to live with someone who didn't care about anything? He hadn't wanted his mother to beat him. But he'd wanted to force her into displaying some sort of reaction. Yelling, screaming, or cursing him out. Yeah, he wouldn't even have minded a punch. Anything, anything at all, except for her vacantly staring out the window and her constant refrain: "I don't know what to do with you, Jack."

"Not abuse. She's scared, feeling lost. Her parents died, and she lost that secure wall. She's pushing you because she wants you to set boundaries," he said.

"Which I do."

"Not firmly enough, obviously. I guarantee you, if I grounded Jason, he'd stay grounded. He wouldn't be sneaking out, getting into mischief, and causing me grief."

"It's different with teenagers."

"It's not that different. Kids need boundaries. They need consistency. I set the boundary, and it stays put. Jason knows he can walk right up to the edge of it, but if he steps over it, he gets a time-out. Every time. No exception. He knows what my expectations are regarding his behavior, and he knows the penalty for not meeting those expectations. Didn't you ever rebel against your parents' authority?"

"Once." Her voice contained a sadness. "I paid a

high price for it, too. No matter what Madison does, I'm not going to stop loving her."

Her answer surprised him. Like Madison, he'd always pictured Kelley as perfect, obedient, a little too good. "What did you do, Kelley?"

"It's not important, it's in the past."

"You've got this hangup about discussing the past—not just me but everything."

"I believe in moving on." She straightened in the seat as they neared the house. "She's here. On the porch. Thank God."

Before he'd come to a complete stop, Kelley was out the door and rushing up the walk. As he climbed out of the truck, he hit a number on his cell phone and waited for the officer on duty to pick up. "It's Morgan. Call off the search. We found Miss Gardner."

He hung up and clipped the phone back onto his belt. As he got closer, he could see Kelley kneeling in front of Madison. The porch light they'd left on had burned out, leaving only the corner streetlamp to provide light.

"You don't know who he was?" Kelley asked. Her relief at finding her sister home was apparently short-lived.

"Some guy. Chill. I'm okay."

"Chill? Did you leave your common sense in Dallas?" Kelley twisted around and looked up at Jack. "She hitched a ride with someone she didn't know." She turned back to her sister. "Madison, what were you thinking?"

"That I wanted to leave that boring scene. It wasn't until I got here that I remembered you hadn't given me a key."

Kelley stood and began searching through her purse. "I honestly don't know what I'm going to do about you, Madison."

Madison glared at Jack, defiant even in the darkness. "Guess you want to chew my butt."

"I think you know what you did was reckless. You don't need me to tell you that. I'm not trying to take her away from you, kid."

At his announcement, Kelley spun around. Madison snatched the keys from her hand, bolted for the door, unlocked it, disappeared inside, and slammed the door.

"What made you say that?" Kelley asked.

"She was engaged in an attention-getting ploy. Why do it unless she thought she needed to reel you back in?"

"Reel me back in?"

"She didn't like that we were dancing."

"She didn't like the whole situation. I should have left as soon as I realized that."

"You can't live your whole life around hers."

"Right now, I feel that I have to—for reasons you wouldn't understand. If you'll excuse me, I need to go deal with Madison."

"No. I won't excuse you."

In one smooth movement, he had her in his arms, and his mouth covered hers with a desperation that came from wanting too long, needing too badly. Her body sank against his in surrender, and it was the only encouragement he needed to deepen the kiss.

She tasted much as he remembered, her sweet fragrance filling his head with images of them writhing on the sheets, limbs entangled. He wanted to carry her to that bed he'd taken apart this afternoon, hauled over here, and put back together. Sheets or no sheets, he'd gladly take her there. Hell, he'd take her here if she were willing.

He'd been able to get every other female in his life out of his system—except for her. Even when it was over between them, even when he'd lost all hope of ever having her again, he hadn't been able to exorcise the memories of her, the desperate wanting of her.

Breathing harshly, his heart pounding, he drew back. "I know my timing is lousy, but I've wanted to do that since you first walked into my office."

Her breathing was equally labored, her sad eyes focused on him as she nodded. "You're right. It is lousy timing. But then it always is with us, isn't it?" She took a step back. "I'm sorry, Jack, I really have to deal with Madison right now."

She opened the door, stepped inside, and looked at him over her shoulder. "I appreciate all your help today."

She closed the door, leaving him with no choice except to head to his truck. She'd been hesitant to get involved with him nine years ago. She was reluctant now—although her kiss had certainly belied her words.

She was interested. She might not want to admit it, but she was definitely interested. And so was he. Unfortunately, he didn't have a clue about what he should do with that bit of knowledge.

Kelley was gripping the handle, her cheek pressed to the front door, listening for the indisputable rumbling of Jack's truck to fade down the street. She hadn't meant to let the kiss happen. Even in the shadows, she'd seen the intent in his eyes one second before his mouth had followed through.

She was still trembling from the impact.

Jack Morgan had certainly not forgotten how to kiss. If anything, like fine wine, he'd improved with age. He'd tempered his urgency with mastery.

He'd been totally in command, seducing every aspect of her being with nothing more than the patient, questing sweep of his tongue, the hot, pliant movement of his lips. His hands hadn't roamed. But she'd felt the strength in them as they'd pressed her body against his.

How easy it would be to fall under his spell once again.

But what they'd had before had only touched the surface of who each of them was. They were older now, more mature. What she needed was a deeper love, a more committed love, and that required delving deeply beneath the surface. Being completely honest. Accepting another's faults. Revealing insecurities, failures, mistakes.

She hated to admit it, but she'd never viewed them as equals before. She'd always seen herself as being in charge of the relationship, issuing demands, establishing guidelines that they needed to follow. To become involved with Jack now, she'd have to recognize him as an equal, a partner. The implications terrified her.

With Jack, she didn't think she could be completely honest. Nor did she think he had the capacity to accept her faults.

Not when he'd accepted absolute responsibility for raising his son.

She shoved unsettling thoughts of Jack to the back of her mind. She had more immediate, pressing concerns, and although she really had no desire to deal with them, she knew she had no choice. She'd put off the inevitable long enough. She walked through the living room to Madison's bedroom. She rapped once and opened the door.

She'd liked this house because none of the rooms—except for the master bedroom—had a lock on the door. Madison couldn't shut her out if she wanted to.

Madison already had her red lightbulbs in place, which gave the room an unnatural, eerie feel. She sat on the floor, her legs tucked beneath her as she rummaged through a box.

"What about respecting my privacy?" Madison muttered, her hands stilling although she refused to look at Kelley.

"How about respecting me? Madison, what you did tonight was another action in a long list of reckless behaviors. I know you've experimented with drugs. You dress up and go to bars. Get arrested. Walk away without letting me know you're leaving. I don't know what to do. You're sixteen, and I can't seem to make you understand that I worry about you, I love you more than is humanly possible, and I'm terrified of losing you. I've lost two fathers and my mother. You're all I have left."

Madison hung her head. "I hadn't thought about it like that."

"You don't think at all." Kelley dropped to her knees so she was closer to Madison. "You speak and act impulsively. Everything we do affects at least one other person. The world isn't made up of only you."

"Now you're getting preachy."

"Damn it, Madison, what do you want me to do?" She lunged to her feet and began to pace. "You tell me that you don't want me to be your mother, and then you do childish things. Running away tonight was incredibly stupid." Madison had put herself at risk for horrors that Kelley didn't even want to think about. She glanced around the room, looking for a weapon—and then she spotted it.

She took a deep, calming breath. "If you question my authority again, if you leave without telling me, if you don't straighten up—and I think you're smart enough to know exactly what I mean by that—I'm taking away your phone and your computer for a month."

"You can't do that! You can't cut me off from my friends in Dallas. I'll go insane."

"You can keep in touch the old-fashioned way: with pen, paper, and postage stamps. Or you can straighten up your act and keep your privileges. Your choice. But I'm warning you, I'm not kidding this time. This house was supposed to be a new start. Don't blow it."

Three seconds after she walked out, she heard Madison slam the door shut. Fine, let her stew for a while at the injustice of it all.

It was nearly midnight when Kelley crawled beneath the covers, weariness finally settling in. She'd been so wired after her confrontation with Madison that she'd had to work off some of her energy. She'd closed herself off in her bedroom and unpacked boxes, setting up her knickknacks, striving to feel more comfortable in the new house. Like Madison, she sometimes felt overwhelmed, needed to escape.

But right now, nothing felt like a sanctuary. Maybe that was part of Madison's rebelliousness. She didn't have a sanctuary, either.

Who was Kelley kidding? Jack was right. She was irritated that he could see so clearly what she couldn't. Irritated that he'd kissed her. Irritated that she'd let him and that she'd enjoyed it.

Irritated that part of her inability to settle into sleep had nothing to do with Madison and everything to do with Jack. She snuggled down deeper beneath the covers and, with a finger, outlined the lips he'd kissed. She could swear they still tingled.

Closing her eyes, she drifted off to sleep thinking about the one night they'd shared . . .

When the doorbell rang a little after midnight, Kelley knew who it was. She turned off the muted television, leaving only the flickering flames of the vanilla-scented candles to softly illuminate the apartment. The images on the TV had served as company while she'd waited, but she had music playing faintly in the background. Her expectations for this evening were probably far different from those of the young man who waited on the other side of her apartment door. From him, she expected neither flowers nor wine—he was, after all, underage—so she'd taken it upon herself to create the ambience she wanted. Moments like she imagined this one would be were far more important to women, anyway.

With her stomach fluttering, she walked across the living room. She'd been waiting, anticipation mingling with anxiety, not certain if the path she was about to travel was the right one, almost certain that it wasn't, but knowing that she really had no choice in the matter. Her heart had long ago decided her course.

Earlier in the evening, she had sat in a special section designated for the Hopeful High faculty and watched the procession of graduating seniors, with their black robes flapping at their calves and their yellow tassels swaying on one side of their black graduation caps. They'd paraded toward the front of the high school auditorium. The music teacher had enthusiastically played *Pomp and Circumstance,* and Kelley knew that she wasn't the only one clutching a tissue she'd pulled from her purse, hoping she could go a few more minutes without having to use it.

With the announcement of each senior's full name, the bittersweet moments had touched her more deeply than she'd anticipated they would. Applauding, she'd watched with swelling satisfaction and tears stinging her eyes as each student marched up the steps, crossed the stage, shook hands with the principal, and received a hard-earned diploma. Students she had taught. Students who had sat in her classroom, completed her homework assignments, and taken her exams.

She was incredibly proud of each and every one of them, had never felt more like a teacher, hoping she'd added to their lives in some small measure, knowing they'd permanently touched hers. She'd remember each and every one of them with fondness. Even the troublemakers, the difficult students, the ones who had challenged her with poor study habits.

Then Jack Morgan's name had been called, and the tears stinging her eyes spilled over onto her cheeks. Her greatest accomplishment. Her most satisfactory achievement. He'd actually managed to pass her class with a B average the last six weeks and had made an A- on the final exam.

And as impossible as it seemed, as wrong as it was, he'd somehow managed to capture her heart.

Following the ceremony, she'd come home to her apartment, knowing he'd be out celebrating. She wanted him to have this night of revelry, something he'd worked hard to earn.

And now he was here. She popped her knuckles and rubbed her damp palms over her jean-clad thighs. She'd considered wearing a silky nightgown, but she couldn't quite embrace the role of seductress, especially when she couldn't completely discharge the notion that she was corrupting him.

She almost laughed at that. Jack Morgan was the corrupting influence. He wasn't an innocent boy. She had a feeling his experiences went far beyond hers. With one more deep breath to steady her nerves, she opened the door.

The porch light cast a halo around him as he stood before her, his black graduation cap pressed against his chest, the yellow tassel dangling across his hand. The rebellious boy had doubt written all over his face.

She couldn't have sent him away if her life had depended on it.

In a silent invitation, she opened the door farther. He slipped through. With her heart thudding, she closed the door and turned to face him.

His familiar, cocky, confident grin slowly eased across his face as he extended his graduation cap toward her.

Hugging it against her chest, she felt the hot, stinging tears once again threaten. "I was so proud of you, Jack."

"Wouldn't have done it if it weren't for you." He cradled her face between his large, work-worn hands. "That day you came to the trailer, I'd made up my mind a few hours before you got there to drop out of school, go to work full-time, and make my way without a diploma. I thought nobody cared. Didn't think anything I did made a bit of difference to anyone." He pressed a kiss to the corner of her mouth. "But it mattered to you."

He kissed the other corner. "I didn't think graduation night would ever get here."

She heard the impatience in his voice, but she didn't want her time with him rushed. They'd waited too long, held too many emotions and too much desire at bay. She wanted tonight to be special, to be perfect in every way.

"I have a gift for you," she said, stepping away, watching his hands fall to his sides, aware of every nuance of his movements.

His grin increased, and pleasure sparked his eyes. "I'll just bet you do. I can't wait to get into it."

She didn't know whether to laugh or cry, supposed she should have expected his single-minded purpose. "No, a real gift."

She walked to the dining-room table and picked up the box, wrapped in blue paper decorated with graduation caps and scrolls. She now realized that the white bow was probably a little too feminine for Jack, but she'd wanted the package to look nice for him. Taking another deep breath to clear her nervousness, with hope against hope that her gift would please him, she extended it toward him.

She'd spent hours trying to determine what to give him. She'd wanted something special, something no one else would think of. Something not easily lost or given away. Something he might always possess to remind him of her when he wore it.

He stared at her offering as though he thought it might bite. "You didn't have to do that."

"I know. But I wanted to." She shook it at him. "Open it."

Worry and concern etched his brow. "I didn't bring anything for you."

"You're not supposed to give me anything. This is your graduation gift."

He stood there with his gaze flickering between her eyes and the wrapped package. He shoved his hands into the back pockets of his jeans.

She laughed lightly. "Jack, didn't you send out graduation announcements, get graduation . . ."

She realized then—with his uncomprehending stillness—that he hadn't. That he had no one, other than her, who cared one whit that he'd walked across the stage to receive his diploma. She thought her heart might shatter on the spot.

"It's just a little something I wanted you to have," she assured him, desperately wishing she could have done more for him.

He still appeared unsure as he took her gift. He gave her one more doubtful look before he tore off the paper she'd placed around the gift with such care. He opened the box, his confusion apparent by the deep furrowing of his brow.

"It's your class ring," she explained. "I noticed that you didn't have one. I ordered it special from the jewelry store in town. If it doesn't fit, they can adjust the size. Look." She removed the ring from the box and set the box aside. "I had your initials engraved inside."

He took the ring and slipped it onto his finger. "It fits." He lifted his gaze to her. "It means a lot to me that you . . . you know, gave me something."

Suddenly feeling bold in light of his discomfort, she wound her arms around his neck. "You're probably thinking a box of condoms would have been more practical."

One corner of his mouth hitched up. "Yeah, as a matter of fact, I was."

"It's waiting on the nightstand by my bed."

Suddenly, his mouth was on hers, his tongue sweeping through her mouth, his hands roaming over her back, up her sides, the heels of his palms pressing against her breasts. Then back down, cupping her bottom as though he wanted to touch all of her desperately.

His eagerness she'd anticipated. Hers took her by surprise. But then, they'd engaged in a sort of secretive foreplay for weeks now, like two strangers who slowly got to know each other through nontraditional means. Watching him in the hallways, knowing he was watching her. Listening as he read poetry with impatience, her reading it to the class as she imagined it had been written to be read.

Finding common ground in the most common of things. Music. A CD left in a drawer in her desk, a note indicating which song she was supposed to listen to. Wildflowers standing in a cracked earthen pitcher by her apartment door. Small things that always managed to startle her. And please her.

She suspected that he hadn't intended to romance her. Rather, he'd simply wanted to leave no doubt that he was in charge of the situation. Since he couldn't blatantly pursue, he'd taken a more subtle, but equally effective, approach. And he'd managed to win her over. Slowly, deliberately, persistently. She was probably insane, reckless, and out of her depth.

She had a feeling that tonight, he would be the teacher, she the student.

She felt the warmth of his hands against the skin beneath her shirt, felt the strength as he bracketed her body, felt the resolve as he drew her nearer and deepened the kiss with purpose.

She knew a moment's hesitation, a moment's doubt. A niggling at the back of her mind that maybe they were rushing into this night without a clear understanding of what it meant and where their actions might lead. She'd fallen into that trap once before, with another boy. When she'd been younger, more innocent.

This time was different. Her reasons were different. She felt for Jack what she'd never felt for another.

But were her feelings as strong as love? Or were they only infatuation? Knowing that the bad boy of town, the one every girl fantasized about and wanted, desired her.

As he pulled her shirt over her head, she no longer cared. He wasn't her student any longer. She'd accomplished the impossible. She'd given him a reason to pour his efforts into graduating. And if his reward was to be hers as well . . . so be it.

He was breathing harshly, staring at her, his eyes taking on a fevered glow. Slowly, he trailed his finger over the red lace of her bra. "You're so beautiful," he rasped.

She hadn't realized how much she'd wanted to meet with his approval.

He took hold of the clasp on the front of her bra. "I love front loaders."

She laughed for the joy of his predictability. His was the sort of comment she expected of Jack Morgan. Not flattery or sweet nothings but honest words with no hidden agenda. He'd always been upfront about what he wanted of her. She didn't blame him now for continuing in that vein.

With one quick twist of his fingers, she was free of the restraint, and his sturdy palms had replaced the frilly cloth. He dipped his head, outlining a nipple with his tongue.

She moaned, her limbs grew weak, and she tugged on his shirt. "Jack?"

He tore off his shirt and pulled her close, his

mouth plundering, his hands roaming, as he backed her into the bedroom, all the while maintaining as much contact as possible, exploring feverishly.

They tumbled onto the bed. Only then did he break away from her.

"Get your jeans off," he ordered as he quickly removed his. Sitting on the edge of the bed, laughing, he reached for the wrapped box on the nightstand. "Is this my other gift?"

He didn't wait for her answer but simply tore off the wrap, opened the box, and quickly put the first condom to use. He turned to her, his brow furrowing. He tugged on her jeans. "Don't go shy on me now."

She licked her lips. "Jack, I want this. I want you. I just don't want you to be disappointed because I don't have any real experience."

"Is this your first time?"

She shook her head. "But I've only done this once, and it was in the backseat of a Toyota. It was a night I've tried to forget."

Something darted into his eyes, something she would have never expected from this brazen boy who had defied her in the classroom: compassion.

"I promise it'll be good, Kelley," he whispered. It was the first time her name had rolled off his tongue. There was something seductive and warm in the way he spoke it, intimate, secretive.

He slid his hand beneath her hair, cupping her neck with his hand, his thumb stroking the soft underside of her chin. "Trust me."

She wanted to, she truly did. But she'd trusted someone else once before, and her trust had been misplaced. "I'm afraid, Jack."

He rolled over onto her until his body half covered hers. Lowering his head, he kissed her tenderly, hungrily. Above her waist, he stroked her bare skin; below her waist, he stroked her through her jeans. His hands were strong, his fingers sure. He rubbed his chest over her breasts, and she found herself arching toward him, striving to get closer.

"Trust me, Kelley," he repeated. "I'll never hurt you. I swear it."

The candles she'd lit earlier lent a soft, romantic touch to the room, causing shadows to dance over his face, over his body. There was so much tenderness in his voice that her heart melted. She nodded, and he gave her a slow, sensual grin.

"Now, these have to go," he whispered as he unzipped her jeans and began tugging them down.

She wiggled, pushing on them as he pulled. When her clothes were free, she lay there in the shadows, baring not only her body but her heart and soul. He ran his hand up her leg, across her hip, along her side, over her stomach. "So beautiful."

Then he stretched out, half his body covering hers, and his mouth blanketed hers with more heat than before, more determination, more skill. As though now he was holding nothing back, when she'd never realized he'd been holding anything back.

She scraped her fingers along his back, up his neck,

into his thick, curly hair. He growled, and she felt the rumble of his chest against her breasts. His hands seemed to be everywhere, touching her, fondling, kneading. Working her body into a fevered frenzy as she imagined he worked on cars to keep the engines purring.

She thought she might have purred herself. Her own sighs and moans mingled with his groans. They became a tangle of arms and legs, touching, reaching, exploring.

Then she felt the pressure between her thighs as he began pushing himself inside. She was aware of her body stretching to accommodate him, and then she was aware of nothing but the rightness of it as she tilted up her hips to welcome him fully, as she wrapped her legs around his waist, her arms around his shoulders.

He raised himself above her, his strokes long and sure, deep and strong, his gaze holding hers. As they found their rhythm, she moved against him, watching as his gaze intensified, his jaw clenched.

He pistoned into her, faster, faster, faster, as sensations within her began to mount. Pleasure spiraled outward as he carried her to the edge.

When she plummeted over, he followed.

Kelley jerked awake, her heart pounding, her breathing ragged, her skin damp. She was in the same bed but a different room, another time.

Another time. A different time.

Jack's involvement with Stephanie, their marriage, their child, Jack's custody of that child . . . all those different aspects had come together to create a barrier between them in ways she was only just beginning to understand.

She slipped her hand beneath her nightgown, her fingers stopping a little above her hairline. She couldn't feel the scar. It had faded over the years, but she knew it intimately, knew what it looked like without seeing it. She'd always thought it resembled a slight smile that someone would give over a joke that wasn't quite so funny.

If Jack discovered the scar, understood its ramifications, would he forgive her?

She doubted it. Not when she couldn't even forgive herself.

Chapter 10

Kelley sat at the table in the bay window of the kitchen, with the blinds raised so she could see the street, the intersection, and the houses on all the other corners and beyond. The scene, along with the hush of early morning, made for an extremely peaceful and calming atmosphere.

And she needed that tranquility after spending most of the night tossing and turning, growing hot and damp, dreaming of Jack. The morning following graduation, she'd awoken with him wrapped around her and her body sore. To her surprise, he'd been considerate, content simply to hold her that morning.

He'd wanted them to go out, but she still hadn't been comfortable with them being seen together. She didn't think anyone would believe she hadn't been involved with her student during the school year, and she'd had no desire to put her theory to the test.

"Maybe by the end of summer," she'd told him.

After accusing her of being ashamed of him, he'd left angry. By the time he'd returned the following night, she'd already heard the tentative rumors floating around town that he'd gotten Stephanie Townsend pregnant.

One look at his face when she'd opened the door, and she'd known that the rumors were true, that their relationship was over before it got a chance to fully begin. She'd been devastated by what she perceived as a betrayal.

The sound of bare feet on the tile had her turning her attention back to the present. She smiled at Madison. "Good morning, sleepyhead."

Madison grimaced, ran her hand through her short hair, and opened the refrigerator. "We need to go to the grocery store."

She brought out the orange juice, one of the few items that remained. Kelley had let the groceries dwindle, thinking it foolish to pack up and move replaceable items.

"We need to do a lot of things today."

Madison poured her juice and joined Kelley at the table, sitting across from her, placing her feet on the chair opposite the one that Kelley's feet rested on. Two women still needed four chairs at their table.

"How'd you sleep?" Kelley asked.

"Pretty good. When the wind blows, the limbs from the tree scratch up against the window. That was a little scary. I kept seeing skeleton hands."

"I'll see about hiring a tree trimmer."

"Who's going to mow the yard?"

"We'll need to get a lawn service. There are a lot of hidden expenses when you live in a house."

"I guess there's no point in fixing things up too much, since we'll be moving soon."

Kelley sighed. "Madison, we'll discuss moving in the spring. Until then, this is our home."

"What are we going to do with the front rooms?"

"For the time being, nothing. I don't think it's worth it to move any more furniture out of the storage unit in Dallas. I'm going to use the other bedroom as an office. We can divide it between us if you want."

"No, my bedroom is big enough. Much better than the apartment."

"I wasn't that crazy about the apartment, either. I think living here is going to be nice." She looked out the window, sipping her coffee.

"Kell?"

"Mmm?"

"I'm really kinda sorry about last night. I mean, I know I was a total butt, leaving without telling you and everything."

As far as apologies went, Kelley had heard more sincere ones, but she decided it was at least a start when the apology wasn't prompted.

"How about truly, absolutely, completely sorry?" Kelley suggested.

"If I'm *that* sorry, could Ronda come spend next weekend with me?"

Ronda Barnes was Madison's best friend. Kelley had never been able to determine how much Ronda's influence had been responsible for Madison's change in behavior. The only child of very wealthy parents,

Ronda tended to think the world revolved around her wants.

"Apologies shouldn't be conditional, Madison."

Madison rolled her eyes. "All right. I'm totally sorry about last night."

Kelley nodded. "I accept your apology."

"So, can Ronda come visit?"

Why did Kelley have the impression that her apology had still been conditional?

"Please? Yesterday, the guys were talking about the county fair. It's next weekend, and I was kinda thinking about going, but I don't want to go alone. It's probably lame, not nearly as good as the state fair. But it's something to do."

"Actually, the county fair is a lot of fun. I went when I was living here before."

"So, can we go? Can we invite Ronda? Please? I won't give you any more grief. I swear."

Kelley had told Madison that this house was a new beginning, for both of them, a chance to bond. She nodded. "All right. You can invite her, and we'll go to the fair."

"Yes!"

It was so rewarding to see Madison happy. "The airport is about forty-five minutes from here. Have her fly in Friday night, and we'll pick her up."

"Great! You're the best."

Funny how she didn't feel like the best. The best wouldn't still be trying to reconcile all the shameful things she'd done in her past.

Madison suddenly bolted upright, her feet hitting the floor. "Was that a black truck?"

"Sure looked like it." Kelley's heart had kicked up a notch when she spotted it driving by.

"Think it's the sheriff?"

Kelley shook her head. "Probably not. Haven't you noticed? Three-fourths of the vehicles in this town are black trucks."

"Right." Madison eased back into a lounging position, feet on the chair.

Then a bit of a mean streak hit Kelley. "Maybe it's Rick."

Madison stiffened. "No way." Her brow creased. "You think?"

The doorbell had them hopping out of their chairs, looking guilty and terrified at the same time. Then they broke into nervous giggles.

"We're a mess," Kelley acknowledged. "It's probably the neighborhood welcoming committee."

"On a Sunday morning?"

"Could be."

The doorbell chimed again. She tightened the sash on her robe, hastily combed her fingers through her hair, and walked to the front door. She peered through the peephole. At the sight of Jack standing on the other side, she didn't know whether to be pleased or angry. He really could be pushy when he wanted to be.

She glanced over her shoulder at Madison, who was anxiously awaiting the verdict. "It's Jack."

Madison rolled her eyes and did her little body shrug. "What's he want? I'm not apologizing again."

Kelly didn't know what to say to that declaration. She was certain Jack wasn't there for an apology. If anything, he was there because he'd slept as poorly as she had. She could only hope he wouldn't say anything in front of Madison about his parting kiss. She opened the door.

"Morning," he said before she could speak.

She had no luck at all suppressing the gladness that swept through her with the rumble of his deep voice and the slow smile that eased across his face like dawn easing over the horizon.

"What are you doing here?" she asked.

He held up a huge plastic dog dish. "I was sent out on doughnut reconnaissance, and I thought since I was in the neighborhood, I'd drop by and install your temporary security system."

She didn't try to keep the skepticism out of her voice. "First of all, there are no doughnut shops in the neighborhood. Secondly, what are you talking about?"

"Invite me in."

As if he were going to give her a choice. She opened the door farther and stepped back.

He walked through. "Hey, kid."

Kelley heard the censure in his voice, and, based on the way Madison was squirming, she had a feeling she heard it as well.

"I already apologized to Kelley, okay?" Madison said.

"Okay." Jack extended the dog dish toward her. "I brought you a security system. Fill this up with water, and put it out on the back patio."

"Why? We can't have pets here."

"Yeah, but a would-be burglar wouldn't know that, now, would he? He's going to choose the path of least resistance. He sees a dog dish in your backyard—a big dog dish—and not in your neighbors', where's he gonna go?"

"That's your security system?" Madison asked.

"Temporarily, although I imagine it works just about as well as the real thing."

Reaching out, Madison took the dish. "You know what I think? I think you just wanted an excuse to come see Kelley."

"Madison!" Kelley felt the heat rush to her face.

"You got a problem with that, kid?" Jack asked.

"Jack!" Kelley scolded.

Madison grinned. "I think Kelley does."

"Madison, take care of the dog dish," Kelley ordered.

Madison flounced into the kitchen. Then Kelley turned to Jack. "I appreciate how much you've helped us get settled in, but Jack—"

"Wanna hear about my dream?" he interrupted.

She could well imagine what it entailed. Their hot, damp bodies intertwined . . . She shook her head. "No, Jack, I really don't."

Madison walked past them and headed for the back door to put the dish on the patio.

"I appreciate your stopping by," Kelly began.

"Got any coffee?"

Unless the man was suffering from a severe case of allergies, he knew the answer, because the aroma still wafted through the house. She planted her hands on her hips. "I thought you were on a mission to retrieve doughnuts."

"I've got a few minutes."

"Okay. The trap is all set," Madison said as she came back into the living room. She plopped onto the arm of a chair, where she was visible and could look into the hallway where Jack and Kelley still stood. "So, how come you're doing so much for Kelley? I'd never go to this much trouble for one of my teachers."

Jack moved farther into the room as though an invitation had been issued. "You've never had a teacher you liked?"

Liked? Kelley thought. He liked her? Well, she'd known that, hadn't she? No, not really. She knew he'd been attracted to her physically back then—still was, apparently. But liked?

"I liked Miss Johnson," Madison admitted.

"There you go," Jack said, stepping farther into the room.

"But I wouldn't haul furniture for her and bring her a dog dish."

"You might when you get older," Jack said. "You'd be surprised how things change when you get older."

He has that right. Kelley moved past him. "Come on into the kitchen. I'll get you some coffee."

"Nice view. I didn't notice it yesterday," he said as he took the mug she offered him and leaned against the counter. "How's the unpacking coming along?"

"We're making progress." No tiny island in the middle of the kitchen to sit at, no way for him to lean over and tempt her. "Did you want to sit at the table?" she asked.

"No, I really can't stay very long. I am the dough-nut brigade."

"I miss Krispy Kreme," she admitted.

"You ought to try Karl's Bakery. They have these doughnuts that still have the hole in the center, and they plop this glob of chocolate icing on top of it. Jason's crazy about them."

"They sound sinful."

"Only a woman would associate food with sin."

She lowered her gaze, sipped her coffee, and tried not to think about what Jack would probably associate with sin. "You told Madison you liked your teacher. . . *me?*"

"You doubt it?"

She lifted her eyes to his. "I don't know, Jack." She bent forward so she could see through the doorway. Madison was nowhere to be seen. She looked back at Jack. "I just thought it was . . . hormones, I guess."

"A lot of it was," he admitted.

"On top of that, you're sexy as hell, and you know it. I always felt out of my league around you. As though you had something to prove, and I was the prize."

"I did. You were."

She should have taken satisfaction in his answer, in knowing she was right, all those years ago, when she'd been falling in love with him, worrying the entire time that she would end up being nothing more than a notch on Jack Morgan's bedpost. The only time she'd ever gotten drunk was the night he got married. Giving him up forever, thinking of him being in bed with another woman on his wedding night had hurt so damned much.

He set the mug aside and crossed over to where Kelley stood. She held his gaze, strengthening her resolve not to fall for him again, to maintain her distance. With the palm of his hand, he cradled her cheek and touched his thumb to her lips.

"You don't get it, do you?" he asked quietly. "I've still got something to prove. And you're still the prize."

Before she could stammer a protest, he'd walked out of her kitchen.

"So long, kid," he called out.

"Hey!" Madison said. "I was thinking you should have brought a dog to go with that dish."

Kelley heard Jack's laughter.

"Thought you said pets weren't allowed," he challenged.

"Yeah, but you're the sheriff. You can break laws and get away with it."

"I'll think about it."

She heard the door close. What did Jack have to

prove? And why did she suddenly feel twenty-two again, honored that Jack Morgan would deem her worthy of his attention?

"Are you sure there's nothing between you and the sheriff?" Madison asked from the doorway.

Kelley picked Jack's mug off the counter and dumped his coffee into the sink. "I'm sure."

With a sigh, she rinsed out his mug. Who was she kidding? There would always be something between her and Jack. A history, without a future.

Chapter 11

There was something enchanting about a Texas county fair. From the Longhorn cattle housed in paddocks on either side of the entryway gates to the people sporting their best cowboy hats and their polished snakeskin boots. It just seemed wholesome and, if not immaculate, at least fun, Kelley thought as she handed Madison and Ronda their entry tickets.

"Are we going to split up?" Ronda asked.

They'd picked her up at the airport yesterday evening. She and Madison were still laughing and talking when Kelley had gone to bed at midnight. They'd been laughing and talking most of the day. Kelley was so relieved to see Madison enjoying herself.

"Let's stay together until I get familiar with the layout of the fairgrounds, and we can figure out where to meet up later," Kelley suggested.

Following the crowd through the gates, they were immediately greeted with another ticket booth, this one selling individual tickets for the various games and rides. "Looks like we have to purchase tickets for the rides and games," Kelley told them.

"Just like the state fair," Madison said.

"My dad says they do that so you'll spend more money," Ronda announced. "You won't hesitate to give the guy at the Tilt-a-Whirl six tickets, but you'd think twice about handing him a dollar fifty."

"Well, since this is Madison's first county fair, I think we should go hog wild. Let's start with twenty dollars' worth." While she stood in line to get the tickets, the girls moved a short distance away. She so enjoyed seeing the excitement on Madison's face. She wished she knew how to keep it there, short of moving back to Dallas. The week had gone remarkably well, though: no tantrums, no late-night phone calls, no arguments. Maybe they were finally settling in; maybe Madison would be content now.

After she bought the tickets, Kelley walked over to the girls and divided the tickets among them, keeping only a few for herself. She wasn't into the games or the rides. For the most part, she simply enjoyed the atmosphere, being part of it, watching the people. "Where shall we start?"

"The Midway," Ronda said.

"You don't want to visit the livestock?" Kelley asked.

"Why would we want to go through stinky buildings?" Ronda asked.

"How about the crafts?" Kelley asked.

Both girls shook their heads as though she were suggesting a fate worse than death. "The Midway it is," she conceded.

Maybe she was getting old, but going through the arts-and-crafts buildings really appealed to her. And she wouldn't have minded looking at the livestock, either. Some of her students had entries there.

Twilight was easing in. Madison had wanted to make sure that they'd be there when it got dark. Kelley had to agree that the lights of the Midway at night carried a special magic. She could hear the music of the carousel and the barking of the carnies as they neared the entrance to the Midway. The atmosphere was very different from the rest of the fair. Not nearly as relaxing. Unconsciously, she wrapped her fingers around the strap on her fanny pack. She always worried in crowds that someone could unsnap it and run off with it before she was aware of what was going on.

The sheriff's department was out in full force, along with many police officers from neighboring towns. Their presence was reassuring, and yet a part of her resented that people behaved in such a way that law-enforcement personnel were needed for what should have been nothing more than a night of fun. She wondered briefly if Jack were working there, then decided if he was working anywhere, he'd be working in Hopeful.

Besides, she really didn't want to run into him there. It was her night with the girls—even though she had the impression that they wanted to get rid of her as soon as possible. She couldn't blame them for wanting to be off by themselves—they were young, in tune with each other, obviously wanting to experience aspects of the fair that she wasn't. Once they parted ways, she'd simply spoil herself with the crafts and the animals and the cotton candy until it was time to meet up again. The important thing was that Madison was enjoying herself, not that Kelley was feeling a little left out because she didn't have a best friend nearby to share the night with.

She didn't think she'd developed a deep friendship since high school. Ever since Madison had been born when Kelley was fifteen, she'd wanted to spend whatever free time she had with her. She'd been a marvel to watch, discovering the world around her. Her parents had adored her. With everyone doting on Madison as much as they had, was it any wonder that she'd turned out to be a bit spoiled and accustomed to having her own way?

"Oh, let's do this!" Ronda cried. "I want one of those big bears."

Madison tugged Kelley toward one of the booths where the entertainment involved throwing baseballs at milk bottles. It looked so easy, but Kelley knew looks at a carnival were greatly misleading. She'd tried this particular game long ago and come away with nothing but a handful of cheap keychains.

"Those things are somehow rigged," she told the girls as they approached. "They're impossible to knock over."

"So? Let's try. Let's all try," Ronda said.

Not wanting to be the spoilsport, Kelley reluctantly handed over four tickets for three balls, trying not to think about how easily she'd given up a dollar for what she knew would result in failure. After all, the object of the game wasn't necessarily to win but to have fun trying.

Madison squealed as she knocked over one bottle. The man set the bottle back on top, grinning at her with stained, crooked teeth. "You have to knock all three bottles over with one ball to get the big bear."

"That's not fair," Madison protested.

He handed her a keychain and winked at her. "Don't throw the ball so hard."

Two throws later, she had two more keychains. Ronda's luck wasn't any better. The girls were busy tearing off more tickets, getting more balls, when Kelley tossed her balls. One missed completely. The next caused a bottle to rock and settle back into place. The third one grazed the top bottle and made it topple. She took her keychain with grace.

"You still throw like a girl," a deep voice whispered near her ear as warm breath skimmed along the side of her neck.

Jack. How long had he been watching her? She spun around, her heart pounding with the force of the adrenaline rush his nearness caused. "That's because I *am* a girl, in case you haven't noticed."

"Oh, I noticed."

His eyes held a predatory gleam. Nothing subtle about Jack's intentions. When he was interested, he made sure they were known. She could so quickly stumble out of her element with him—again.

He was wearing jeans, a denim jacket over a cambric shirt, and a black hat. Not in uniform. Obviously, he wasn't working, unless they had some officers working undercover, which she seriously doubted.

"I didn't expect to see you here," she said.

"I brought the boys." He tipped his head to the side. "That's them shooting BB guns at metal ducks and rabbits."

She looked toward the nearby shooting gallery. She saw two blond-haired boys who looked to be about eight. Like Jack, they both wore denim jackets. They were shooting, laughing, pointing at each other's successes and misses. She'd expected Jack's son to have hair as black as Jack's, to resemble his father to such a degree that she'd spot him right off.

"Which one is Jason?" she asked.

"The one on the right."

She heard the pride and love reflected in his voice. The boy was the paler of the two, his blond hair almost white. He looked so incredibly happy. Why couldn't Madison laugh with such abandon?

"Oh, Jack, he's precious."

"He's a good kid."

Having apparently used up all their shots, the boys turned away from the booth at the same time. She couldn't get over how cute Jack's son was. But seeing him completely and not from a disadvantageous angle, she was surprised by how little he resembled Jack. Her memory of Stephanie was faulty, because she didn't think she saw much of Stephanie in the boy, either.

The boys rushed up to Jack.

"We're all out of tickets, Dad," Jason said. "Can we get some more?"

"Sure," Jack said as he reached into his back hip pocket and brought out his wallet. "Jason, this is Miss Spencer."

The boy's dark eyes were alight with joy. It was silly, but she'd expected to see Jack's startling blue eyes within that young face.

"Hi," Jason said without apparent discomfort, as though having his dad introduce him to women were par for the course.

"Hello," Kelley said.

"This is Riker," Jack said, pointing toward the other child. "I mentioned him before."

"Yes, I remember. Hello," Kelley said.

The boy nodded, bounced on the balls of his feet, nudged his friend.

"Dad? Tickets?" Jason reminded Jack impatiently.

Jack handed him a twenty. "Straight to the ticket booth and back, no detours."

"Yes, sir," the boys said in unison before scampering away.

Jack turned his intense blue gaze on her. "If I could bottle their energy, I'd be rich."

She was struck with the thought that he might be richer than he realized.

"Hey, Sheriff," Madison said.

"Hey, kid, fixing to open up a keychain shop?" Jack teased.

"Ha ha," Madison said. "Don't suppose you'd care to try and win us one of those big bears?"

"Not on your life. I managed to do it once about nine years ago, and it cost me nearly a hundred dollars for something I could have bought in the store for less than twenty."

Madison jerked her attention to Kelley and then back to Jack. "It wasn't a purple bear, was it?"

"Don't remember what color it was."

"Kelley has a big purple bear she keeps in the corner of her room. You didn't see it when we were moving because she'd already packed it up."

"Doubt that was it. I gave my bear to a girl I was trying to impress."

But it was the same bear. He'd run across her at the fair. It was before she'd ever gone to his trailer, before she'd tried to get his mother involved. He'd had a girl nestled up against his side, his arm slung across her shoulders. Kelley had been trying to win a big bear at a bottle toss similar to this one. Her luck had been just as atrocious then as it was tonight. When she'd gone into her classroom the following Monday morning, the bear had been sitting in the chair at her desk. And she'd known who'd put it there—even though it came with no note, no message.

The boys returned with their tickets, hopping from foot to foot, obviously anxious to move on to the next bit of entertainment.

"Can Ronda and I go off by ourselves now?" Madison asked. "We can meet you at the entrance to the Midway when it's time to go."

"Okay. Midnight," Kelley said. "Meet me at the front ticket booth."

"No!" Both girls groaned and looked like twins as they did a similar body shrug.

"We want to stay until it closes," Madison said.

"That's two o'clock," Kelley reminded her. "Way past your curfew. Meet me at the front ticket booth at midnight."

"But, Kell—"

"Midnight, or we can leave now, Madison. We had an agreement."

Madison rolled her eyes. "You're being unreasonable. Sheriff, what do you think?"

"If you were with me, you'd be leaving at ten."

Madison groaned. "You never take my side. All right, Kelley, we'll meet you at midnight." Her voice left no doubt that she was being coerced into agreement.

"We've got our cell phones, so call me if there's any problem."

"Chill. There's not going to be any problems."

Refraining from adding another caution to be careful, she watched the girls wander away. She didn't want to be overprotective, but it was so hard not to worry.

Turning, she found Jack still standing there. She thought she detected a spark of admiration in his eyes, probably because she'd stood her ground with Madison. She hated to admit to herself that if he hadn't been standing there, she might have caved and allowed the two o'clock departure that Madison wanted.

"Want to tag along with me and the boys?" he asked.

Nodding distractedly, she looked back in the direction where Madison had disappeared. "It's so hard to let them go."

"She'll be fine," Jack said quietly. He put his arm around her. "How'd you like for me to impress you by winning you a big bear?"

As the night wore on, he did impress her. Not so much because of the big blue bear she carried—he'd won it throwing baseballs at milk bottles—or the enormous stuffed pink poodle nestled beneath *his* arm— he'd won that tossing darts and graciously offered to cart it around for her.

He impressed her simply because he was a great deal of fun to be with. They'd never had an opportunity to date, and although they were trying to keep up with two boys who seemed to have boundless energy, Kelley couldn't help but feel a little as though they were shifting away from the past and tonight she was seeing a side to Jack that had eluded her before.

Jack insisted they try every game that was offered. He didn't care if the games were rigged, if the chances of losing far exceeded the opportunities to win. "Just for the fun of it," he'd say.

And it was fun. They'd get competitive with the boys, competitive with each other. She couldn't remember the last time she'd laughed until her sides hurt or smiled until her jaw ached.

When they weren't throwing balls, tossing darts, or picking up floating ducks from the narrow pond, they were eating. Hot dogs, corn dogs, candied apples, caramel apples, cotton candy. She didn't know where the boys and Jack put it all.

"Hey, Dad, is it time for us to do the rides yet?" Jason asked just before he shoved a billowy cloud of cotton candy into his mouth.

"Not yet," Jack said. "Let's go see the livestock, then I'll take everything out to the truck. *Then* we'll do the rides." He teasingly snitched some of Kelley's cotton candy. "If that's all right with you."

"I was wondering what you were going to do with all these stuffed animals."

In addition to the two huge ones he'd won for her, he'd helped each boy win a smaller one of his own. Riker had a gorilla, and Jason had a green, big-headed thing that she thought was some sort of alien.

"There is a method to my madness," he assured her. "I think the guys in the booths let people win more easily early on in the evening. We're a walking advertisement for the odds of winning."

"You're like a big kid here."

His bright smile subtly turned into one that carried adult promises. "I'm far from being a child."

Shaking her head slightly, she tore her gaze from

his powerful one. He had eyes that could hold a woman captive and melt her resolve, make her realize that being with him was where she wanted to be.

After darkness completely descended, the lights of the Midway beamed a little more brightly, warmed and excited, and invited in the fun. After Jack had taken all the stuffed animals to the truck, he, Kelley, and the boys had shored up their energy with salted pretzels, more cotton candy, and another round of corn dogs. Then they'd headed for the rides.

They'd walked through the crazy house, where floors and walls moved, mirrors reflected distorted shapes, and flashing lights created strange illusions. They'd ridden the Tilt-a-Whirl, the twister, and an awful swinging Viking ship that had made Kelley fear she was going to bring up the latest barrage of carnival food that had invaded her stomach. She couldn't decide why carnivals made the most unattractive-looking food appear appealing.

Kelley had determined quite quickly that the big roller coaster was holding the boys' main interest. But it was to be the last ride of the night. A reward for good behavior.

As they stood in line to ride the Ferris wheel, she couldn't help but reflect on Jack's parenting style. He seemed to come by it naturally. While she struggled with every aspect of taking care of Madison, he had a comfortable rapport with the boys. Friendly yet never letting them forget that he was the parent.

"I don't suppose when we're finished here, we could ride the carousel," Kelley said.

Both boys looked as though they might be ill.

"That's a sissy ride," Jason said.

"For babies," Riker concurred.

Jack grinned at her. "If it was just you and me, babe, I'd take you."

And she knew without a doubt that he would. He'd ride the sissy ride with her. When the breeze had begun to turn cooler, he'd given her his denim jacket. And they were holding hands.

"Is the coaster next, Dad?" Jason asked.

Jack gave a long, slow nod. "If you boys are ready to call it a night."

They looked at each other, a silent communicating that Kelley had seen them do often throughout the evening. It was almost as if they were twins, so in tune with each other.

Finally, Jason turned his attention back to Jack. "Yeah, we're ready for the coaster."

"All right. Soon as we're done with the Ferris wheel," Jack said.

The boys did a little knuckle-knocking thing that Kelley figured represented a high five—the popular means of expressing oneself in her day.

"They are so cute," Kelley said.

"Give them a few years. The teen years are hard on guys."

"Oh, and you think they're easy on girls?"

"I think adolescence sucks. Period."

The Ferris wheel began its slow unloading-and-loading process. The boys clambered onto the bench seat.

"No craziness, now," Jack called out to them. "I'll be right behind you, so I can see everything you do."

Grinning, they waved as the wheel carried them up. The next compartment fell into line. Kelley slid onto the cold metal seat. Jack joined her. The metal bar was slammed into place. A jolt, the seat swung slightly, and she watched as the ground moved away from her.

"Have I mentioned that I'm afraid of heights?" she asked.

He placed his arm around her. "I won't let you fall."

He said it with confidence, as though he had the power to save her if the seat came loose—while he absolutely couldn't.

"It's silly, I know it's silly," she said as she took a deep breath.

"So why'd you agree to go on the ride with us?" he asked.

"Just caught up in the moment, I guess."

The ride jerked to a stop, and she slammed her eyes closed. "I hate this part."

"Think about something else."

Opening her eyes, she turned to him. "I can't believe the patience you have with the boys."

"I'm sorta reliving my own childhood through them, I guess. I always wanted to come to the fair but never had anyone interested in taking me. The year I turned sixteen and got my driver's license, I came every night. I barely had enough money for a ticket to get in, but that didn't matter. I just liked being here, being part of it all."

"Did you ever think about running off with the carnival?"

"Sure, but I figured working at the carnival wasn't nearly as much fun as playing at it."

The Ferris wheel started up again.

"Did your mother ever return to Hopeful?"

"Nope. I don't seem to have much luck at holding onto women."

"I don't think you should count your mother or Stephanie in that equation."

"Where do you fit in the equation?"

No longer sure, she simply shook her head. "I don't know." She turned the conversation away from her and back to the boys. "You seem to have given Jason a strong foundation."

"I tried to. My old man bailed out when I was born. Took off for parts unknown. At least, that's what my mom always said. I didn't want that for Jason." He held her gaze. "But sooner or later, he's going to start asking questions that I'm not going to know how to answer."

"Is he the reason you took psychology courses?"

"No, I actually took them to help me with law enforcement."

"Where did you find the time?"

"Correspondence courses, classes, and summer school. Serena was a big help, watching Jason whenever I needed her to."

She grinned. "Sounds like a lot of psychology classes."

"They weren't all psych courses. I earned a degree in criminal justice."

Surprised by what he'd said, she stared at him. "You earned a degree?"

"BA. But you want to hear the real kicker?"

She nodded.

"I'm thinking of going for my master's."

"Oh, Jack." She was beginning to think she hadn't known him at all. He'd accepted the responsibility of raising his son as a single parent. And from what she'd witnessed tonight, she knew beyond a doubt that he was a good parent. He'd gotten a higher education, had achieved far more than she'd ever expected of him. "I'm so proud of you. I wish I'd been there to see you get your diploma."

"I wish you'd been there, too. I worked my butt off for the damn thing."

She could well imagine that he had. A single parent, working, going to school. While she'd recognized that Jack had a strength of character that he kept hidden, she hadn't realized he had such a driving need to succeed, a determination to better his life to the extent that he had. "You're a remarkable man, Jack."

"Still scared?" he asked.

She nodded slightly. She was terrified. Not of the

ride but of where her heart was leading her—toward this man.

He cupped her cheek, tightened his hold on her, and drew her closer. "I'm in a damned-if-I-do, damned-if-I-don't place," he said roughly just before he lowered his mouth to hers.

He tasted of cotton candy, strange considering that the heat of his kiss could melt sugar. He boldly swept his tongue through her mouth. She thought his kiss alone would have made her dizzy, but with the breeze flowing around her and the big wheel circling, she was certain it was only her imagination that made it seem as though the ride were spinning out of control.

More than likely, it was she. With one hand, she clutched his shoulder, while fisting the other around his shirt. She leaned into the kiss as though they weren't adults, circling high above the ground in a creaking, swaying metal seat.

The wheel jerked to a halt. Dazed, Kelley leaned back, her lips swollen and tingling. Jack slowly stroked the edge of his thumb over her bottom lip.

"The ride's almost over," he said.

She had a feeling it was only just beginning.

Chapter 12

"Home sweet home."

Jack shifted his gaze to Kelley. Even with the street-lights, the porch light, and the outside light, he couldn't see into her eyes, couldn't tell what her first impression of his home was. Within the truck, her face was nothing more than shadows.

His one-story house represented middle-class America. For him, it had been a gigantic leap up the social ladder. But for Kelley, it probably wasn't too impressive. She'd always had this air about her that spoke of wealth, a subtle thing that indicated an absence of hard times.

"Let me get Riker to his mom, then maybe you'd like to come inside while you're waiting for Madison. See what I've done with the place."

"I'd like that," she said softly.

He climbed out of the truck, walked around to the passenger side, and opened the door for her. Once she'd stepped out, he opened the half-door and lifted a sleeping Riker into his arms.

The poor kid had hurled chunks after the roller-coaster ride. Plans had changed at that moment.

Kelley had offered to ride shotgun in case either of the boys got sick on the way home. She'd called Madison with the change in plans and instructions to pick Kelley up on the way home—at midnight.

Jack turned in time to see Serena flying out of her house, wearing her robe and fuzzy slippers as she tore across the front yard, a woman with a purpose. Jack had felt obligated to call her and tell her about her son's upset stomach. He should have known she'd react as though he'd called to announce that Riker had contracted SARS.

"How is he?" she asked when she got close enough to press her hand to her son's forehead.

"Fine. I think it was just the excitement—"

"*That* followed by a half-dozen hot dogs and no telling what else. I know you, Jack Morgan. Junk food is the bane of your existence."

The last thing he needed was a dressing down, especially in front of Kelley. "Kelley, this is Serena, Riker's mom."

Serena turned as though just realizing Kelley was standing there. When her son was involved, the woman tended to narrow her focus way down, as though automatic blinders suddenly emerged from the side of her head. Jack worried about that aspect of her personality sometimes, even though he knew it was really none of his business.

The women greeted each other, and Jack thought he could sense a subtle sizing up. Men were never that restrained.

"Let me help Serena get Riker to bed, then I'll be back for Jason," Jack told Kelley. Although he hadn't gotten sick, Jason had fallen asleep on the drive home, no doubt a result of the late night and all the excitement.

"I'll keep an eye on him," Kelley promised.

Jack liked the sound of that, her keeping watch over his son. He wouldn't mind making it a permanent arrangement, although he figured she'd bolt if he shared that little tidbit with her. He headed for Serena's house with Serena keeping pace beside him, her robe flapping at her calves.

"I didn't realize there was a new woman in your life. You've been holding out on me, Jack," she scolded once they were no longer within Kelley's earshot.

"Not really. It's a long, complicated story."

"I see. And you think I have a short attention span?"

He chuckled low. "No, I just don't have everything sorted out in my own mind yet."

Serena opened the door, and Jack slipped into the house. From habit, he turned toward the stairs. He was as comfortable in Serena's house as he was in his own.

"Kelley? The name's familiar. She's not the one—"

"Yeah, she is," he interrupted. She knew a little of his past with Kelley. She also knew about his tattoo. Steve had razzed him about it unmercifully.

He made his way into Riker's room. The kid's bed was already turned down. He laid Riker on Spider-

Man sheets that matched Jason's and stepped back, watching as Serena fussed over her only child. Riker moaned, yawned, and squirmed, never opening his eyes while his mother removed his clothes and brought the covers up to his chin.

Jack watched, mesmerized. Sometimes, guilt assaulted him because Jason didn't have a mother to tuck him in at night and to do all the little things moms did that made life special. For all of his and Jason's boasting that they liked being two males living by themselves, Jack had a feeling they'd both welcome the comforts that a woman would provide as a mother to Jason, a wife to Jack.

Serena turned to him. "Thanks for bringing him home."

The original plan had been to let him spend the night with Jason. "Sorry I didn't pay more attention to how much they ate." He followed her out of the room. "So, what'd you do tonight?"

She glanced over her shoulder at him. "Took a bubble bath. Soaked in the tub with candles glowing, devoured a box of chocolates, and read a romance novel."

"These nights when I have Riker, you're supposed to go out and enjoy yourself."

They reached the living room. "I did enjoy myself. It's not often that I can curl up and read a book in one sitting."

She picked a book off the coffee table and extended it toward him. "You're going to love this one."

He looked at the cover. A scantily clad woman leaning into a man who'd lost his shirt somewhere along the way. It screamed romance novel. He patted his jeans pockets, his shirt. No hiding places. "I'll pick it up tomorrow."

She narrowed her eyes. "Because there's a woman waiting by your truck? Jack, Jack, Jack, you've got to come out of the closet, my friend."

Leaning toward her, he bussed a quick kiss across her cheek. "Maybe tomorrow."

"She'd be impressed. You could read the hot parts together. That's what Steve and I used to do." She shook her head quickly and flapped her hand at him. "Go on, get out of here."

He squeezed her hand, knowing that after all these years, it still hurt her when she thought of her husband. "I'll come by tomorrow."

"You do that, because I want to hear all about Kelley."

" 'Night." He turned to go.

"Jack?" He stopped and looked back over his shoulder.

"Is she special?"

He nodded. "Yeah, she is."

Kelley sat in the truck, her arms tucked up against her ribs, her attention focused on the little boy who sat opposite her, his head against the window, his mouth slightly open, his eyes closed. She must have thought of Jack and his child a thousand times over the years.

She hadn't expected in the space of one night for him to steal her heart. In that respect, he'd definitely taken after his father.

She heard movement and turned her head to the side. She saw Jack striding across the moonlit grass. Just the sight of him could make her heart trip over itself with joy, and yet something else was settling deep within her. He'd matured far more than she had, had accepted responsibility for his child, a town, a nation. It frightened her to realize how much she was coming to care for him again.

Only it wasn't really *again*. She'd never felt this strongly toward him, this deeply. Her love for him before had more closely resembled infatuation, an attraction to the bad boy because for the most part she'd always been so sickeningly good.

"He still asleep?" Jack asked as he neared.

"Yes."

He extended his keys toward her. "Can you get the door for me while I carry him in?"

"Sure." She took the keys and stepped out onto the drive.

He leaned into the truck. She heard Jason mumble.

"Shh," Jack murmured. "We're home. Let's get to bed."

When he eased out of the truck, he was holding his son, the boy's head nestled against his shoulder as though they'd both been in this position a thousand times. Kelley led the way up the walkway, stepped onto the porch, inserted the key, and opened the front door.

She followed him inside. On a table nestled between a recliner and a couch, a lamp had been left on to send a soft glow over the room. Along one wall was an entertainment center with a huge television nestled in its center. Boys and their toys. It was obviously important to their existence.

She followed Jack down the shadowy hallway to a room at the end. She waited in the doorway while he laid his son on the bed and switched on a lamp. Spider-Man leaped to life on the comforter, on the curtains, on the wall.

The bed was in the shape of a sports car. Books lined shelves along one wall. Matchbox cars rested on top of a toy box which she was certain was full of other toys. A computer sat on a desk in the corner. In the opposite corner was a rocking chair, and Kelley could well imagine Jack sitting there gazing on his son while he slept.

Model fighter jets and fictional aircraft—the *Enterprise,* the *Millennium Falcon*—were suspended from the ceiling. The room was a boy's paradise.

She turned her attention to Jack and watched as he undressed the child with such gentleness that Jason barely stirred. When nothing remained but Spider-Man underwear, Jack brought the covers up to his son's shoulders, leaned low, and kissed his brow. "Sleep tight, bud."

" 'Night, Dad," Jason murmured with a yawn.

Kelley's heart contracted and expanded. Tears stung her eyes. Of all the things she'd expected of Jack, such fatherly devotion had never been one of them. She'd hoped he'd be a good father, but she'd never truly *expected* it of him because of the harsh upbringing he'd obviously had. But he'd risen above it.

Jack turned off the lamp and joined Kelley in the hallway. "Want a drink while you're waiting?"

"Yeah," was all she could manage to say.

A corner of his mouth hitched up. He reached into the bedroom, grabbed the door handle, and pulled it closed. "So we won't disturb him," he offered.

She wasn't certain how they would disturb him if all they were going to do was some quiet talking.

"What do you think of the place?" he asked as he led her into the kitchen and switched on the light.

Homier than she'd expected it to be. The refrigerator was covered with pictures obviously drawn by a child, held in place with magnets that touted "What I did in school today" or were souvenirs from various vacation spots or outings. A large bulletin board on one wall displayed other schoolwork, reminders about PTA meetings and other school functions, a list of important phone numbers. Jason was obviously the center of Jack's world.

She could see in his eyes that her answer mattered to him, but she didn't know how to sum up everything she was seeing, all she was feeling. "It's a very male house," she said. "But there's a lot of love here."

He opened the refrigerator. "Beer okay?"

"It'll be fine. Madison will be the designated driver."

He uncapped a bottle and handed it to her. "Overall, the house doesn't have all the little frilly gewgaws that women like."

She grinned. "I think the picture in the dining room of the dogs playing poker is very classy."

He grimaced. "Serena gave me a hard time about that one."

"You two seem very close," she said. The depth of their friendship was obvious. Although she'd sensed that Serena had been surprised by her presence, she hadn't thought the woman felt threatened.

"We've been through a lot together," Jack said. "Let's go sit in the living room."

She wasn't quite in the mood to sit—not just yet. She wandered around the room, looking at photos in a haphazard assortment of frames. None of the frames matched, leaving her with the impression that he cared more about displaying the photo than having any sort of decorative scheme. Jason was the center of every picture: alone, with Riker, sometimes with Jack. Always smiling, always happy. What a legacy to hand down to a child, a legacy she wasn't giving Madison.

She felt Jack come up behind her.

"I've never been good with the photo album thing," he said quietly. "Don't have the patience for it, so we always pick a favorite out of the roll and frame it, stick it on the shelf."

"I like it. It's . . . real. It's so obvious that you enjoy being together." She turned to face him. "That's a wonderful gift to your son, Jack. I don't know if you realize that."

"It's mutual. He's a great kid." He tugged on her hand. "Now, come on, come sit down."

She joined him on the couch, took one sip of the beer, decided she wasn't really in the mood for it, and set her bottle aside.

"Not thirsty?" he asked.

"Not really. I was just being polite." She shifted on the couch until she was facing him. "I enjoyed tonight, Jack."

"I liked having you with us," he said quietly, running his hand along her arm, threading his fingers through hers, and bringing her hand to his lips.

She felt the dew of his heated breath against her skin. "I'm scared, Jack."

Stilling, he held her gaze. "Of what?"

"Nine years ago, we were both incredibly young. I didn't feel young then, but looking back from where I now stand, I can see that I was remarkably . . . innocent, naive. Although neither of those descriptions is exactly right. I was just young.

"When I heard that you'd gotten Stephanie pregnant—" She pulled her hand free of his and balled it against her stomach. "You'd told me you loved me, Jack. And then you turned around that very night and took her to bed. It hurt so damn much."

"I'd bared my heart, and you told me that you didn't want to hear it, because you were my god-damned teacher. 'Don't say that, Jack,' you said. 'I don't want to hear *that*. You shouldn't be saying *that*.' "

She remembered her words all too clearly. The

elation of knowing he loved her, the anxiety because she knew he should never have had the opportunity to fall in love with her. Her emotions had been in turmoil, her culpability in question, her shame intensified, because she'd become involved in his struggles, couldn't turn her back on him when his mother had, and had unwittingly led him on—a student. She'd allowed a relationship to develop. No matter how unrequited it might have been, the potential for harm was there.

So she'd turned him away in the darkened stairwell that night, turned him away and straight into Stephanie's arms.

"I wanted to be with you. We were six weeks from graduation. I didn't think it mattered."

"But it did matter, Jack. You were still my student."

"I'll concede, now that I'm older and have a few years behind me, that you were right. But when I was nineteen, I got angry. I was hurt. I didn't understand. Stephanie was mad, too. She'd had a fight with her old man. So we were two frustrated kids, parked out by the creek . . . one thing led to another. Regardless of my reasons, regardless of the final outcome of my marriage to Stephanie, on prom night, when temptation came knocking, I opened the door." He trailed his finger along her chin. "Maybe I did it because I *did* want to hurt you."

"Well, you succeeded."

"And I'm sorry as hell that I did, but I'm not the same guy that I was that night."

"Don't you think I can see that? But neither am I the same girl who opened the door. You're projecting what you experienced back then onto the present: the excitement, attraction—"

"Are you saying there's no attraction on your end?"

"No, I'll admit there's plenty of attraction. But you're not going to get into my pants as easily this time."

"It wasn't easy before. You made me graduate from high school, for God's sake."

Reaching out, she combed her fingers through his hair. He'd jumped through every hoop she'd put before him. He'd grumbled enough while doing it, but still he'd done it.

"Jack, before you, there was someone else. I got hurt badly. It was a long time before I was willing to trust again, and when I did—"

"You trusted me, and I hurt you."

She nodded.

He slid his hand around, cupping the nape of her neck.

"So, tell me," he said in a low voice. "What do I have to do to make you forgive me?"

He pressed his mouth against hers, not with the heat that had always accompanied his kisses but with a tenderness that spoke of remorse, opportunities missed, roads not traveled.

The confident, demanding man—she could hold him at bay. But the man revealing his vulnerabilities, who tucked his son in beneath Spider-Man sheets, who expressed regret for the pain he'd caused her . . . that man was close to being irresistible.

He ended the kiss and placed his forehead against hers. "Any chance you'll forgive me?"

She nodded.

"Anytime soon?"

Leaning back, she held his gaze and nodded. "I think we both made mistakes."

She heard a horn honk. For once, Madison obeyed her, and Kelley wouldn't have minded if she hadn't arrived exactly on time. "There's my ride."

"Bad timing."

It always was with them.

He stood and pulled her to her feet and wrapped his arms around her, pulling her close until they were hip to hip.

"I want to see you again. What are you doing tomorrow?" he asked.

"The girls and I are going to Houston for lunch, to do a little shopping. Then we're taking Ronda to the airport."

"Come by afterward. I'll grill steaks for you and Madison."

Rising up on her toes, she kissed him quickly before easing out of his hold. "We'll see you tomorrow evening."

She hurried outside to where Madison was waiting for her. Seeing more of Jack was probably a bad idea . . . or just maybe it would be the best decision she'd ever made.

Chapter 13

Jack thrived on recipes that involved quick and easy food preparation. As a rule, he didn't go into desserts much, but for some strange reason, he wanted to offer his guests more than a steak and a baked potato. He had two recipes that required nothing more than dumping items into a bowl and stirring: a seven-fruit salad that went right into the fridge and brown-sugar brownies that went right into the oven.

"So how come Mrs. Hamilton isn't making the extras like she usually does when you cook steaks?" Jason asked as he rinsed and put the spoons used for stirring the brownie mix into the dishwasher.

"Because I didn't think it would be right," Jack explained. Opening the oven door, he peeked inside. He never could remember how long to cook the brownies. The recipe said twenty minutes, but they were always still gooey after that length of time. He added time in ten-minute increments until the knife he inserted in the center came out clean. He'd already gone into at least two overtimes. Wouldn't be much longer. Someday, he was going to remember to keep track of exactly how long they baked.

"How come?" Jason said.

Closing the door, Jack straightened and faced Jason. "You remember the lady you met last night at the fair? Miss Spencer? I invited her and her sister to join us. Since they're my guests, I felt like I should prepare everything."

"How come you invited them?"

Had his son suddenly reverted into an inquisitive three-year-old? Jack's patience had been tested back then when Jason's favorite word had been *why*.

"She's my friend."

Jason closed the door to the dishwasher and leaned against the counter with a stance that mimicked Jack's usual kitchen pose. "You know what me and Riker were thinking?"

"Riker and I," Jack automatically corrected.

"Right. Riker and I. We were thinking you should marry his mom."

Jack knew a part of him should have seen this coming, but he still felt as though he'd been blindsided by a freight train. "Jason—"

"Dad, it's perfect," Jason interrupted, stepping closer, earnestness in his face. "I mean, I could start calling her Mom, and Riker could call you Dad. We do everything together anyway, so we're really like a family. We just live in two houses."

Jack shook his head. "Son, Mrs. Hamilton and I are friends."

"Which makes it even better. That means you like

each other. Shouldn't you marry someone you like? Someone you're friends with? I mean, you wouldn't want to marry your enemy."

Jack rubbed the back of his neck, trying to ease the tension that was suddenly knotting his muscles. "Jason, when a man marries a woman, he needs to feel something more than friendship."

"I know. You gotta love her. Don't you love Mrs. Hamilton? I mean, you always give her something nice at Christmas and take her out for her birthday and change the oil in her car and fix her stuff that breaks. I love her. And Riker loves you."

Shit. How could he explain the reasons he and Serena would not work as a married couple?

"I do love her and Riker. But for a marriage to work, there has to be a little bit more to it than that."

"Like what?"

"It's hard to explain—"

"Sex?"

So there it was. Hanging out there, so to speak. He wasn't surprised Jason had said the word so casually. It was discussed on almost every television show Jason watched. It was alluded to in commercials. Still, Jack hadn't expected his son to draw the correct conclusion for Jack's hesitancy to marry the lady next door.

"Yeah, a man needs to *want* to have sex with the woman, and as much as I love Mrs. Hamilton, I just don't think of her in that way."

"What way?"

Jack decided that questions containing *what* were

more difficult to answer than those containing *why*. How could he phrase it delicately?

"I don't think of her as someone I want to have sex with."

"How come?"

"It's hard to explain."

"Don't you think she's pretty?"

"I think she's beautiful."

"She's nice."

"Definitely. Very nice." He felt as though he'd dropped into a *Seinfeld* episode.

"So, how come you don't want to have sex with her?"

"Because she's a friend."

Jason's brow puckered. "You don't have sex with friends?"

"Look, Jason—"

"The friends on *Friends* have sex with each other."

Jack stared at his son. "When did you watch *Friends?*"

"Wasn't really watching it. Mrs. Hamilton was watching it, and me and Riker just sorta watched it. But they were friends, and they were having sex."

"Well, that show's made up. In real life, a man has to feel something for a woman—"

"Love?"

"No, not necessarily. Attraction. When he looks at her, he wants her." He sighed at his ineptitude. He was going to attend the next school board meeting and propose they start teaching sex education in kindergarten. "You'll understand in a few years."

"You don't want Mrs. Hamilton?"

"I don't want to marry her."

"How come?"

His frustration level was climbing. How could he explain tactfully, clearly, concisely, that he simply had no sexual interest in Serena? If she stood before him nude, he probably wouldn't react. All right, he would react. He was, after all, a man. He just wouldn't follow through on the message his body was sending, because when he looked at her, he saw Steve standing beside her with that possessive grin that always made it seem that his buddy thought he'd walked away with the grand prize.

"Because—"

The acrid stench assailing his nostrils saved him from uttering another inadequate explanation and brought the awkward conversation to a grinding halt. Jack spun around, jerked open the oven door, swore under his breath when he really wanted to curse out loud, and reached for an oven mitt. So much for the uncomplicated brownies.

He carried the darkened remains across the kitchen, dropped the pan into the sink, and turned the water on full force. Water shot up, splattering him, the counter, the floor. Great, just great. He turned off the faucet, grabbed a nearby dishtowel, took a quick swipe at his shirt, the counter, and the floor.

"Throw that into the washer," he ordered as he tossed the towel at Jason.

Jack didn't understand why he still had this irrational, overpowering need to impress Kelley. Grilling a steak was a manly endeavor, fraught with danger, primal. It involved fire. He didn't need to provide anything more than that.

"Mrs. Hamilton could make dessert," Jason suggested as he walked back into the kitchen. "All you gotta do is ask her. I love her desserts. She never burns anything."

From his son's mouth to his neighbor's ears. A knock on the back door sounded a split-second before it opened. Jack and Serena had become so familiar with each other over the years that they no longer waited to be invited inside. A knock gave warning, and then they simply entered.

With Riker in tow, Serena wrinkled her nose. "Ew! Smells like you have a problem."

"Yeah," Jack admitted glumly. "I didn't keep a close enough watch on the brownies."

"Dad won't marry your mom," Jason blurted out. "He doesn't want to have sex with her."

"Jason! I didn't say that," Jack insisted, wondering why he hadn't realized the conversation had yet to die.

"You do want to have sex with her?" Jason asked, his voice filled with hope.

"No, I . . . geez." He shifted his gaze to Serena, grateful to see her fighting to hold back her laughter. "Help me out here."

Smiling, she shook her head. "But it's so much more fun to watch you squirm."

"Mom said she can't marry your dad," Riker said.

He looked at Serena. She shrugged. "I think the boys are up to no good."

"Jason, Riker, go play outside," Jack ordered.

The boys dashed through the back door, out into the yard where their fort awaited them. Serena crossed over to the sink, edged Jack out of the way, and began working to get his charred dessert out of the pan.

"You really don't want to have sex with me?" she asked.

He thought he detected hurt in her voice. Surely not. They were friends. The thought of anything more between them had never occurred to him.

"It's not that . . . I just . . ." He shook his head. "Why don't you want to marry me?"

"Because you haven't asked."

Damn. He hadn't realized she felt that way. "Serena—"

She held up a hand. "I wasn't expecting you to ask, Jack. I'm just giving you a hard time."

But something in her voice told him that she might have been considering the possibility. He slid his arm around her shoulders, drew her up against his side, and hugged her. He liked her so much; he didn't know why he didn't find her sexy as hell.

"You know, I've always thought you were a terrific lady. I've never been able to figure out why I never wanted more with you."

"I have a feeling that I just heard the reason drive up."

• • •

"I don't know why I have to be here," Madison grumbled just before she slammed her car door closed.

Kelley climbed out of the car. "Because Jack invited both of us to dinner." And she still needed the little buffer zone that Madison could provide. She wasn't exactly sure where things might have ended up last night if Madison hadn't been on time.

"I don't want to stay long," Madison mumbled.

"We won't. We'll just have dinner and be on our way." Kelley reached into the car and brought out her gift for Jack.

"I can't believe you bought him that," Madison said.

"It's just a little something for his house." On the way back from the airport, she'd stopped at a nursery. "I just noticed last night that he didn't have any plants."

She and Madison were halfway to the house when the door swung open. Kelley's heart picked up its tempo as Jack stepped onto the porch. In spite of the cooler temperature that remained from last night's winds, he wore a blue polo shirt. If her fingers were cold, she was certain that she'd only have to press them against that wall of chest to warm them.

"Did you get Ronda to the airport okay?" Jack asked.

"Without a hitch." Kelley extended her gift.

"What's that?"

"A kalanchoe. I noticed that you didn't have any plants. It's very hardy."

"I've never had much luck with plants."

"You just water it," Madison said.

Jack grinned. "Then I should be able to handle it. Come on in."

Kelley walked into the house with Madison following closely behind.

"I was thinking the plant would do well in the kitchen." She strode into the kitchen and came to an abrupt halt at the sight of Serena standing by the sink, running a kitchen towel over a cake pan. Kelley's insecurities shot to the surface with the velocity of the tower ride that had hurtled them toward the sky at the fair the night before. Only to drop them down, down, down.

Her feeble attempt to add her own personal touch to Jack's house seemed silly and inconsequential when another woman stood in his kitchen, cleaning his pots. She suddenly felt awkward, as she had her first day of teaching, not sure what to do but desperately trying to appear cool and in control.

"Is that for Jack?" Serena asked.

"Yes, I thought the kitchen . . ." Clearly, she was neither cool nor in control.

"Right over here at the window by the sink would be a great place." Smiling, Serena took the plant and settled it inside the tiny bay area that looked out toward another house.

Feeling small and petty, Kelley desperately fought not to resent the woman's taking over her gift to Jack, but, as with all the battles she'd faced of late, she lost. Serena seemed far too comfortable in her surroundings.

Serena didn't wait for Jack to gather his manners around him but took it upon herself to introduce herself to Madison. In any other situation, any other place, Kelley probably would have seen his neighbor as friendly, making everyone feel comfortable and welcome. Only this wasn't Serena's home. It was Jack's, and Kelley couldn't help but wonder if Serena had designs on making it hers.

"Jack, I'm going to pop next door and see what I can scrounge up for dessert," Serena said.

"You don't have to do that."

Serena flapped a hand in the air. "It'll just take me a minute." She disappeared through the back door.

"Well, she's very Martha Stewartish," Madison said, leaning against the counter, her arms folded over her chest. "Is she your girlfriend?"

"No," Jack said. "We're just good friends, neighbors."

"I'll just bet."

"Madison," Kelley warned. Honestly, sometimes she wanted to enroll Madison in etiquette school.

"Aren't you a little young to be quite so suspicious?" Jack asked Madison.

"I just don't want to see Kelley get hurt," Madison said.

Kelley couldn't have been more surprised if Madison had suddenly announced she had no desire to move back to Dallas. Where had her concern for

Kelley come from? Every time Kelley thought Madison was self-centered and only aware of her own little world, Madison would toss out a comment that made Kelley reevaluate her.

"Well, then, you and I have something in common," Jack said.

The doorbell rang.

"Serena wasn't kidding when she said she could whip up a dessert quickly, was she?" Kelley asked.

"That won't be Serena. She doesn't ring bells. She just comes on in. It's probably the guys," Jack said as he turned to leave the kitchen.

"The guys?" Madison asked, her voice a little too high.

"Yeah, I offered to cook them a steak to thank them for helping with your move," Jack threw over his shoulder before he disappeared from sight.

"I hate it when he does this," Madison mumbled, wrapping her arms around her waist and hunching her shoulders as though she suddenly had a tummy ache.

Kelley walked over to her and slipped her arm around Madison. "It'll be all right, sweetie. They're nice guys."

"Yeah, but I would have worn something a little more hip. And fixed my hair."

She meant color and spike it. Kelley was glad the boys were a surprise.

Jack chose that moment to stride back into the room, Chris and Rick in tow.

"Bryan couldn't make it," Jack said. "Why don't we head out back so we can enjoy this cool autumn weather?"

Sitting in a comfortable chair in front of a chimenea that had a fire keeping her warm, Kelley acknowledged that Jack's backyard was a male paradise that even she could appreciate. The incredible workmanship on the cedar deck he'd designed and built himself impressed her beyond measure. She was itching to try out the hot tub he'd installed off to the side.

Hanging from four trees, spaced closely together, were two hammocks. Madison was lounging in one now, Chris was in the other, and Rick was leaning against the tree near Madison's feet, gently pushing the hammock so it swung ever so slightly.

The boys were playing in a fort that Jack had also designed and built over the fence that separated his yard from his neighbor's, with half of the fort on one side, half on the other. She was absolutely amazed by the extra effort he went to in order to include his neighbors in his life.

Shifting in her chair, she watched as Jack turned the steaks sizzling on the nearby gas grill. The tantalizing aroma of cooking meat and burning mesquite teased her nostrils, made her stomach rumble and her mouth water. He closed the lid and dropped into the chair beside hers, farthest away from Madison.

"I'm impressed, Jack. I can't believe you built all this."

"Why not? You know how skilled I am with my hands."

As though to bring home his point, he inconspicuously skimmed his finger from her elbow to her wrist, sending a delicious shiver of warmth tripping through her. How easily she could lose herself with him again.

She gazed over at the hammock. "I'm not sure you should be encouraging those boys to spend time with Madison."

"Why not?"

She looked back at him. "I told you that I haven't let her start dating yet."

"She has to start sometime."

"I'd like for her to be a little bit older."

"How much older?"

She shrugged. "Twenty-five, twenty-six."

He grinned. "That's not going to happen."

"You just wait until you have a daughter, Jack Morgan."

"She's not your daughter. She's your sister. Cut her some slack."

"She's my responsibility. Besides, last week, you were all for locking her up and tossing away the key."

"You just need to pick your battles."

"Well, her not getting pregnant is one of the battles I intend to fight."

"Guess I can't blame you for that."

Considering their past, she was relieved to hear it.

"How do you know those boys, anyway?"

"Rick I picked up for shoplifting. Chris and Bryan I got for underage drinking and drunk driving."

She stiffened. "They're criminals?"

"I prefer to think of them as misguided youths."

"That's great, Jack," she hissed. "That's just great. The last thing Madison needs—"

"Hey. That was three years ago. They've walked the straight and narrow ever since."

"As far as you know."

"I keep a tight watch on them. Their family situations aren't the best in town, but they're good kids. I wouldn't have introduced them to Madison if I thought they'd be a bad influence on her. People can change, Kelley. Those boys have worked hard on changing."

"That's why you get along so well with them."

"Been there, done that. Trust me, Kelley. Those guys didn't have a big sister to step between them and me. Now that they're on my good side, they want to stay there."

"I just want her to be safe."

"She is."

She released a deep sigh. The boys had certainly seemed nice enough. They were polite, and she couldn't recall any of them getting in trouble at school. Chris was an honor student. In thinking about it, she realized that she wouldn't have introduced Madison to Jack as a youth, and he hadn't turned out so badly. "All right, Jack, I'll trust your judgment here."

He took her hand and kissed her fingertips. "Good. That's a start. By the way, I should warn you that Jason is campaigning for me to marry Serena."

"Is that a possibility?"

"After our discussion last night, what do you think?"

"Not even remotely possible?"

"Not even. As a matter of fact, Jason and I were having a very uncomfortable discussion about sex before you arrived." He continued to stroke her arm lazily with his finger.

"Oh?" she prodded.

"I was trying to explain what it is about a woman that makes me want to go to bed with her."

She widened her eyes. "You were explaining this to your son?"

"Mostly I was stammering around."

"So, what is it that makes you want to go to bed with a woman?" she asked.

He shook his head. "I can't identify it. I only know the second I laid eyes on you nine years ago, I wanted you. And my feelings haven't changed."

He rolled out of the chair, lifted the lid on the grill, and began turning steaks again.

"Medium well work for you?" he asked.

"It works fine," she answered distractedly. It was totally unfair that he'd drop a comment like that in her lap and then move on to ask her about steaks. Had he really felt that strongly, that quickly?

He lowered the lid.

Kelley got up and moved closer to Jack. "What can I do to help?" she asked.

"Kiss the cook?"

She rolled her eyes. "I was thinking of something a little more practical."

"Then I guess staying the night is totally out of the question."

"Totally."

"Can't blame a guy for trying."

"Sure I can. I'm serious, Jack. What can I do to help?"

"Well, we actually have a policy around here. The one who cooks doesn't clean."

Kelley stood at the kitchen sink, rinsing the dishes and placing them in the dishwasher. Dinner had been delicious, the company fun. Madison had even enjoyed herself. Jack seemed to know exactly how much attention to give her, how to keep her from dropping into one of her funks.

Kelley couldn't remember when she'd last had such a pleasant evening. During dinner, it had quickly become apparent to her that Serena's relationship with Jack more closely resembled that of a sister to a brother. Having seen Jack's life nine years earlier, Kelley was grateful to see that he had so much now.

Speak of the devil. He opened the door and strode toward her. "Tongs need washing."

She tilted her head to the side as she rinsed off the next plate. "Just set them on the counter."

He did, and then he placed his arms around her and put his hands under the rushing water.

"I could move out of the way, you know," she said.

"I kinda like this." He squirted dishwashing liquid onto his hands, lathered them up, rinsed them off—all the while allowing the insides of his upper arms to stroke the sides of her breasts.

"Smooth move, Morgan," she teased.

"I thought so."

Keeping himself folded around her, he reached for a dishtowel and dried his hands. Then he slipped them beneath her top, stroking her stomach while he lowered his mouth to the curve of her neck.

"I like having you in my kitchen," he said in a low voice. Drawing her earlobe into his mouth, he nipped at the sensitive flesh. "Stay the night."

It was tempting, he was tempting.

"Jack, I can't. Not with Madison—"

The door opened, and Jack eased back. It was all Kelley could do not to jump guiltily away from him.

"Sorry to interrupt," Serena said, a stack of bowls in her hands. Her apple cobbler topped with ice cream had been a hit.

"You're not interrupting," Kelley assured her.

"Yes, she was," Jack said.

"Then I'll just drop these off and get out of here," she said with a wink.

Jack's cell phone rang. He unhooked it from his belt. "Morgan."

Turning from the sink, Kelley watched as hardness

and determination came into his eyes. "I'll be right there."

He closed his phone, and Kelley realized that he'd slipped into police mode. The easiness and relaxation she'd enjoyed with him the past two evenings was gone.

"It's Cindy," he said.

Serena waved a hand. "Go. Kelley and I will finish up and see to Jason."

"I'm sorry," he said to Kelley just before he kissed her quickly, abruptly turned on his heel, and headed out the door.

She wasn't sure if he was apologizing for the kiss or for leaving. She looked at Serena. Kelley had heard him mention Cindy before. "Cindy. She gives Jack massages—"

Serena shrugged. "I wouldn't know about that. I just know since he got laid off, her husband uses her as a punching bag."

"What will Jack do?"

"Intervene. Stop him. Threaten him." She sighed. "Welcome to Jack's world."

"Does he get a lot of calls like this?"

Grabbing a dishtowel, Serena began wiping the counter as though she simply needed to be doing something. "The craziness comes and goes. He's on call twenty-four seven. The only time he really gets a chance to relax completely is when we go away for the weekend."

Kelley's stomach instantly knotted up with the implications. She forced herself to relax, not to read more into the comment than was intended. "You go away often?"

"Not as often as I think we should," Serena said.

She stopped rubbing the counter and looked at Kelley. "But we are going away next weekend. My family has a beach house at Surfside that we all share. It's on the bay side of the island, quiet, peaceful. Why don't you and Madison come with us?"

Kelley leaned against the counter. "We wouldn't want to impose."

"It's no imposition. It's four bedrooms, plus the crow's nest, which is where the boys usually sleep."

A weekend away at the beach sounded lovely. She wondered how Madison would react to the idea. More, she wondered how Jack would take to the idea. "I guess we could check with Jack—"

"No need to check with Jack. I'm not blind, Kelley. He's not going to object."

"You know Jack really well."

"We've been through a lot together. I was numb for the longest time after Steve was killed, and I'll admit that in the past couple of years, it's occurred to me that maybe Jack was the one to replace Steve. But I don't think that thought ever occurred to Jack. So my invitation is sincere."

"Thank you, Serena. I'll check with Madison and let you know."

She turned back to the sink to rinse the remaining dishes, surprised to discover her hands trembling. She remembered Jack telling Madison about the dangers of being a cop, the ease with which a bullet could find him, an angry husband with a gun.

"Be safe, Jack," she whispered. "Please be safe."

Chapter 14

Kelley was curled on the couch, reading a romance novel. She'd found Jack's stash of novels when she opened a cabinet on the entertainment center expecting to find videos. He was a continual source of surprises.

The room was dark except for the lamp illuminating the words. She wasn't sure why she hadn't gone home as soon as she and Serena had finished cleaning the kitchen. She only knew that she wanted to make sure Jack was all right when he got home.

With a promise to be home by eleven, Madison had gone to a movie with Chris and Rick. As the minutes ticked closer to ten, Kelley was beginning to think she'd been silly to stay. She'd need to get home to Madison soon.

Her heart kicked up a notch when she heard a key go into the lock. Setting the book aside, she stood and walked into the entryway as the front door opened.

"What are you still doing here?" Jack asked.

She did feel like a fool then. There was no joy in his voice, no pleasure. As a matter of fact, he sounded extremely irritated.

"I just wanted to make sure you were all right."

"Yeah, I'm peachy. I need a drink. You want one?"

"Sure."

He strode into the kitchen, with her following in his wake. He opened a cabinet door above the refrigerator, reached in, and grabbed a bottle of Jack Daniel's. Then he retrieved two small glasses and filled one halfway, the other to the rim. He handed her the one that was half full.

"What happened?" she asked.

"Son of a bitch beat the crap out of her before we could get there."

He carried the glass to his lips and downed its contents in one long swallow. Reaching out, she touched his bruised and scraped knuckles.

"You're hurt."

He turned his hand toward himself as if only now noticing the damage. "Not as badly as he is."

"You hit him?"

"Yeah, I lost my temper. Look, Kelley, I'm not at my sociable best right now."

"I wouldn't expect you to be." A part of her said she should leave, give him room to deal with his feelings. A part of her wanted to be there to help and comfort him. "Do you only want me around when you're in a good mood?"

He slowly shook his head. "But if you've still got doubts about us, then you probably should leave."

"And if I stay?"

With his hands, he bracketed either side of her

face, angled her head, and lowered his mouth to hers,* hot and determined, his tongue delving deeply, sweeping away any doubts that might have lingered.

She placed her hand on his chest and felt the steady, rapid pounding of his heart beneath her fingers. She was a grown woman, old enough to know her own mind, still exploring the maze of her own heart. Regardless, she was certain that she wanted to be here now, with him, this moment.

He tore his mouth from hers, desire and hunger in his eyes, his breathing labored. "You've got two choices. You open the front door and walk out, or we close the door to Jason's bedroom."

"Jason's at Serena's. She and I thought it best. We didn't know how late you'd be or if he'd be comfortable having someone he only recently met take care of him."

"Then your choice is to walk out through the front door or walk through my bedroom door."

In answer, she rose up on her toes and pressed her mouth to his. His guttural groan echoed throughout the kitchen before he broke off the kiss.

"Be sure, Kelley. Be damned sure."

"I am."

He lowered his mouth to hers, kissing her leisurely, deeply, as though moments weren't ticking by, as though they had all night, as though they were the only two in the world and nothing, no one, would intrude on them.

He kissed her chin, her neck. "I need a shower first. Join me?"

Without waiting for an answer, he took her hand and led her toward his bedroom. Not with the over-eagerness and zealousness of his youth but with a maturity tempered by resolve.

With the outside lights peering around the edges of the curtains, the room wasn't in total darkness. He was as neat here as he was elsewhere, his needs met with a large four-poster bed, nightstands framing each side of it, and a dresser.

He slid his arm around her and guided her through the shadows to another door, another room, illuminated only by a night-light. She didn't mind the intimacy of the darkness, preferred it really. Secrets were more easily kept here.

Moving away from her, he crossed the room and turned on the shower. He walked back to her, settled his mouth over hers, and bunched his hands around the hem of her shirt. He lifted it, breaking off the kiss only long enough to get her shirt over her head.

And it was as though the floodgates on his desire had been unleashed. His mouth turned hot, hungry, demanding, his tongue thrusting to reclaim territory with a feral possessiveness. His hands, equally demanding, removed his clothes, helped her to remove hers.

When he was completely nude, she wondered why she'd bothered to fight the attraction. He was more gorgeous than she remembered, muscles corded and defined. She skimmed her fingers over the light covering of hair on his chest that arrowed down toward his belly. She considered journeying downward, but she wasn't nearly as bold as he. She feathered her fingers over his chest, over his hard nipples, felt the rumble of his broad chest against her palms as he groaned.

His eyes darkened with intent as he took her hand, brought it to his mouth, and kissed her palm. Tightening his hold, he walked backward and pulled her with him into the shower.

He took the brunt of the pelting water against his back while his mouth descended on hers, to continue the assault he'd begun earlier, sending her senses reeling, her passions soaring. It was sweet surrender to rise up on her toes and loop her arms around his strong, sturdy shoulders. The warm water ran over them, between them, pooling at their feet. She was vaguely aware of his hands near her but not touching her, and she desperately wanted him to touch her. She parried her tongue around his mouth, wanting him closer, as close as he could get. She released a frustrated mewling sound, which caused him to chuckle even as he continued the kiss.

Then his large soap-covered hands were gliding over her back, her buttocks, around her sides to her stomach, over her breasts. They lingered there, his palms cradling the weight while his fingers taunted her nipples. She hadn't expected a leisurely shower. Yet it was as sensual as anything she'd ever experienced.

He broke off the kiss, lathered up more soap, and, holding her gaze, with barely an inch separating them, he went to work on his own body—not with the slow, careful, gliding motions he'd used on her but with a hurried scrubbing that spoke of his impatience.

She pressed her palms flat against his chest, which was so different from what she'd touched before. She was amazed that nine years could bring so many changes. He'd truly been a boy on the cusp of manhood, and now he was a man to be reckoned with. Her hands became as soapy as his. Lowering them, she cupped him before slowly, leisurely stroking him. He emitted a guttural groan, slammed his eyes closed, and dropped his head back.

She relished the power she had over him, discovered that it ignited her passions with a fervor equal to his. He opened eyes that had deepened to midnight.

"You little witch," he rasped. "Keep that up, and I'm not going to make it to the bed."

She gave him what she truly hoped was a seductive smile. "I am keeping it up."

Chuckling low, he bracketed his hands on either side of her hips, pulled her to him, and kissed her. Then his hands were gliding over her again, directing the water, removing the lather until none remained. Dipping his head, he trailed his mouth along her throat, down lower to her breasts, kissing, suckling, lapping up droplets of water that were quickly replaced.

He moved her as effortlessly as the sun pushed back the night, until her back was pressed against the tiled wall. Its coolness sent a shiver through her that was in direct contrast to the heat caused by his slick hand caressing her breasts, her stomach, before moving lower. Moaning, she clamped his shoulders as his fingers skillfully parted her silken folds, as his thumb circled and stroked. Her body hummed, her knees grew weak.

"Jack, I can't hold on much longer."

"Then don't."

He increased the pressure, slipping his finger inside her as a shattering orgasm swept through her. He cupped the back of her head with his other hand, covered her mouth with his, and captured her cry of ecstasy.

She loosened her hold on his shoulders; her quivering body wanted to melt to the floor of the tub. And if he hadn't snaked his arm around her and drawn her up flush against his taut body, she thought she might already be on the floor, limp and sated. He shut off the shower, wrapped a towel around her, and lifted her into his arms.

"Been a while?" he asked as he carried her into the bedroom.

She wound her arms around his neck, nestled her face against his shoulder, and laughed lightly. "You have no idea."

He laid her on the bed, quickly ran the towel over her relaxed body, then over his own, before tossing it aside and stretching out beside her, a satisfied male grin on his handsome face. She ran her fingers up into his damp hair, wondering why it wasn't until this moment that she realized the one thing that Jack Morgan had never been was selfish.

Cradling his face between her hands, she pulled him down, kissing him with as much enthusiasm as her sated body would allow. She couldn't believe how quickly he'd ignited her passion, how easily he seemed to be doing it again. It seemed his nearness was all she needed in order to ignite. She once again found herself hot, bothered, and turning toward him.

He kneaded her breast, his thumb circling her nipple which had already tightened into a hardened pearl. With his knee, he nudged her thighs apart. Then he nestled himself between her legs and scooted down, kissing her chin, her throat, her breasts, while she did little more than run her fingers through his hair, over his shoulders, and along his back. She stroked his calves with the soles of her feet.

He slid lower. With his tongue, he circled her navel, dipping inside. He lapped at the hollow of her hips. Then he moved lower still, his heated breath wafting over her flesh, sending shivers shimmering up her spine. He kissed the inside of her thigh, and warmth poured through her.

"I wanted to do this before," he whispered huskily. He pressed his face to her curls.

"Why didn't you?"

He lifted his gaze to hers. All they had was the light from the bathroom, but it was enough for her to see the earnestness in his face. "I was scared. Scared you'd say no. Scared I'd do it wrong."

She couldn't imagine Jack Morgan being afraid of anything. Jack Morgan, who had sauntered confidently through the hallways as though he'd owned them. Jack Morgan of the heated looks and the knowing grins. Jack Morgan, who had stood before her with his graduation cap pressed against his chest. She thought she'd known him so well, and yet the boy in her classroom never would have confessed to fearing anything.

She trailed her fingers along the jaw of this complicated man who could excite her and humble her with the same look. "Are you afraid now?"

"Yeah, but not for the same reasons. Aren't you?"

Not waiting for her answer—she wasn't certain he expected one—he spread her legs farther apart, opening her up to his eager mouth, his questing tongue, silk against velvet.

"Oh, God," she murmured on a breathless sigh.

Incredible sensations dipped and swirled through her, mimicking his skillful actions. Sliding his hands beneath her quivering hips, he lifted her slightly. The pleasure increased, intensified, rippled through her, curling her toes, curling her body. She hadn't expected to peak again, not so soon, not with such force.

Her body bucked, her back arched, and he wasn't there this time to capture her cry as her climax cascaded through her in undulating waves. She lay there breathing heavily, gasping, wondering if her body might simply dissolve into the sheets.

He kissed the inside of each thigh, her stomach,

her ribs, her breasts, her throat. Leaving her, he leaned partway off the bed and opened a drawer in the night-stand. He tore open a foil packet and slipped on the condom before rolling back to be with her.

Resting on his elbows, he cradled her face between his large hands and kissed her with a languid power that hinted he wasn't finished with her yet. Then he rose above her. She watched the emotions wash over his face as he entered her, inch by inch, moan by moan, sigh by sigh.

With another groan, he pushed with more insistence until she'd completely taken his full, glorious length. She wrapped her legs around his waist as he began to pump his hips against hers. Long, sure, determined strokes.

She met each thrust, matching his rhythm, her body in tune with his as though they'd been made for each other. The sensations began to build, to escalate, to intensify. She hadn't expected that he had the power to bring her to full force again, and yet here she was hovering on the brink, digging her fingers into his tight buttocks, hanging on for dear life while the pleasure spiraled out of control.

When she catapulted into ecstasy, he followed right behind her, his back arching, his final thrust burying him deeply within her, his feral groan of satisfaction echoing around her.

Lying on his back with Kelley nestled against his side, Jack breathed heavily while his hand lazily stroked her arm, belying the hard pounding of his heart, the loud rushing of blood still thrumming through his ears.

Replete and exhausted, he thought he'd be content to lie there forever. His release had been more intense than he'd experienced in a good long while. More gratifying. The fine sheen of sweat covering his body didn't seem to bother Kelley as she trailed her finger over his chest. But then, she was equally damp.

Tonight for the first time since he'd moved into the house, he felt as if his backyard had been exactly as he'd imagined it when he built the deck. Oh, he'd had Serena and Riker over countless times on autumn nights with a fire in the chimenea, steaks on the grill, a beer in hand, and pleasant conversation. Still, always before, there was that sense of being alone, of not truly belonging. Of being that kid staying up all night Christmas Eve, staring out the window, desperately hoping that bicycle would miraculously appear. The year he'd given up, the year he'd crawled into bed and pulled the blankets over his head so no one would hear him cry, that was the year he awoke and found the bike resting against the side of the trailer.

Just like tonight. Not too long ago, he'd given up hoping that the loneliness would ever ease. And then Kelley had walked back into his life and filled it so full that he almost couldn't remember what it was that he'd thought he was lacking.

Glancing down at the top of her head, he combed her hair off her face. "Can you stay the night?"

She tilted her head back until he could look into her eyes. The dim light from the bathroom gave her a soft glow. "No, Madison went to a movie with Rick and Chris. I need to get home to check on her."

"Kids are a pain."

"Not always." Softness touched her eyes as she rose up on her elbow and traced her fingers around his face. "I found your stash of romance novels."

He groaned. "Serena got me hooked on them when I was recovering from a wound."

"While you were in the army?"

"Yeah."

"Where were you wounded?"

"Took a bullet in the leg."

"I hate thinking of you wounded. You could have been killed."

"But I wasn't."

"There's so much about your past that I don't know."

"All that matters is now."

An emotion touched her eyes that he couldn't quite figure out.

"Do you mean that, Jack?"

"Yeah, I do."

She looked doubtful, and he couldn't imagine why.

"Serena invited us to spend next weekend with you at the beach. I don't know if that's such a good idea now."

"Why?"

She released a tiny, self-conscious laugh and swept

her hand across the length of his body. "Well, for one thing, this. We'd have to behave—"

"I can behave. I want to spend more time with you. At the beach, I won't have to duck out because of a phone call. It'll give you a chance to get to know Jason better."

"All right. I'll let her know." She looked past him to the clock on his nightstand. "I need to get home."

He rolled over until he was covering her. "My gas tank isn't nearly empty enough. How about one for the road?"

Chapter 15

❧

"God, this is so boring. I can't believe we're wasting the whole weekend here."

"Madison, can't you at least try to enjoy it?" Kelley asked, grateful that Serena was lost in the pages of a romance novel—or pretending to be—and wasn't giving any attention to Madison's constant deep sighs and eye rolling. The three of them were sitting on towels spread over mesh lounge chairs while Jack and the boys were fishing a short distance away at the edge of the bay.

They'd arrived late last night in Serena's minivan. True to her description, the house had a peaceful element to it. Raised on stilts, the lower section was nothing more than a storage area and the entryway to the inner stairwell that led to the second floor.

The second floor had a kitchen and a living area with windows all around, a balcony, and a large bedroom.

The third floor was three more bedrooms and narrow stairs that led to the crow's nest. Serena had her own room. Kelley and Madison were sharing a room.

The boys ran up and down between their bedroom and the crow's nest, which was so small it barely had room for their sleeping bags.

"I mean, honestly, who comes to the beach in the fall?" Madison asked. "It's totally lame. The water is too cold for swimming, and it's not hot enough to sunbathe."

"Madison, it's all about relaxing, getting away—"

"It's all about boredom."

Kelley gnashed her teeth. She could tell Madison to behave, but she had yet to figure out how to make her enjoy herself. "Go fish with Jack and the boys."

"Ew! I don't think so. He's using live critters. Worms or shrimp or something that make an awful sound in the bucket while they're waiting to be selected. It's barbaric."

"I'm sure he'll bait your hook."

"Boring."

"Madison, can't you at least try to be a good sport about this? It was nice of them to invite us—"

"I'd rather go to a funeral."

"That can be arranged," Serena said.

Madison's eyes popped wide open, and Kelley bit back her smile. Why did it seem so much easier for others to put this child in her place? Kelley had no trouble managing a class of thirty students, but one sixteen-year-old who was now her complete responsibility seemed beyond her capabilities. Probably because she wanted so badly to be a perfect mom to Madison, and instead she was a constant failure.

Jack turned away from the boys and strode to where Kelley, Serena, and Madison were sitting. Like the boys, he was dressed in jeans, a white T-shirt, tennis shoes, and a gimme cap that had the Houston Texans' red and white bull emblazoned it. He and the boys were a matching trio, about as relaxed as three guys could get.

"Everybody having fun?" Jack asked.

"Yes!" Kelley and Serena said at the same time, a little too enthusiastically, Kelley thought, as though they both anticipated a complaint from Madison and wanted to drown it out.

Madison slunk down farther on her lounge chair, her arms shoved up beneath her breasts.

"What's the matter, kid, aren't you having fun?"

"There's no one around here."

"There usually aren't many people on the bay side. That's why we like it. But you can walk up the road to the surf side. There's bound to be a few people out."

"Maybe you haven't noticed, but this isn't exactly summer."

"So? Fun isn't seasonal."

"You wouldn't know fun if it bit you on the butt."

"Madison—" Kelley began, but Jack held up a hand.

"You know, kid, I've had about all of your attitude that I can take. If you're not having fun by the time I count to three, I'm tossing you in the bay."

Madison scoffed. "Yeah, right."

"One."

She scrambled to her feet. "You're not going to toss me into the bay. That water is cold."

"Two."

"You're bluffing."

"Three."

Madison shrieked and started running with Jack hot on her heels. She tried a couple of fancy twists and turns, but he quickly caught her and tossed her over his shoulder.

Screaming, Madison pounded his back as he strode toward the water.

"Kelley! Make him put me down!" Madison ordered.

Kelley got to her feet for a better view but did nothing more than give Madison a helpless shrug. Jack was doing what Kelley had been contemplating doing with Madison since she'd joined them out there.

"You wouldn't dare throw me—"

"No?" Jack asked as he got to the edge of land. "Just watch."

With a little jerk, he repositioned her so he had her in his arms, cradled like a baby.

"You wouldn't dare!" Madison repeated.

He dared.

She was out over the water when she screamed, terror in her voice, "I can't swim!"

Jack's harsh curse filled the air before he hurled himself from the bank, hitting the water almost at the same time Madison did, intent on rescuing her.

Madison's laughter echoed around them as she kicked away from him and swam to shore. "Sucker!"

She scrambled up the embankment. Jason and Ryker were lying on the ground, laughing, holding their stomachs, rolling back and forth.

"Oh, that was great," Serena said, chuckling.

"You're gonna pay for that, kid!" Jack threatened, but his voice held no heat. "You guys, stop laughing, or you're next."

Madison turned around, trudging backward. "Jerk!"

"You had fun, though, didn't you?" Jack called after her as he began to make his way up the embankment.

"You wish! I'm going to take a shower and use all the hot water." She quickened her step, reached the lounge chair, and snagged her towel.

"Madison, are you all right?" Kelley asked.

"Sure." She was smiling brightly. "He is such a jerk. I *am* going to use all the hot water. He can shiver all afternoon, and I'm not going to feel a bit guilty."

Watching in amazement as a seemingly happy Madison ran to the house, Kelley picked up the towel she'd been lying on. The least she could do was offer it to Jack. The beach house only had one shower, and Madison *would* use all the hot water.

Shaking her head, she walked to Jack. "I don't know how you did that, but you actually had her smiling."

"I don't put up with her BS."

He started to peel off his drenched T-shirt, revealing toned muscles inch by inch. What a fine specimen of maleness he was. His arms bunched as he wrung out his shirt.

"Little brat will use all the hot water, though." He nodded toward the towel Kelley was holding. "I'll switch with you."

"Oh." She laughed self-consciously, embarrassed she'd been caught staring at him. "That's why I brought it over."

He dried his chest and arms, dipped to get to his back. Something appeared on his left shoulder and disappeared.

"What was that?" Kelley asked.

He stilled. "What? Oh, nothing." He returned to drying himself off.

She shook her head and moved closer. "No, I saw something. Was that a tattoo?"

"It's nothing. Something I got when I was in the army."

She hadn't noticed before because they'd been in the shadows, and she realized now that he'd always remained facing her. She hadn't thought anything of it at the time, having her own secrets that she preferred to keep in the dark, but now she wondered if he'd done it on purpose. "Jack, let me see your back."

"I said—"

"Let me see."

With a deep sigh, he turned slightly, presenting her with his left shoulder, and she immediately understood why he hadn't wanted her to see it. She trailed her finger over her name inscribed within a heart—split down the middle with jagged edges.

"It must have hurt," she said quietly, not certain if she was referring to getting the tattoo or the broken heart.

"I don't even remember getting it. I got drunk one night, woke up the next morning, and there it was."

She eased back until she could hold his gaze. "Does the broken heart represent yours or mine?"

"Does it matter?"

"I suppose not. Stephanie must not have been too pleased with it."

"She couldn't have cared less what I did. The only person who cared was a guy in my outfit whose last name was Kelley. He wasn't real bright, and he took the tattoo to mean I was trying to make a pass at him."

"Really?"

He hitched up a corner of his mouth. "Really."

She placed her palm against his chest where his real heart beat. "Sometimes, Jack, I forget that maybe I wasn't the only one who got hurt."

He cradled her chin and circled his thumb around her mouth. "You know, we have a rule around here that if a person isn't smiling, she gets tossed in the bay."

She couldn't stop herself from grinning. "You wouldn't dare."

Lowering his head, he whispered, "Try me. Then we could take a shower together to conserve the hot water."

"You promised to behave," she reminded him.

"Yeah, but I'm finding that promise difficult to keep. Maybe we could meet out under the stars tonight."

"Maybe not," she said, easing away from him. "Madison is a light sleeper."

"Two or four, two or four, two or four," Madison chanted.

Sitting at the card table, Jack shook the dice in his hand. The boys had wanted to play Monopoly. Although, at eight, they didn't quite grasp the strategy of empire building, they understood they wanted the colors of their properties to match and lots of houses on the properties. Serena served more as their guide than a true competitor, although she was still in the game, holding on by the skin of her teeth with the ownership of all four railroads. Kelley had gotten tossed out of the game early on. Jack had never known anyone to go around the board three times without landing on any property other than the utilities. She was a magnet to Chance and Community Chest.

Madison changed her chant. "Park Place or Boardwalk."

"Ain't going to happen, kid," Jack said. He tossed the dice. A pair of twos.

"Busted!" Madison yelled. She punched at the air, more animated than Jack had ever seen her. "Boardwalk. Hotel. Two thousand." She snapped her fingers. "Hand it over, dude."

Rubbing his hands together, Jack looked at his meager pile of money and his mortgaged properties. "Looks like I'm out."

Madison took his seven dollars and his properties and began arranging everything on her side of the table as though she were some tycoon. Jason and Riker were whispering, and Jack knew from experience they were plotting their strategy. They would form an alliance, sacrifice one for the other if they had to. It was the boys against the adults, and the adults had yet to win a game.

"There's a new sheriff in town, boys," Madison announced.

Chuckling, Jack got up from the table and approached Kelley. She was curled in a chair, reading.

"It'll be dark soon," he said. "I need to gather some driftwood for the fire we'll build later. Want to come with me?"

With a soft smile, she held out her hand and he pulled her to her feet. On the way down the stairs, Jack grabbed a burlap sack he'd used to carry the driftwood in. He didn't need much. They had a cord of firewood stacked against the side of the house. He shoved open the door, waited while she walked through, then followed her out.

Taking her hand, he led her to the sandy road that would wind its way around to the Gulf side of the island. Strange how intimate it seemed to have their fingers threaded together, their palms pressed against each other's. He'd always slung his arm around a girl's shoulders, tucked her up against his side. It had always made him feel powerful, in a protective sort of way. Laying his claim, staking out his territory.

For some reason, simply holding Kelley's hand felt incredibly right.

"So, when are you going to tell Madison about us?" he asked.

She glanced over at him. "I don't know."

"She's sharp, Kelley. It's not going to take her long to figure it out."

"I know. I just don't know if she'll be happy with the news."

"Sometimes kids aren't happy."

She laid her head against his arm. "I know, but my relationship with Madison is important. Things have been going much more smoothly lately, and I'd like to keep them that way for a while longer. I'm not like you, Jack. You seem to have natural parenting skills. You're so good with the boys and Madison. You're like the perfect father, and I'm such an inept mother."

"Don't be so hard on yourself," Jack said. "You're Madison's sister, not her mother. You probably fixed her hair and let her borrow your makeup when you were younger. Then, suddenly, bam, you're the one in charge, and she has a hard time seeing you as an authority figure. Whereas her relationship with me, from the get-go, has been that I'm the authority. Why do you think she calls me Sheriff?"

"I thought she did it to irritate you."

"Some of that, too, I'm sure. But the day she calls

me Jack is the day I'm in trouble. I'll have lost my power over her."

"I think it's more than what she calls you. I think she has a grudging respect for you."

He glanced over at her. "What about you?"

She lifted her gaze to his. "I've always had respect for you, Jack. No grudging to it. I'll admit the respect has grown. Now, when I see you with Jason, I'm so impressed with the way you handle him. I always thought abused children were supposed to be abusers."

"I was neglected, not abused."

"Neglect is a form of abuse. You're kidding yourself if you think it isn't. I took a couple of psych courses myself, you know."

They'd reached the main stretch of shoreline where the waves washed over the sand. The breeze picked up with no dunes to act as buffer. It brought the scent of the sea, not always pleasant but reminiscent of life.

He looked off toward the horizon, where the sun was beginning to set.

"She wouldn't hold him, Kelley." He turned and faced her. "Stephanie. After Jason was born. She wouldn't hold him. How can you not hold a baby?"

She squeezed his hand. "You held him."

He nodded. "I was so afraid I'd break him, but he'd look at me with those unblinking dark eyes. There was trust in those eyes, and at the time, it was more powerful than love. He made me feel invincible." He held her gaze. "I really tried to make it work with Stephanie."

Tears sprang into her eyes, and she blinked them back. "I'm glad you did. I'm just sorry it didn't work out."

"I'm not. She had these moods—they were a bitch. The doctors said she was depressed. Nothing I did seemed to make her happy. Maybe she was bipolar. I don't know. The day she packed up, I thought I should have felt the burden of being a single parent. Instead, I just felt relieved. Strange, huh? To feel relieved because someone walks out on you?"

"I think Stephanie was a fool."

Maybe they were all fools. He picked up a seashell and hurled it into the sea. Some things were easier to say when he wasn't looking at the person. "I never forgot you, Kelley."

All he heard was the roar of the ocean and the whisper of the wind. Then he felt her arms coming around him. She slid around to face him and lifted her gaze to his. "I never forgot you, either, Jack. I tried. God knows, I tried."

Gathering her in his arms, he kissed her. The past was behind them. He was beginning to have hope for the future.

Chapter 16

Kelley sat on a blanket on the ground with her feet tucked up beneath her, trying to remember the last time she'd felt so relaxed or at peace. The cooling wind blew at her back, and the low fire danced in front of her, warming her hands, roasting her marshmallow.

Madison sat beside her, and even she seemed content. Jack sat within easy reach, his arms bracketing Jason as they roasted two marshmallows on one straightened coat hanger. They were so at ease, so comfortable, that she knew without a doubt that they'd done this often. On the other side of them, Serena and Riker were in the same position.

The boys had simply climbed onto their laps, without prodding, without asking, as though it were an understood ritual.

The sight caused an ache to form within Kelley's chest for moments she'd never had with Madison. Jack was right. She'd shifted from being Madison's sister to being her mother without the foundation that type of bond required.

Was it any wonder they were constantly butting heads, trying to understand the dynamics of their new relationship? She found herself feeling ashamed that Jack was a far better father than she'd ever be a mother.

She wondered if the heat she saw in his eyes every time he looked at her would cool if she told him why she found dealing with Madison to be such a struggle. Or would he offer to lighten her burden? She was unworthy of him for so many reasons—the main reason nestled within his lap.

"That's perfect, Dad," Jason said as he and Jack studied the browned marshmallows.

"Let 'em cool off a bit," Jack reminded him, as he did every time they finished toasting their dessert.

Kelley could hardly take her eyes off them. They could have been a Norman Rockwell painting, and she thought she'd remember this night for as long as she lived. The serenity. The perfection. A father and son who obviously adored each other.

The sight was bittersweet, moments previously denied to her. She wanted to draw Madison onto her lap, hold her close—all that remained of her family— go back in time to when Madison was younger, more innocent, and wouldn't have objected to being cuddled.

She watched as Jack popped the gooey confection into his mouth, slid his gaze over to her, and very slowly licked his finger and thumb. She had a feeling that if they hadn't had an audience, he would have offered to let her do the licking.

"Can I have another, Dad?" Jason asked.

Jack turned his attention back to his son. "Nah, I think we've had enough."

Jason groaned. Jack groaned.

"Ah, Dad."

"Ah, bud."

Jason snuggled more closely against Jack. "Wish we could stay here longer."

"Can't," Jack said. "Got school on Monday."

"We could play hooky."

"I don't think so. State law would require me to arrest myself if I let you play hooky."

Jason groaned again. "That's a dumb law."

"Still, it's the law."

"When I grow up, I'm gonna change laws."

"Thought you were gonna fly fighter jets."

"That, too."

Grinning, Jack ruffled his hair. "I don't think you know what you're gonna do, and that's just fine for right now."

"Me and Riker—"

"Riker and I—" Kelley said at the same time Jack did. He looked over at her, his grin broadening.

"Gotta watch how you talk," Jack said. "We have an English teacher sitting here."

"Since you were so quick to correct him, I don't think you really need me here."

"Oh, I need you here," he said, his voice lowered a notch, an undercurrent and another meaning shimmering in his voice.

"Riker and me—I mean I—are going to stay up all night tonight, okay?"

"Sure," Jack said, surprising Kelley with his answer. She'd assumed even if he didn't adhere to a strict bedtime on the weekend, he wouldn't be quite that lenient.

Jason leaned over and tapped Riker's knuckles, then settled back into Jack's lap.

"So, what now, Sheriff?" Madison asked as she tested the coolness of her blackened marshmallow. "Scary stories, campfire songs?"

"Scary stories!" both boys cried.

"I wouldn't be able to sleep if we told scary stories," Serena said. "But I have a new wizard story."

"All right!" Again, the boys in unison.

As Serena began weaving her tale, Jack leaned toward Kelley and whispered, "Serena's the storyteller."

"Are you really going to let him stay up all night?"

He shook his head and mouthed, "Half an hour. Tops." He tipped his head to the side and closed his eyes, indicating what he expected to happen. His son was going to fall asleep in spite of his desire to stay up all night. Then Jack opened his eyes. "I pick my battles. No sense in butting heads over something that's a moot issue."

The words of Serena's story washed over her as she studied the profiles of father and son. As hard as she looked, she could see no similarities in any of their features. Jason's dark eyes began fighting to stay awake. Dark eyes. When Jack's were so blue. And Stephanie's had been . . . an even lighter blue.

No, that couldn't be right. She was remembering wrong.

Just as Jack had predicted, about twenty minutes into her story, Serena quieted and sighed. "J. K. Rowling, I guess I'm not."

In the dancing firelight, Kelley could see that the boys' eyes were closed, their jaws slack.

"Don't take it too hard," Jack said. "They've had a long day. I'll take Jason up to the crow's nest and come back for Riker."

"I think I can manage if Kelley and Madison will help me get up."

Although Jack didn't seem to need any help, Kelley did grab his arm and give him a little support as he worked his way to his feet. Then, with Madison, she helped Serena rise.

"Wait here," Jack ordered. "Keep an eye on the fire. I'll be back once I tuck him in."

Nodding, Kelley shoved her arms beneath her breasts and watched with bittersweet longing for what might have been, as Jack and Serena walked toward the beach house.

"I don't think it's fair that she stopped the story just because the boys fell asleep," Madison grumbled. "The rest of us were still awake."

"Were you interested in the story?" Kelley asked. Sometimes Madison seemed so old, and at other times, the child within her still managed to peer out.

"Not really. I mean, it was a kid's story, but I was sorta wondering how the hero was going to escape from the sorcerer. I mean, it was sorta interesting."

Kelley rubbed her shoulder. "Maybe we can get her to finish telling the story when she gets back." She sat on the blanket and patted the space beside her. "Sit down. We haven't had any time alone since we got here."

When Madison dropped down beside her, Kelley leaned over, wrapped her arms around her, and hugged her. It felt so good.

"What was that for?" Madison asked, working herself free.

"I just needed a hug," Kelley said. Everyone else had kids to hug. Why not her?

Madison tossed something into the fire—a rock or a twig, Kelley wasn't sure. She just saw something small soar through air and land within the flames with a pop.

"Kell?"

"Uh-huh?"

"I know you said there's nothing between you and the sheriff, but I find it totally weird that he's suddenly in our life twenty-four seven."

"It's not twenty-four seven," Kelley protested.

"Almost. I mean, ever since that night . . ." Her voice trailed off.

"Ever since that night you got hauled to jail?" Kelley prodded. "I guess you should have stayed home that night."

Madison started picking at some threads on the quilt. "I don't care what you say. There *is* something between you and the sheriff . . . and I think it started before that night."

There was such honesty in Jack's relationship with his son. Complete trust. Kelley couldn't imagine Jack ever lying to Jason. She desperately wished she could say the same about her relationship with Madison, but there were promises she'd made to her parents that she was honor-bound to keep, even though they were no longer there. If she couldn't be completely honest with Madison, she thought maybe she could be more honest. She popped her knuckles and took a deep breath. "I like Jack. I've always liked him. Even when he was my student."

Madison turned her attention completely away from the fire and focused it fully on Kelley. "So, when he was your student, you and he—"

"No." Kelley shook her head, deciding she could be honest while easily glossing over the details and leaving out the heart of the matter. "I'll admit that I was attracted to him, but I wasn't willing to step over ethical boundaries to satisfy that attraction."

"Miss Goody Two-Shoes," Madison countered.

"I have to be able to live with myself, Madison." She'd learned long ago how difficult it could be if she made a stupid decision. Part of her concern over Madison's behavior of late was that she'd do something equally irresponsible—and payment was always a bitch. Some decisions couldn't be undone.

"So you followed the rules, and he got away," Madison said.

"I suppose that's one way of looking at it. I forced myself to keep a distance between us while he was my student. Shortly after he graduated, he got married, so we didn't have a chance to develop anything lasting. Now he's not married, our paths have crossed again—thanks to your little stunt a couple of weeks ago—and I'm finding it more difficult to keep my distance."

"I think you'd be smart to keep your distance. I mean, why start something when we're going to move back to Dallas?"

"That's not definite," Kelley reminded her.

"You said if I didn't get into any trouble—"

"And we're making progress."

Madison released a burdened sigh, drew her knees up, wrapped her arms around her legs, placed her chin on her knees, and stared into the fire. "You know, the sheriff's kid doesn't look anything like him."

So she wasn't the only one who'd noticed. "I think he has Jack's smile." Which Kelley thought could possibly be learned behavior, imitating the smile that he'd always seen when he was small.

"I guess. We're studying heredity in biology."

"Genetics isn't exact—"

"Sure it is, Kelley. It's an exact science. That's why genetic scientists can manipulate genes."

"I simply meant the process isn't as simplistic as biology books make it out to be. Just like you were talking about baldness being passed down through the mother."

"That's true. But you know, you and I look a lot like Mom. My hair's a little darker, but we have her eyes. You'd think with different dads that we wouldn't look so much alike."

"But we do," Kelley said, at a loss for anything else to say.

"Yeah, we do. So I guess the sheriff's kid doesn't have to look like him. His mom's genes could have been really dominant."

"That's probably what it was."

Madison turned her gaze back to the fire. "Kell, have you ever done anything you shouldn't have?"

Kelley's heart lurched, and she swallowed past the lump that suddenly rose in her throat. She couldn't confess to Madison about all the things she'd done that she shouldn't have. "Sure. We all have moments of weakness or display bad judgment."

Madison looked over at her. "What did you do?"

Kelley sensed that this was a bonding moment, a reaching out of younger sister to older. She wished she knew what Madison was searching for: absolution or affirmation. She wished she could reveal her own imperfections, unburden her sins—but she couldn't, not to this precious person sitting beside her.

"I smoked a cigarette in the girls' bathroom my sophomore year in high school."

Madison groaned. "That is so lame."

"I know," Kelley said. "I was so scared I'd get caught—"

"No, I mean, that was a stupid thing to confess as

your awful sin. I thought maybe you'd done something really bad."

"What would be really bad, Madison?"

"If you have to ask, then you obviously didn't do it. I'm going for a walk." She started to get up.

"I'll go with you," Kelley said.

"I need some time by myself," Madison said.

"Where are you going to go?"

"Just up to the water."

It seemed safe enough. Kelley nodded. "Don't go too far."

"God, Kelley, I wish you'd stop trying to be my mother."

She watched Madison disappear into the darkness beyond the fire. She wished she could stop trying as well. It was just all so damned hard.

She heard heavy footfalls behind her. She glanced over her shoulder. Jack was walking toward her.

"Where's Madison?" he asked.

"She went for a walk. Do you think it's safe?"

"Sure."

He dropped down behind her, bracketing his thighs on either side of her, wrapping his arms around her, and pulling her back against his chest.

"You're warm," she said.

"You're chilly." He pressed his hot mouth against the nape of her neck, sending shivers of anticipation down her spine.

"Where's Serena?"

"Inside, reading, keeping watch over the boys."

"I'm not sure you should be sitting this close to me," she said. "When Madison comes back—"

"I'm just keeping you warm, offering you a little support for your back. Relax against me, Kelley."

She did, burrowing her head into his shoulder, folding her arms over his. It was nice, really nice. Having him hold her, having him near. She snuggled closer against him. "I love watching your rapport with Jason. I see you in his smile."

"That's about the only place you'll see me, and I figure that's learned."

She twisted around slightly until she could look at him, the firelight dancing over his chiseled features but unable to reveal the color of his eyes hidden by the shadows of the night.

With featherlike touches, he combed her hair back from her face. "I'm surprised you haven't figured it out yet. I'm not the one who got Stephanie pregnant," he said quietly.

Although stunned, she didn't doubt his words, not when Jason had eyes the color of chocolate. "But she said—"

"I think she thought I was the one."

With tears in her eyes, she wound her arms around his shoulders, pressed her face against his neck. "Oh, Jack, I'm so sorry."

"For what?" he whispered near her ear.

"I hated you, I hated you for what you did . . ."

He tucked his fist beneath her chin and tilted her face up until she was looking into his eyes.

"Jason's parentage doesn't change what I did on prom night, Kelley."

"But you didn't have to marry her. And I insisted—"

He pressed a finger to her lips, silencing her. "If I hadn't married Stephanie, I wouldn't have Jason. He's one of the best things that ever happened to me. I put him right up there beside you. Kelley Spencer, who always follows the straight and narrow, no matter how rocky the road gets."

"No, Jack, don't put me up on a pedestal."

"Why? Because you're having a little trouble managing your sister?"

Shaking her head, she wound her arms more tightly around him. She couldn't tell him the truth, couldn't tell him of her sins. So, instead, she drew comfort from the sturdiness and warmth of his body, knowing she was so undeserving of his nearness, of this remarkable man who'd *chosen* to be a father while she'd chosen not to be a mother.

With the flames dying and the fire slowly losing its heat, Jack rocked Kelley. He didn't understand her tears. He supposed he could have DNA testing done, confirm his suspicions that Jason didn't come from his loins, but the truth of the boy's origins had ceased to matter the first time he wrapped his tiny infant fingers around Jack's index finger and looked at him with unblinking dark blue eyes.

Jack knew most babies were born with blue eyes.

He figured Jason's would eventually turn and more closely resemble his than Stephanie's. And they had turned, slowly but surely, into brown.

By then, they could have turned purple, and Jack wouldn't have cared. He loved the kid. If Stephanie knew who'd fathered the boy, she wasn't saying, always insistent that Jack had gotten her pregnant. Then she'd announced that she didn't want the baby or Jack, so that gave him and Jason something else in common: mothers who hadn't wanted them.

Jack had been determined that Jason wouldn't do without all the things that Jack had done without growing up. He could give Jason all the things he'd never had.

The one area where he'd failed was in securing a mother for Jason. Jack had searched. He'd dated, he'd considered a couple of women as potential candidates, but in the end they'd fallen short—

Because none of them had ever looked at him the way Kelley had. That day in his trailer, she'd looked beneath the calculated grin, the cocky stance, the hard eyes—she'd seen the vulnerabilities, and, instead of offering him pity, she'd challenged him.

She'd never cut him any slack, and he'd loved her for it.

He cupped the back of her head and lowered his face to hers, touching her cheek with his. "Hey, it's not a bad thing, you know. He's a terrific kid."

She lifted her face. "He's a wonderful kid. And you're a wonderful dad. I wish I had your strength."

"Are you kidding me? You're tough as nails."

She wiped at her cheeks. "Not where Madison is concerned. She's my Achilles' heel."

"Don't be so hard on yourself. You're still trying to get your bearings."

"This weekend helped."

"We'll have to do it again sometime. Next time, though, I think we'll leave all the chaperones at home."

She laughed lightly and nipped at his chin. "It's all about sex with you, isn't it?"

"Damn right. And I've shown remarkable restraint."

"I think that deserves a reward."

"Yeah?"

"Yeah."

Her lips touched his, a butterfly caress, more of a tease than a commitment.

"If you're going to do it, do it," he ground out. "Because if you don't—"

She covered his mouth with hers, accepting the dare he was on the verge of issuing. She tasted of marshmallows and carried the scent of an open fire— or maybe he was simply inhaling the fire she was blazing through his body with each bold stroke of her tongue.

She was intoxicating and sexy as hell. He stroked his hands along her back, lower, cupped her backside. Nice and firm. Just the way he liked it. A tight little ass that had been melted and poured into her jeans— which he'd give anything for her not to be wearing at the moment.

Holding her in place, he shifted and rolled until he had her on the ground with his body stretched over hers, never breaking the kiss, never stopping the sensual assault. Her hands were in his hair, as though she were striving to keep him from leaving.

When leaving was the last thing on his mind.

He wanted her as he'd never wanted anything in his life.

Breathing heavily, he trailed his mouth along her throat, down into the V of her shirt, so tempted to loosen the buttons and take his exploration further.

"Jack, Madison—"

"What about her?"

"She could come back any time."

"Send her to bed. It's way past her bedtime."

Laughing, she braced her hands on either side of his head and lifted his gaze to hers. "I don't want her to see us like this."

"We're just kissing."

"But if we don't stop now—"

"We might not stop."

"Exactly."

"Spoilsport."

He covered her mouth, kissing her deeply, taking a kiss with him that he figured would keep him up most of the night. With regret, he drew back, rolled off her, and pulled her to a sitting position.

She snuggled up against him, looked toward the fire, and released an ear-splitting scream that had him reaching for the gun he wasn't wearing.

Chapter 17

"That wasn't funny, Madison. It wasn't funny at all."

"I thought it was hilarious," Madison insisted.

"You shouldn't have snuck up on us like that."

In the bedroom she was sharing with Madison, Kelley yanked down the covers on the bed. She'd looked toward the fire and seen an apparition that scared the holy crap out of her. It had taken several rapid heartbeats to recognize that it was Madison standing beside the fire, arms crossed over her chest, staring at her and Jack.

"I didn't sneak. You were just too busy playing tonsil hockey to notice I was back. I thought you were going to pee in your pants," Madison said.

Kelley had thought so, too. She opened her suitcase and pulled out the tank top and boxers she'd brought to sleep in. "Exactly how long were you there, anyway?"

"Long enough." Madison dropped onto the bed. "You're not keeping your distance anymore, are you?"

Since Madison had obviously seen her sprawled over the ground with Jack's firm body covering her, Kelley could hardly pretend otherwise. "No."

She found relief in the single word but also a sense of sadness. Being around Jack confirmed her own failings as a parent, her own shortcomings where Madison was concerned. She thought it ironic that with his past reputation, there were probably those who might have thought he wasn't good enough for her, when the truth was that she wasn't good enough for him.

"That sucks," Madison said.

Kelley released a bubble of laughter in disbelief. "Why?"

Madison held up a finger. "You'll want to stay in Podunk."

Although she knew the chances of their moving back to Dallas were extremely slim, Kelley wasn't in the mood for a full-blown discussion or fight, so she compromised. "Maybe. Maybe not. Madison, I don't know what the future holds for any of us. It's been a long day, and I'm really tired. Let's go to bed, okay?"

"Okay."

She let Madison use the bathroom first. By the time Kelley was finished with her nightly ritual of brushing her teeth, cleaning her face, and brushing her hair, Madison had turned out the lights and crawled into the bed they were sharing.

Kelley tiptoed across the room and slipped beneath the covers. The screened window was open. The breeze ruffled the curtains and brought in the scent of the sea. The house was situated close enough to the bay that Kelley could hear the water. A foghorn sounded in the distance. A lonely sound that seemed to echo in her heart.

She had friends, but even with them, she had a protective barrier that never allowed them to get too close. Close friendships resulted in secrets eventually being shared, and Kelley had some secrets she preferred to keep locked within her heart. Decisions made that she constantly questioned.

"Kell?"

"Yes?"

"Do you love him?"

"I admire him, Madison." He possessed a strength of will and determination that she wouldn't have expected in a man with his past. A man who'd barely graduated from high school but went on to get a degree in higher education while working and raising a child without help from a wife. A man who held a position of respect and responsibility in the town. A man who was an exemplary father to a child who probably didn't carry his genes. A man who tried to guide her when she made mistakes with Madison. A man who was willing to make room in his life for both of them. "Yes," she continued quietly. "I think I might love him."

Kelley felt the bed bounce as Madison rolled over.

" 'Night, Kell."

Kelley had expected more questions, had thought Madison would wonder if Jack loved Kelley. She was glad Madison hadn't asked, because she feared the answer.

Not that he didn't love her but that he did . . . and that she could lose that love again if she weren't careful.

Guilt swamped her. Nine years ago, Jack had been adamant that he hadn't gotten Stephanie pregnant, and Kelley had been too hurt to listen. That child was the proof. How he must have resented her for not believing him, for holding him to a high standard, for insisting he marry the girl. He'd hate her that much more if he knew everything she kept from him. She'd thought he'd betrayed her, and only tonight had she come to realize that she'd betrayed him.

Kelley awoke as dawn's fingers barely eased through the window. Madison lay still beside her, lost in sleep.

Kelley eased out of bed, padded to the window, and looked out on the bay. She saw a silhouette standing where the land jutted into the water. As quietly as she could, not wanting to disturb Madison, she gathered up her clothes and trotted to the bathroom. Quickly, she changed into jeans and a sweatshirt.

Her shoes barely made a sound as she crept down the two flights of stairs and outside. The morning was cool, a stronger breeze blowing off the water than had been blowing the day before. The sky was only just beginning to lighten as she made her way across the wide expanse from the house to the shore, to the man standing at its edge.

He didn't move as she came to stand beside him but continued staring outward.

"I love standing here, watching the day begin," he said quietly.

"It's peaceful."

"The sounds are all hushed, still there, but muted." He slid his gaze over to her. "Doesn't this feel right to you?"

And she knew he wasn't talking about the dolphins playing in the bay or the water lapping at the shore. He was talking about them, standing there together.

"I'm still scared, Jack, but not as much."

"So there's hope for us?"

Smiling, she nodded. "Yes, there's hope."

He drew her into his arms and kissed her, with dawn bursting over the horizon.

Chapter 18

It was to be their first official date. Kelley could hardly believe it.

Jack had called earlier in the week to let her know that Serena was taking the boys to her parents' for the weekend. Although he'd be on call, he'd be free Saturday night. What was she doing?

What she decided to do was send Madison to Dallas to spend the weekend with Ronda.

"I'll pick you up at seven," Jack told her. "Wear something nice."

Something nice. She'd liked the sound of that. So far, everything they'd done together had been casual. She was looking forward to dressing up.

She'd spent the afternoon making herself ready. She put on a red, satiny dress with a flowing skirt that danced around her calves. It was long-sleeved to accommodate the cooler weather, but the neckline dipped down to reveal the barest hint of cleavage. She thought it would drive Jack wild.

And just to be sure he noticed the cleavage, she selected a pearl teardrop necklace that hung down low enough to end where her cleavage began. She dotted perfume on erogenous zones. And applied more makeup than she'd ever worn before.

She couldn't remember the last time she'd spent this much time getting ready for anything.

When the doorbell rang and she opened the door, she felt underdressed.

"Oh, wow." She'd never seen Jack in a sport coat.

"I've waited years to take you out on a real date," Jack said. "Did you think I was going to wear jeans?"

She nodded. "Jeans and a nice shirt."

"This is a nice shirt."

"So is the jacket." She lifted her gaze to his. "When you say dressed up, you mean dressed up." She took a step back. "Come on in."

He lifted his wrist to glance at his watch. "We don't really have time. Our reservations are for eight."

"There's someplace in Hopeful that takes reservations?"

"We're going to Houston. Thought we'd take your car. It's a little more romantic than my truck."

"Let me get my purse."

She hurried inside and snatched her purse and keys off the couch. She walked outside, closed the door, and locked it. Then she handed him the keys.

Leaning down, he kissed her.

"I was afraid if I did that before you locked the door, I'd cancel our reservations."

"You can still unlock the door."

He shook his head. "We've waited too long for this."

Threading his fingers through hers, he walked her to her car and opened the passenger-side door for her. After settling in, she watched him walk around to the driver's side and slide behind the wheel.

"Ready."

Smiling, she nodded.

He slipped the key into the ignition, turned it on, shifted into reverse, and looked over his shoulder. It was then, with his hand on the steering wheel, that she noticed he was wearing the ring she'd given him.

Reaching out, she touched his finger. He applied the brakes before looking back at her.

"You still have it."

He smiled warmly. "I haven't worn it in a long time. I was surprised it still fit."

"I was afraid maybe you'd hocked it somewhere."

"Why would I do that?"

"I don't know. A way to get rid of it and make some money at the same time."

"I don't think you realize how much you mean to me, Kelley. Tonight I intend to show you."

He backed out of the driveway while she settled back against the seat. "Isn't it risky for you to head to Houston when you're on call?"

"We'll be a little over an hour away, and they'll only call me if it's something they can't handle. We're usually a pretty quiet place, as I'm sure you know."

"But if you get called—"

"Then we'll cut the evening short."

He drove toward Main Street and then on toward Houston.

"So, where are we going?"

"A nice little restaurant someone recommended to me. I've never been there before, but if the prices are any indication, the food ought to be good."

"Jack, you don't have to take me someplace expensive."

"I'm not taking you there because it's expensive. I'm taking you there because it's nice. You deserve nice, Kelley."

She wasn't so sure. She wished the gearshift wasn't between the seats so she could snuggle up against him. She contented herself with reaching across and laying her hand on his thigh.

"When does Madison get back?" he asked.

"Tomorrow afternoon. What about Jason?"

"Same. Guess that means we can sleep in late."

She offered him a suspicious smile. "And where are you planning to do this sleeping in late?"

"Thought I'd leave that decision up to you. Your bed or mine?"

She realized there was no point in pretending that tonight wasn't going to end with them going to bed together. She wouldn't have minded if he'd canceled dinner and simply taken her to bed. But she was also enjoying the thought of being wooed. "Mine."

Reaching into his jacket pocket, he brought out a CD. "Why don't you put this on?"

She wasn't surprised to see that it was Whitney Houston's "I Will Always Love You." The song they'd danced to in the stairwell.

"I'm surprised you could find it," she said as she opened the case, took out the CD, and popped it into the player.

"I've had it for a while."

"What's a while?" she asked.

"Oh, about nine years."

His admission made her feel warm, special, cared for. "I'm beginning to believe that you're a sentimentalist at heart."

"Only where you're concerned. Play it."

She punched the CD player's on button, and the song filled the car. She wondered what other surprises he had in mind for the evening.

Jack didn't think he'd ever walked into a place with a woman as beautiful or graceful as Kelley on his arm. He wanted the night to be special for her, for them.

The restaurant was everything that Mrs. Lambert had promised him it would be. He and Kelley sat at a white-cloth-covered table in a darkened corner. A candle surrounded by flowers flickered in its center. The atmosphere was refined, quiet. Romantic.

He'd ordered the wine that Mrs. Lambert had suggested, and, to his surprise, he even liked the way it tasted.

"This is nice, Jack," Kelley said.

Taking her hand, he pressed a kiss to her palm. "I'm glad you like it."

"You're spoiling me."

"That's the plan."

He'd never been much for fancy restaurants where the prices weren't included on the menu, but he'd wanted something they'd never had together. A night to remember. Hopefully the first of many.

When the dessert dishes were cleared away and he'd taken care of the bill, he led her upstairs, where a live band was playing the slow kind of music that older people danced to. They found another corner table, ordered drinks, and simply sat for a while, holding hands, watching others dance.

"How did you discover this place?" she asked.

"Mrs. Lambert. She's a virtual fountain of information."

"I've never been anywhere this nice," she said. "I feel as though I should have worn an evening gown."

"You're beautiful just the way you are."

"Flattery will get you everywhere, Jack."

He kissed each of her fingers. "It's not just flattery, Kelley. I mean everything I say."

She squeezed his hand. "I know you do."

"So, you know I mean it when I say I want to dance."

She smiled. "I thought you were never going to ask."

He led her onto the dance floor, smoothly taking her into his arms and holding her close.

The dance was different from their dance at the Broken Wagon. Here they weren't surrounded by her students. They weren't dealing with Madison.

It was only the two of them, moving slowly to the rhythm of a song that seemed to weave its way around them. She placed her head in the nook of his shoulder. She'd had too much wine, too many drinks, while he'd been conservative. She was certain because he intended to drive them home. One glass of wine. One whiskey sour.

She was sure Jack Morgan wasn't perfect. But whatever his flaws, they were minuscule, not readily apparent. He was an exemplary father. A good man.

He offered her guidance in her dealings with Madison, and while they might not always agree, she had to admit that she respected his opinion, was even on occasion willing to concede that he was right. She liked the way he handled Madison, with just enough firmness. She'd give anything to be able to imitate his style.

But her relationship with Madison was vastly different from his—just as he'd pointed out. And even then, there were facets to it that he didn't know about.

Madison was so very important to her, but she was beginning to see that perhaps she was putting Madison first a little too often. Sometimes Kelley needed to reach for the things that she wanted.

And she wanted Jack.

The music ended, and Jack whispered, "Another dance or home?"

"Home."

Home where her bed waited. Home where she could have what she wanted.

Kelley thought the ride home would never end. She wanted Jack, wanted him now, wanted him as if she'd never wanted him before.

It was more than the wine and the music, the dancing and the dinner.

It was the way he looked at her. As though she were precious. As though she'd never made mistakes, as though her past didn't exist.

It was the way he continually touched her as though he couldn't get enough of her. A kiss on her palm, her fingers. A combing back of her hair. A touch of his finger along her cheek. A brush of his lips over hers.

Tonight he was restrained, passion leashed, and it was driving her crazy.

She was used to the sensual looks, but she was accustomed to a hot kiss following them. All his innuendos and hints of longing were absent.

It was as though he wanted to provide the setting and leave the passion up to her.

She wanted to drive him wild, make him hot with desire, force him to be all she needed.

He'd barely closed and locked the door to her

house before she was in his arms, running her hands through his hair, pressing her mouth to his. His low growl, his hands urging her closer, alerted her to the fact that she'd either misjudged his complacency or unleashed his desires.

His mouth was as eager as hers. His hands as demanding. She shoved his jacket off his shoulders. It dropped to the floor.

She took two steps back. He followed and unzipped her dress. It pooled at her feet.

Another two steps back as she unbuttoned his shirt. It hit the floor.

She kicked off her shoes. He did the same.

Then he had her against the wall, their breathing harsh, their goals the same: removing clothes as quickly as possible.

He trailed his mouth along her throat. "Damn, I thought tonight was never going to end," he rasped.

"I thought you wanted it to be special," she said, nipping at his shoulder.

"I did. But I can only be civilized for so long."

She laughed, the sound echoing between them.

He dragged her to the bedroom. By the time they tumbled onto her bed, neither wore a stitch of clothing. Their bodies were hot and ready. Their hands caressing, stroking, igniting.

"Damn." He bolted upright.

"What?" she demanded.

"I need my wallet. Condom."

"Drawer in the nightstand."

He jerked it open too hard, and it fell to the floor. "Sorry."

"Doesn't matter."

She pressed her breasts to his back as he sorted through everything that had tumbled out.

"Got it," he finally said.

When he turned, rolling them both back onto the bed, he had protection in place, and his mouth was once again devouring hers. Hot, steady, insistent. Pulling her to the brink. Pushing her back from the edge.

She was writhing beneath him, wanting what he could give her.

She felt as though her nerve endings were on fire, sensitive beyond anything she'd ever experienced before. Her body was coiling, seeking release, threatening to ignite.

He entered her with one sure thrust that had her calling out his name. They moved in rhythm, his body pumping into hers. The pleasure built, then spiraled out of control, sending her over the edge. Her body tightened around his.

Her orgasm ripped through her, leaving her barely aware that his powerful body was trembling with the force of his release. Their harsh breathing echoed around them.

He lowered his glistening body to her. "Damn, I'm going to take you out to a fancy restaurant more often."

He rolled off her and tucked her up against his side.

"Did I empty your gas tank?" she asked.

"I think so. Yeah. Definitely."

She lay there, her heart slowing as his hand lethargically stroked her back. She had a feeling that tonight neither had held anything back—not physically, not emotionally.

There had been no guilt, no doubts, no reservations.

She knew that tomorrow they would return. But as she drifted off to sleep, she was content to remain within the shelter of his arms.

Kelley awoke lethargically, completely relaxed, the sun shining in her face and a familiar finger drawing circles on her stomach, figure eights around her navel. With a slow, happy smile of contentment, she opened her eyes. Jack was resting up on an elbow, his dark head bent. She could see sworls in his hair from where he'd lain on it. She stroked the back of her hand along the side of his bristly cheek. She loved the rasp of rough stubble. His hand stilled as he turned his head toward her, his blue eyes intense and penetrating.

"Morning," she whispered in a low, sultry voice.

Ignoring her greeting, he said, "Do you know that I've never seen you naked in the light?"

She widened her eyes as realization dawned more brightly than the sun outside her window. Jerking upright, she searched for the sheet, but he'd moved it off to the side, beyond reach. He splayed his large hand and strong fingers over her stomach.

"Too late," he said in a silky voice. "I saw the scar, Kelley."

She sank back. It was just as well. This wasn't a secret she wanted to keep from him anymore. Let him pass judgment.

"Stephanie had a scar like yours," he said quietly. "Hers was a result of the C-section she had when she gave birth to Jason."

She tried to swallow but discovered her mouth had gone incredibly dry. She simply nodded.

"Was it my baby?"

"Oh, God, no." Reaching out, she cradled his face. "It was long before I met you. I was fifteen."

"You had a baby when you were fifteen?"

She nodded. "A result of that one night I told you about."

A shadowy expression that she couldn't read crossed over his face. "What happened to the baby, Kelley?"

Tears burned her eyes, scalded her throat. Sitting up, she scooted back against the headboard and wrapped her arms around her drawn-up knees. "Jack—"

"Tell me about your baby," he demanded.

Your baby. No one had ever called her that before. No one had ever let her be Kelley's baby.

"I gave her up," she confessed. The tears she'd been fighting to keep in check flowed over onto her cheeks. "I put her up for adoption."

Even though she was certain he'd expected her to reveal exactly what she had, he lay there stone still, as though he couldn't quite determine what to do with the words she uttered.

"You put her up for adoption?" he finally muttered as though he were waking up from a long sleep.

Pressing her lips together to stifle her cry, she nodded.

"You put your baby up for adoption but *insisted* that I marry Stephanie and do right by *mine*—who, by the way, turned out *not* to be mine?"

Oh, God, this was hard, almost unbearable. She'd insisted because she knew how difficult, how heartwrenching, it was to give her child up. She hadn't wanted Stephanie to have to suffer through that torment, hadn't wanted Jack to look back in later years and wonder where his child was or how it was doing. She nodded jerkily. "I was trying to spare you both the anguish of giving up a child."

"The anguish of giving up a child? What about the anguish of giving up the only woman I ever loved?"

She wrapped her arms around her bent legs, trying to draw herself into a tight, comforting ball. "Oh, Jack—"

He rolled off the bed, presenting her with his back. His tattoo filled her vision, and for the first time she realized whose broken heart it represented. His. And she realized with startling clarity that she'd been the one to break it.

"Jack, I'm so sorry."

He faced her. "Sorry?" He shook his head as though to clear it. "Was this a case of do as I say and not as I do? Why didn't *you* get married? Why not practice what you were preaching?"

"I was fifteen. I had no job. No education. Limited possibilities. And the baby's father"—she pressed a hand to her mouth, remembering the pain of his accusations—"wouldn't marry me. He told people he wasn't the father." She searched his face, trying to find a spark of understanding, a hint of compassion. "My parents believed him, Jack. They believed *him*. Not me. And they were so ashamed. I was lost, so confused, wanting to do the right thing but not knowing what that was."

Staring at her, Jack plowed his fingers through his hair. His head was filled with a riotous confusion of conflicting emotions. Part of him wanted to be sympathetic, understanding. She'd only been fifteen. Part of him wanted to lash out. He could see now how she'd been totally irrational when he'd told her about Stephanie's pregnancy. He'd always assumed it was because of her disappointment in him. Now he wasn't so certain. Now he wondered if it stemmed more from disappointment in herself.

"You weren't happy with your choices, and my situation was the opportunity to do the right thing," he said.

"No, it's not that simple. I know realistically that I had no choice except to give her up. But you and Stephanie had a chance to be a family."

He laughed harshly. A family. All he'd been was miserable. "You know what I think? I think you projected me onto that scum who got you pregnant or him onto me." He shook his head, trying to get things straight in his mind. He'd suggested getting DNA testing done to prove the baby wasn't his. She'd shot that idea down. He'd said he wasn't the father. She wouldn't listen to his arguments. "You didn't want Stephanie going through what you went through. To hell with Jack, let's protect the mother."

"No, it wasn't like that. She said you were the father. Why would she lie? I didn't lie about Randy. I didn't think Stephanie would lie about you."

"Well, you sure had that wrong, didn't you? And I loved you so damned much, Kelley, I would have done anything to keep you from being disappointed in me. Anything. Marry the girl, you said. And so I did. Do right by the baby, and I did. When were you planning on telling me?"

"Never."

He scoffed. "So, we were going to make love in the dark for the rest of our lives?"

It didn't escape Kelley's notice that he was talking in the past tense now. He'd *loved* her. Possibly no more. They *were* going to make love. Probably no more.

And what hurt most of all was that he didn't know the worst of it, and she couldn't bear to tell him, couldn't stand to see the complete disgust in his eyes. Couldn't reveal her darkest secret for fear that in his anger, he'd reveal it to Madison, Madison, who would never forgive her for the deceit.

As though reading her mind, he said, "Madison doesn't know, does she?"

"No!" She scrambled to her feet, his word a catalyst. She had to protect Madison from the truth at all costs. "And you can't tell her. My parents did everything they could to protect me, to protect Madison."

"What were they protecting Madison from?"

"The scandal."

"We don't live in the Victorian era. It's not as if unwed mothers are labeled and shunned."

"The times may be modern, but my parents weren't. They didn't want anyone to know about the pregnancy. It's always been my dirty little secret. Hidden away, not talked about."

Dropping the sheet, he snatched his jeans up off the floor and jerked them on.

"What are you doing?" she asked.

"Getting dressed."

"Are you leaving?"

"Yep. My son will be home in a little while." Looking over his shoulder, he glared at her. "You know, the *son* I didn't abandon."

"I didn't abandon my daughter."

"Really? What do you call it? You didn't keep her. What makes you any different from my mother? From Stephanie? The going gets rough, and so you go."

"That is so unfair, Jack."

"Unfair or not, everything I thought about you is

crumbling. You deliberately kept this information from me. You ran away from your responsibility as a mother. I think you ran away from me. I think you were afraid to commit to me, and so you foisted me off on Stephanie. Convenient. You can't handle Madison. Rather than stand your ground, you run back here. And here I am again. I'm starting to think excuses are all you're good for. That and a great romp in bed."

Tears blurred her vision. "You bastard."

"That's right, Kelley. That's exactly what I am. My mother wasn't married, either. Took her seventeen years to abandon me, but you know what? Abandonment is abandonment. So, this time, I'll spare you having to come up with any excuse to leave me. This time, I'm the one who'll do the walking."

Stunned by his words, his anger, his resentment, she could do little more than watch him gather up his things and stride from her room. She heard the front door slam shut. Heard his truck start up. Heard him drive away.

Everything within her was screaming—at the unfairness, at his failure to understand, at the betrayals. The betrayal by her baby's father. Jack's betrayal nine years ago and now. But most of all, screaming because her parents had betrayed her as she'd never anticipated.

She walked into her closet, stood on her tiptoes, and grabbed the metal box that housed her most precious possessions. Returning to her bedroom, she took a key out of her jewelry box and crossed over to the bed. Sitting, she laid the box beside her hip, twisted slightly, and inserted the key.

The fireproof box was where she kept everything of value. Inside was the letter that Jack had written her, a letter she'd never opened. Since returning to Hopeful, she'd been tempted countless times to read it, to discover exactly what he'd written nine years ago, but in hindsight it probably wouldn't have the same meaning it would have had nine years ago. She'd view the words differently, through the eyes of a woman who had changed. And the words were probably not ones that the Jack Morgan of today would write.

But it wasn't his letter that had drawn her into the closet. It was the secret photos. Only half a dozen. Taken by her best friend in high school, taken and secreted away because her parents would have never approved of her keeping them. But how could she not?

Taking out the pictures, she ran her finger over the image of her holding her little baby girl. She'd been so tiny, her face all scrunched up. Kelley had thought her heart would burst with the love swelling within her. All she'd wanted was for the baby to grow up happy, healthy, and wiser than her mother.

She'd truly believed she was doing the right thing. But now, seeing Jack with his son, she was no longer so certain. Jack hadn't wanted responsibility for a child. And yet he'd taken it. A child whom he hadn't fathered.

While Kelley had handed over the child of her womb to others. She understood Jack's anger, knew he would never forgive her. How could he when she'd never forgiven herself?

Chapter 19

Hammering the cedar plank into place, working on an addition to his deck that he'd been contemplating for several months, Jack was mad at the world, women in particular, Kelley specifically.

And when he was angry, he built. Based on the depth of his fury, he figured he could add a second floor to his house. A third and a fourth. Several decks.

He'd awoken this morning with his arms wrapped around Kelley and the sunlight pouring in through the windows, the draperies never having been drawn closed the night before. He'd taken his time studying all the lines and curves of her face in profile. He'd eventually moved his gaze down to her neck, her shoulders.

Then, with a soft sigh, she'd rolled onto her back, her palms against the pillow, her fingers curled. She'd looked sweet and innocent, and he'd thought he wanted to wake up to this every morning of his life.

He'd begun slowly trailing his finger over her warm flesh, around her breasts, between them, under them. He'd outlined every rib. Then he'd gingerly moved the sheet aside and begun exploring lower, relishing her perfection, feasting his gaze on that which until this morning had been denied his eyes.

And then he'd spotted the scar, and his brain had engaged in some sort of mind warp, replacing Kelley with Stephanie. He could see his ex-wife, see her scar, hear her bemoaning the imperfection. She'd loathed every change of her body that her pregnancy had brought. She'd despised every diaper she had to change, every feeding she had to provide. Jack had wondered many a time if maybe she lacked some sort of motherhood gene.

His mind had warped back, and he was with Kelley. Kelley, who had insisted he get married.

With a curse, he buried the nail into the wood. He thought of Madison and tried to envision her a year younger and pregnant. Rocking back on his heels, he superimposed Kelley over her sister. They looked so much alike, it wasn't difficult to imagine Kelley as Madison was. But he didn't think she'd have Madison's attitude.

No, she would have been sweeter. How had she managed to get herself into that situation? He hadn't even bothered to ask. He'd simply jumped down her throat because she'd taken the easy way out and had expected him to take the hard way.

He slammed the hammer against another nail. Only maybe her way hadn't been so easy after all. Was her way responsible for the haunted look he sometimes saw in her eyes? Was her way the reason she kept such a tight rein on Madison—because she didn't want her to have to go through giving up her child? She was trying so damned hard to be to Madison what she hadn't been to her own child.

He hefted another board, set it in place, and began pounding another nail. His muscles bunched and stretched with his efforts. He'd gotten angry this morning because he'd always thought she was perfect. And he'd wanted her to look at him and see someone of value.

Only she wasn't perfect. She was flawed like everyone else. She'd made a mistake in her youth, and he had a feeling she was still paying for it. Otherwise, why wouldn't she face it? Why had she felt the need to keep it from him?

And she had felt the need. They'd made love only in low light or the dark. She'd hidden from him in the shadows. She was hiding from Madison as well.

If she'd open up to Madison, explain why she was so overprotective, maybe she could hit an accord with the kid. Or maybe Madison would react as Jack had and throw out accusations. He'd reacted from the gut, which he wasn't particularly proud of right now.

He briefly wondered how Madison could not know that her sister had been one of the statistics, a teen pregnancy. But if Kelley was fifteen when she had the baby and she was thirty-one now, sixteen years had passed. Madison would have been born shortly afterward. Kelley and her mother would probably have been pregnant at the same time. What a thing for mother and daughter to go through together. And when the babies were born: a joyous moment for one, a shameful moment for the other.

He stilled. Sixteen years. Shouldn't she have accepted that she'd given the child up for adoption by now? Or did a mother never accept that, was she always wondering about her child?

He shook his head, remembering how quickly tears had sprung to her eyes, as though he'd gouged a raw wound. Slowly, he stretched to his full height, the hammer thudding to the ground near his feet. All he'd seen when he looked at her was abandonment. He hadn't wanted to see a mother's struggles. He'd wanted to be the aggrieved party, because it was so much easier to be the one hurting than to be the one who needed to offer comfort to the one who was hurting.

She wasn't his mother. She wasn't Stephanie. She hadn't abandoned her child. Every day she lived with her choice. Just as every day he lived with his.

"It was awesome, Dad," Jason said around a mouthful of pizza.

The boys had been starving the minute Serena drove into the driveway. They'd barely given Jack time to wash off the dirt of his labors before they'd persuaded him to take everyone out to Vinnie's Pizzeria.

Jason swallowed and continued. "The puppies were so tiny. And their eyes were closed, but they still found the milk. So maybe when they get old enough, we could go back to Grandpa Larry's and pick one out to keep."

Jack exchanged a knowing glance with Serena. He

should have known where this conversation was leading. He'd always liked Serena's parents. They'd made him and his son feel welcome the first time they'd ever visited, had insisted everyone call them Grandpa Larry and Grandma Mary.

"A dog is a big responsibility," Jack informed everyone at the table, because he knew if Jason brought a dog home, sure as shooting, Riker was going to bring one home as well. And vice versa. The boys were practically joined at the hip. One didn't do without the other one doing.

"Me and Riker know that," Jason said, confirming Jack's suspicions that he'd been targeted as the weaker link, the parent who would be easier to crack.

"What's your mom think about you having a dog, Riker?" Jack asked.

Riker exchanged a quick look with Jason. "She said it depends on what you say."

"I see. Who's going to pay for the vet bills?" Jack asked. "Dogs have to get shots."

"We will," Jason assured him. "We'll wash cars or something to raise money."

"Who's going to feed him, bathe him, walk him?" Jack asked.

"We will," Riker answered. "You won't even know the dog's there."

"Oh, I doubt that. Who's going to clean up the mess he makes before he's trained?" Jack asked.

"Mom," Riker answered quickly, no doubt at all in his voice.

Jack laughed, and Serena chuckled.

"Think again, boys," Serena said, smiling.

"But, Dad, we saw the puppies being born, so it's like they're ours."

Studying his son, Jack understood that feeling. He'd felt it the first time he gazed on Jason. He sometimes wondered who had really gotten Stephanie pregnant, but if she knew, she wasn't saying. Not that Jack would have given Jason up without a fight. For all he knew, the man who had fathered Jason could have been a stranger passing through town.

He supposed there would come a time when he'd have to discuss the truth with Jason, but he didn't see that happening for a long while. Jason was his son. It didn't matter whose genes he carried.

He'd been grateful no one had ever challenged his right to have Jason as his son. The boy gave him roots, and when they were together, neither was an outcast. Kelley's wanting to make up for her past had given him his future.

And he'd thrown it all in her face.

"What about the dog?" Jason prodded.

"I'll think about it," Jack said.

Jason and Riker tapped knuckles, and Jack knew they read him too well. "I'll think about it" was too close to a yes in their young minds. Probably because it usually did turn into a yes.

As soon as the boys finished their pizza, Jack gave them a handful of quarters, and they went off to play the video games, leaving him with Serena.

"They must have worn you out," Jack said.

She smiled softly. "They always wear me out, but I wouldn't have it any other way." She shoved her plate aside and leaned toward him. "I sorta thought you'd have Kelley here tonight."

Sadly, he shook his head. "I think I might have made a mistake where she's concerned."

"You mean, in thinking she was *the* one?"

"No, in making her think she wasn't."

Chapter 20

Jack sat at his desk, his mind wandering from the paperwork he needed to concentrate on. He'd left messages on Kelley's answering machine at home and at the school. She hadn't returned his calls. Not that he blamed her. He'd been an incredible jerk.

He'd considered dropping by the school, but he decided a more private meeting would be best. But how was he going to arrange that? He needed to speak with her when Madison wasn't around. So her house was out, unless he went on twenty-four-hour surveillance, watching for an opportune moment when Kelley was home and Madison wasn't. Who knew when that would happen?

He didn't think he could make Kelley venture across his threshold. Short of arresting her and locking himself in a cell with her, he didn't know how he was going to get her alone. Although his last thought had some merit. Might even be fun. Especially if he took a pair of handcuffs into the cell with him.

On second thought, she probably wouldn't be too receptive to that idea.

As a general rule, he was confident of his place in the world. He'd worked hard to attain it. But where Kelley was concerned, he was never certain exactly where he stood. Even when he thought he knew, something nagged at the back of his mind, something that said she wasn't a hundred percent with him. It was the guy who was supposed to relish the physical and shun the emotional. Kelley seemed to relish the physical as long as he didn't push for a commitment. What was wrong with this picture?

He'd finally determined that what was wrong with the picture was that Kelley didn't have a lot of reasons to trust the opposite sex. She'd gotten pregnant, and the guy had refused to claim her or the child, had left her high and dry, to make do on her own.

So then she took a chance on Jack. And what did he do? Called her late at night, told her she was the only one for him, convinced her of it if the way they'd celebrated graduation night was any indication—and yet he'd betrayed her as well, with Stephanie. Based upon what he knew about Kelley's past now, based upon what he figured she'd faced, how else was she supposed to react when Stephanie had announced she was carrying Jack's baby?

The whole situation had been insane. They'd been too young, gullible, caught up with their own insecurities, to think things through clearly. But immaturity wasn't an excuse. It was simply a detriment. And they'd all paid for it.

In a way, Jack figured he'd come out ahead. He had

Jason. And he did love the kid, would do anything to ensure his safety, keep him happy and healthy. The kid loved him, which he considered somewhat of a miracle. Before Jason, Jack's life had lacked anyone who truly loved him just for being him. He even had doubts about Kelley, doubts that nagged at him and that he hated feeling. Had he simply been a project to her back in high school?

What did it matter what he was then? What mattered was now. How he felt about her, how she felt about him. Once he'd calmed down and was looking at things rationally, he realized he loved her, heart and soul, for better or worse. He just needed an opportunity to tell her, to convince her that nothing from their past mattered. All that mattered was the future.

The sharp rap on his door brought him out of his reverie. "Yeah?"

The door opened, and Mike stuck his head into the room. "Chief, we just got a call that I thought you might want to deal with. It's Mr. Gunther. He says he's caught a shoplifter and has a gun trained on her."

"Shit!" Jack was up from behind his desk and out his office door before his expletive settled into silence. He didn't want to think about the damage Mr. Gunther could accomplish with a gun in his hands.

Feeling as if she were in some bad B movie, Madison stood in the tiny convenience store where people had no choice but to come in to pay for their gas. The pumps were ancient. They didn't even take credit cards. Madison didn't know why people bothered with them. Maybe to get a closer look at the giant inflated gorilla that guarded them. Or, more likely, they dropped by for the same reason she did—the convenience.

She'd been in the store several times since she'd moved to Hopeful. It wasn't that far from the house she and Kelley were renting. She liked the store, even though it had a funny odor, because the old guy behind the cash register always looked as though he were half asleep.

So it had been easy to slip a few items into her purse, undetected. Or so she thought. She'd been heading for the door when he'd come out of his chair with a gun in his hand and told her to reach for the sky. His exact words.

"As if," had been her reply until she'd realized how badly his gnarled hands were shaking. So she'd raised her hands. Whenever she tried to explain, he ordered her to shut up.

Not that there was really anything to explain. And she was grateful she'd gotten caught. She'd been good, so good, just as Kelley wanted, but they weren't going to be moving back to Dallas. Madison was certain of it. Kelley and the sheriff were spending way too much time together.

When Madison had been at Ronda's, they'd talked about her concerns that she was going to be stuck in

Podunk until she graduated. The shoplifting had been Ronda's idea.

If Kelley would just move back to Dallas, Madison would behave again. She'd be with her friends, where she belonged. She'd gotten lost and angry after her parents died, but she was over that now.

She had to make Kelley understand that.

She heard the sirens and wasn't certain if she wanted them to be headed her way or not. If the cops were coming to save her, fine. Let them come. But if they were coming to arrest her, she'd prefer that they just keep driving on by.

The old man grinned, and his hands started to shake more visibly. She remembered the sheriff talking about how easy it was to get shot. She so did not want to get shot.

"Told you the cops would come," he said. "You're in big trouble now, little girl."

"I'm not a little girl."

"You will be in the big house."

The big house? Honestly, could the situation get any worse?

It could. The hinges squeaked and groaned as Jack Morgan jerked open the screen door with the Dr Pepper metal sign across it. And he did not look happy.

Jack swiveled in his chair, then leaned back and tapped his fingers on his desk, all the while never taking his impatient glare from his culprit. She wouldn't meet his gaze, but he could see the tears that kept popping into her eyes and vanishing.

"We've been here before, haven't we, kid?" he asked.

Without looking at him, she lifted both shoulders into a rebellious shrug. "So, are you, like, arresting me or what?"

"What."

She jerked her attention to him. "What's that mean?"

"You asked if I was arresting you or what. Since I'm not arresting you, then the answer is what."

"So you're not arresting me?" she repeated incredulously.

"Nope. But you're not free to go until your sister gets here."

She gave him a fulminous glower. "You're just holding me here so you can see her, and you damn well know it."

"Let's watch the *d* word."

"Fuck you!"

He stilled his fingers. It took more strength of will than he knew he possessed not to jump over the desk and shake her. "Who are you trying to hurt, Madison?"

She shook her head. "You couldn't possibly understand."

"You don't think so? Kid, I did everything you did. Shoplifted, drank, acted tough. Anything I could think of to get my mother's attention. Know what happened? She walked out, walked off. Never looked back."

"Yeah, well, Kelley's not my mother."

"She's trying to be." And it occurred to him that maybe Kelley was trying so hard because she saw Madison as a second chance, an opportunity to be to her sister what she'd never had a chance to be to her own daughter.

"You hurt her," Madison accused.

"That was a long time ago."

"A long time ago? When you were her student?"

Damn. He'd been manipulated. There was a subtle increase of interest in her voice. He remembered now that Kelley had told him that she hadn't told Madison about them. The little hellion was good. Suspicious but good.

A rap on the door, and Mike stuck his head inside. "Chief, Miss Spencer is here."

Taking a deep breath, Jack got to his feet. "Show her in."

There was a sadness in her eyes that he figured he'd put there. He was tired of the secrets, the things not said that needed to be said. And even though he knew she wasn't going to like it, he was going to say plenty in the next few minutes.

Her gaze lingered on him briefly before she crossed her arms beneath her chest, turned, and faced Madison. "What'd she do this time?"

Good for her, he thought. She didn't have the lost look about her this time. And she didn't appear to be in a mood to take any crap.

"She was imitating Winona Ryder," Jack said.

Disappointment seemed to wash through her. "You were shoplifting?"

Madison shrugged.

"Madison, answer me."

"I would have paid him."

"What did you take?"

"Nothing."

"If you didn't take anything, then why are you here?"

"Because *he* doesn't like me."

Kelley looked at Jack. He could see her shoring up her resolve.

"What did she take, Jack?"

"A pack of gum, a bag of candy, and a lighter."

"Is that what you took? Something you could have easily bought?"

Madison stood. "It's no big deal. I don't know why everyone is going so ballistic. Just pay him five bucks so we can go home."

"No, Madison, it's not going to be that easy this time." She held Jack's gaze. "You mentioned before"—she swallowed—"about community service."

Jack propped his hip on the edge of his desk, to lower himself so he wasn't the dominant one in the room. He doubted that anyone other than him would notice that he was recognizing Kelley's authority. "She took the items from Gunther's convenience store. Gunther has a problem with people writing graffiti on his public restroom walls, so we have a policy around here that the punishment for nonviolent crimes that take place in or around that establishment involves painting the bathrooms and cleaning them for a month."

"Bullshit! I'm not—"

"Madison!"

Madison looked as surprised by Kelley's sharp interruption as Jack felt.

Kelley took a deep breath and nodded. "That sounds like a fair punishment. When do you want her to do it?"

"Tomorrow morning, eight o'clock."

"No way," Madison said. "I sleep late on Saturday."

"Not tomorrow, kid. I'll be by to pick you up at seven-thirty. Dress down."

"I'm not doing it. This is so totally not fair. Kelley, it was a pack of gum."

"What you took isn't the point, and you know it. I honestly don't know what gets into you sometimes. You stole, Madison. You broke the law."

"Why are you siding with him?"

"I'm not siding with Jack."

"Yes, you are. You're just trying to impress him."

"This has nothing to do with Jack and everything to do with you. I'm trying to do what's best for you."

"You don't know what's best for me. You're not my mother! I hate you! You're ruining my life."

Madison tore out of the room, brushing past Kelley. Jack had seen that broadsided-by-a-hit-and-run-driver look on Kelley's face before, the first night she'd been in his office, when Madison had said almost the same thing.

"Shit," he ground out, feeling as if he'd taken a kick to the midsection himself. All the varied bits of information that he'd been juggling around his mind suddenly came together with the force of an implosion. The age difference between Kelley and Madison. Kelley's mother hadn't had a baby at the same time Kelley did. Only Kelley had a baby. "Ah, damn, Kelley."

He came off his desk and drew Kelley against his chest. She was trembling as if someone had dunked her in ice water.

"See?" she rasped. "If I try and stand firm, it just makes it worse."

"Sit down."

She shook her head and tried to break free of his hold. "No, I have to go after her."

"No, I'm going to have Mike go after her." He led her to the chair. "I want you to sit."

As soon as she dropped into the chair, he went to the door. "Mike?"

"Yeah, Chief?" Mike got up from his desk and started toward him.

"Go after Miss Gardner. Her car is at Gunther's, so that's probably where she's headed. Pick her up. Handcuff her if you have to. Then take her home, see that she gets inside safely, and watch her."

"Yes, sir."

Jack turned back into his office and closed the door. Kelley heard the click of the door and wrapped her arms around herself. She was cold. So cold. She was vaguely aware of Jack crouching in front of her.

"Madison is your daughter, isn't she?" he asked quietly. "The one you gave up for adoption?"

Tears pooled in her eyes and spilled over onto her cheeks as she shook her head, denying out of habit what she'd denied for so long.

Tenderly, with his thumb, he wiped the tears from her cheeks. "Don't you see? It explains so much. You gave her up for adoption, but she was always within your sight. Always there. How hard it must have been to watch your parents raise her, to hear her call your mother Mommy, to have her believe you were her sister."

Oh, God, it hurt. It hurt to remember. It hurt to know he knew all her flaws. Knew how totally inadequate she was. Pressing her arms against her chest, she began rocking back and forth, back and forth, while little gasps escaped from between her lips. She tasted the salt of her tears, pooling at the corners of her mouth.

"It's all right, Kelley."

"No, it's not, Jack. It'll never be all right. I wanted to keep her," she rasped, the pain almost unbearable.

"I know," he said in a low, comforting voice as he pulled her from the chair and cradled her on his lap.

She clutched his shirt. "I was only fifteen. I hadn't finished school. I didn't have a job. My mom convinced me that letting her adopt Madison was the best thing for Madison. But she made me swear that I could never tell Madison that I was her mother. She said it would destroy my baby."

She buried her face in the nook of his shoulder. He held her close, his large hand rubbing her back. "She was born in Austin. My stepfather got a job transfer to Dallas, so we could move and no one would know the baby wasn't theirs. It was so hard watching her with my parents, being her *sister*. Knowing how much I'd disappointed them. I thought if I could just be really, really good, they'd love me again. Love me the way they loved her. But it was too hard. That's why I wanted to teach here, in a small town, away from Dallas."

"Kelley—"

She shook her head. "When you married Stephanie, I moved back home because I wanted to be near my little girl. I wanted to raise her; I wanted her back. But she was almost eight. How could I explain to her what I'd done? How can I tell her now?"

"I don't know, sweetheart."

She leaned back until she was able to see his face, to see the understanding and the love reflected in his eyes. He kissed her sweetly, tenderly, his hand cupping the back of her head.

She pulled back. "I need to get home to Madison."

"You need to get yourself together first. You can't go home looking like this," he said. "Mike will take care of her. Let me get you some coffee."

Shivering, she nodded. She closed her eyes, wondering how she could stuff her secrets back into the darkened corner where they belonged.

Leaning his hips against his desk, Jack studied Kelley as she drank the coffee he'd handed her.

No wonder she guarded Madison so diligently. No wonder she seemed so irrationally possessive. She was trying to spare Madison from making the mistakes she had, spare her without ever letting her realize she'd made mistakes. Madison saw her sister as a Goody Two-shoes who didn't know what it was to be a teenager. She didn't realize she was looking at a mother who had sacrificed everything for the welfare of her child. She couldn't appreciate what her mother had done because she had no idea she was adopted.

He couldn't imagine anything more unfair—to Kelley or to Madison. And yet he supposed Kelley's parents had been trying to protect both of them—their daughter and their granddaughter. After all, Madison eventually would have noticed that she looked a hell of a lot like her sister. And that would have aroused her suspicions.

He couldn't even begin to imagine how difficult it would be to explain Jason's parentage to him, watching the hurt and confusion take hold. So Jack understood Kelley's fears. How could she tell a sixteen-year-old girl that everything she knew about her past had been a lie?

"So, how'd you find yourself pregnant at fifteen?" he asked quietly.

She rolled one shoulder into a shrug. "More lone-liness than rebellion. When my mother remarried, I didn't take well to having a stepfather. I'd had my mother's undivided attention, even when she was married to my dad, and then suddenly, here was an-other man in the house, and she was always fussing over him. I felt left out. I wanted to feel special, I wanted to be touched, hugged, loved. Having sex with Randy seemed like an easy way to obtain all three."

A corner of her mouth tipped up in a sad imitation of a smile. "I think he thought foreplay was a golfing term. He certainly didn't give me the attention you did. The act itself hurt, but thank goodness he was quick. I've always callously thought of him as the minute man. Afterward, I was embarrassed and just wanted to wash him off. We just had that one time, but that's all it took."

He desperately wanted to put his arms around her, but she was barely holding herself together and looked as if a touch might shatter her.

"And when you discovered you were pregnant?"

She released a deep sigh. "I thought I'd made the biggest mistake of my life. I knew my mom and step-father would be disappointed, angry. I thought they might even kick me out of the house. Some parents still do that, anger and shame blocking out reason.

"They surprised me, though. They were hurt, they were upset. But they were willing to do what they could to make things easier for me, if I was willing to follow their rules. My mother was young when she had a hysterectomy, so she couldn't have any more children. She was my stepfather's first marriage, and he'd gone into it knowing they'd never have children. Mom was in her early forties, my stepfather in his late forties, but they decided that raising a baby together was what they wanted to do. But it had to be *their* baby. They wanted to raise the baby as theirs. They wanted to be a mother and a father.

"Their solution seemed perfect. I was terrified, overwhelmed by the responsibility of bringing a child into this world. So I could give birth to the baby and turn it over to them without guilt. I knew the baby would be in good hands. I could get on with my life."

"But it wasn't easy."

"No, it wasn't easy. Not at all." She sipped her coffee.

He could see the faraway look come into her eyes, as though she were watching the past, reliving the moments.

"My mother was in the delivery room," she said softly. "She held Madison before I did. I hadn't expected to want to hold her so badly. I'd convinced myself that letting her go would be easy. And it was so far from being easy that I thought I'd die. I told myself that it was good that the first person who held her was the woman who would be her mother. My eyes were so full of tears that I probably wouldn't have been able to see her clearly anyway."

Sniffing, she got up, crossed his office, and set her mug on the table where he kept the coffeepot.

"So your mother took her," Jack said.

She faced him. "Yeah. She said it was important that she immediately be the mother and I be the sister. It made sense to begin as we planned to continue. I knew if I'd simply given Madison up for adoption, if strangers had adopted her, I never would have seen her again. But in a way, it was so much harder watching her with my parents. The first time I heard her call my mother Mommy, I thought my heart would break.

"As I got older, matured, I wanted her back. I wanted my baby back, I wanted to be her mommy, but I knew that was wrong, would hurt Madison, hurt my parents. I'd made my choice, had to live with it. I went off to college, buried myself in my studies, came here to teach, had planned to bury myself in my work"—she gave him a wry grin—"until you distracted me from my purpose. And that's the lurid and ugly tale."

Only he didn't think it was a lurid or ugly tale. Stephanie had given up her child as well, but self-love had motivated her actions. The strength of love that Kelley was talking about humbled Jack. Now that he had Jason in his care, would he give him up if he thought it was best for him? Kelley's parents had been convinced they were doing what was best for Madison. But their unexpected deaths had thrown a kink into everything, shifting responsibility back to Kelley.

Jack wasn't immune to the fact that she'd distanced

herself from him as though she feared he might again distract her from her purpose. He was certainly going to give it his best shot. She was back in his life now, and he didn't want her to leave.

"So you moved back home to forget me?"

"Yes. You think you probably see a pattern developing here, that I run away to escape facing things, but when I was running from here, I was also running back to Madison. I realized that I was missing all those precious moments: watching her discover her world, playing soccer, taking dance lessons. I was like a parent denied custody. Whenever she'd come to spend the night, I'd spoil her rotten. Take her to movies, shopping, dinner. We'd have so much fun. But I was always her sister, her friend, never her mother. I'd sacrificed the right for her to call me mother—for her own good. But I'm sure she wouldn't see it that way."

"Tell her the truth and find out."

She stared at him as though he'd just suggested she do something illegal.

"That's an absurd notion," she finally uttered.

"Why?"

"She'd hate me."

"She hates you now."

"Don't sugarcoat it, Jack. Tell me how you really think she feels."

"All right, I will. I think she's feeling lost—"

"And taking away her past will remedy that?"

He stepped toward her, needing to close the distance. "That night I saw her in the bar, with all that piercing, she struck me as a kid who was trying to hold herself together. All these things she does that make you crazy, she does because she's trying to force you to be parental. So tell her the truth. Stop being her sister, start being her mother."

"You make it sound as though it's a simple solution. But it's a complex problem. You have no idea how difficult it's been watching you with Jason, a child who isn't your biological son. Yet you acknowledge him as your own. And here I am, pretending to be my daughter's sister." She sighed softly, and tears welled in her eyes. "My daughter. I've never called her that before. I've never even thought of her as my daughter. I was afraid if I did that I'd slip. That I'd say something to give myself away."

He studied her, the dark circles beneath her eyes, the hollow cheekbones. She was letting Madison worry her to death.

She peered up at him. "You told me that the first time you held Jason, you fell in love with him. From that moment on, he was your son. And now you expect me to tell Madison that I held her in my arms and then gave her away."

He heard the derision in her voice, the disgust. Not with him but with herself, for what she saw as her own failings.

"You held her in your arms, and you did what you thought was best for her."

"I'm on the brink of losing her completely, Jack. I

honestly believe that the truth will send her over the edge. I can't do it. She thinks her parents are dead. She grieved for them. Now, from the ashes of that grief, I'm supposed to resurrect her mother? I don't think so. I made my choice, and now we all have to live with it."

"If you change your mind, give me a call, anytime day or night. I'll be there to lend you support."

She lifted her eyes to his. "Why couldn't you have been her father?"

He grinned. "Other than the fact that I didn't know you, I was twelve and hadn't yet discovered that sex was more fun when you had a partner."

She laughed, a forced sound that bordered on edgy. "You are so bad, Jack."

"I was, and that's the reason I know that she's crying out for help. No one heard my cries, Kelley, until I was a senior and my English teacher gave me a reason to straighten out my act. My God, I thought you were merciless. If I called you after I didn't turn in an assignment, you hung up on me. You ignored me if I didn't raise my hand in class. You were tough as nails and gave me every reason to hate you. Believe me, I tried to hate you. But all I could do was admire you for not backing down. Every decision I made in the past nine years, I've made with one criterion in mind: Would Kelley Spencer be proud of me if she found out that this was the road I'd decided to travel?"

Tears welled in her eyes. He took hold of her chin

and rubbed his thumb over her lower lip. "For what it's worth, after everything you've told me, I love you at this moment more than I've ever loved you. Sometimes I think I've been waiting my whole life for *us*, and if I have to wait a bit longer, I will."

Chapter 21

No way, no how. Madison absolutely was not going to spend her Saturday painting a stinky old bathroom in a dumpy old gas station that should have been condemned years ago. What was it with this town and its refusal to move into the twenty-first century?

Madison knew Jack Morgan's interest in Kelley was deeply rooted, the product of something that had started long ago. There were just too many clues. The sheriff wasn't the only one who could gather evidence.

So now she was going through boxes in Kelley's closet, looking for proof that Kelley and the sheriff had been involved when he was her student. She didn't plan to make the information public. She knew it could hurt Kelley's career. She didn't want to do that. But she could threaten to expose their past.

That's all she was looking for: a leverage tool. So she wouldn't have to paint a smelly bathroom that probably harbored Ebola germs.

So far, her search hadn't yielded anything significant. A black graduation cap that could have been anyone's. Pressed wildflowers. She wasn't exactly sure what she was searching for or what she expected to find. But there had to be something. A note, a diary, a journal. Kelley was an English teacher. She was always making students keep journals, had always encouraged Madison to keep one. Surely, Kelley practiced what she preached.

She seemed to do so in every other aspect of her life. Madison had never seen her drunk, and she'd certainly never caught anyone coming out of Kelley's bedroom. Still, she knew something serious was developing between Kelley and Morgan. Kelley had practically admitted it at the beach house. And Madison didn't care what Jack Morgan said. You didn't do all those things for a teacher, no matter how much you'd liked being in her class.

Which left only one thing. A little hanky panky behind the overhead projector.

Madison put the lid back on the last box she'd searched and stuffed it back into the corner of the closet from where she'd retrieved it earlier. A horrible thought occurred to her. What if any incriminating evidence was still in Dallas?

It wasn't as if Kelley had packed up *everything* and brought it to Podunk. They'd both left anything they could live without in a storage unit. The question was: Could Kelley live without reminders of Jack Morgan? Would she have left things in Dallas?

Getting to her feet, Madison dusted off her hands, considered hopping into her car and heading to Dallas. This plan had the advantage of ensuring that she wouldn't be anywhere in the area at the crack of dawn and therefore would miss her appointment with the paint can and brush. The disadvantage was that it was a temporary solution. Her butt would be hauled back, and the sheriff would probably make her paint every bathroom in town.

With mounting disappointment that her search had failed, she reached up to turn off the closet light. Her gaze fell on a metal box at the farthest corner of the top shelf. Kelley's safe—a fireproof holder where she kept important documents that she'd temporarily moved out of the safety-deposit box because she knew she was going to need them, things like Madison's birth certificate. She'd known she'd need it to get Madison enrolled in school. Madison had never actually looked at her birth certificate. Kelley guarded it as if it were an expensive piece of jewelry. She kept it in an envelope and was always the one to present it when it was needed. Not that Madison really cared.

But that metal box might also contain some personal memorabilia that Kelley didn't want anyone to get their little hands on. Probably not, but maybe . . .

Madison reached for it, felt her fingers close around the cool metal, and brought the box down. She knelt on the floor and placed the box before her. She tried to lift the lid, but the box was locked. Her heart thundering, she carried it into her room, set it on the desk, and grabbed a paper clip. She unfolded it and began digging it into the keyhole.

The box's main purpose was to protect items from

fire, not from burglars. She couldn't understand why the manufacturer even bothered with a lock or why Kelley had gone to the trouble to use it. She heard the click and smiled.

Taking a deep breath, she slowly opened the box. It contained a hodgepodge of items: photos, letters, documents. She began rummaging through them, ignoring anything that was official-looking and giving photos only a passing glance, since none caught her eye with an image of Jack Morgan on them.

Near the bottom, she found an envelope with a return address from J. Morgan, a postmark dated nine years ago. It was addressed to Ms. Spencer. She slowly brought it out of the box, her palms growing damp. With her luck, it would just be a student thanking a teacher.

She turned it over. So, how come it had been kept but never opened?

Sitting back in her chair, she tapped the edge of the envelope against her fingers. Wouldn't a teacher immediately open a letter from a student, unless she feared it would contain something she didn't want to read? She thought about steaming it open but decided against it. First of all, she had no idea how that approach worked. She'd heard of doing it but had never seen it done. Second, it seemed a little dramatic.

She studied the sealing. Time had eroded the glue somewhat. She slid a ruler beneath the edge of the flap and carefully worked the flap free. She hesitated, not certain she really did want to know what the letter said. On the other hand, it could save her from a fate worse than death.

She pulled out the letter, written on notebook paper, unfolded it, and read the scrawled words.

Dear Ms. Spencer,

I tried calling you before I left town, but you weren't answering your phone. Reckon I can't blame you for that. I joined the army. I'm in basic training right now. Not the hardest thing I've ever done, so I don't figure I'll fail here.

I think about you every night when I'm stretched out on my bunk. I know I'm not supposed to. I'm supposed to be thinking about my wife. I know that's what you'd want me to do. But all I can think about is that one night I had with you. It was perfect. Don't know what I did to deserve it. Hope it was more than just graduating.

I know you said you wouldn't wait, but here's the thing. I love you. I've never said that to anyone but you. I know I made a mistake with Stephanie. I'm just kinda hoping that what you and me had was as important to you as it was to me. If you think you can ever forgive me, write me back. And if you can't . . . well, I guess if I don't hear from you, I'll know the answer to that.

All I can say is that I'm really sorry.

Jack

Madison dropped the letter onto her desk as though it had suddenly ignited in her hands. They'd had one perfect night together. But what did that mean, exactly? Did it mean what she thought it did? And what did it prove? What could she do with this information?

It read as if it were written by a kid, and she supposed nine years ago, the sheriff had been almost that. And Kelley had been equally young. And she'd been hurt. Madison was certain of it now. She remembered the stunned expression on Kelley's face when she'd walked into Morgan's office. She hadn't expected to see him there. Hadn't wanted to see him there.

He'd wanted her forgiveness. She hadn't even opened his letter. The jerk had hurt her sister. And here Madison wanted to do the same thing. Kelley hadn't deserved to be hurt back then, and she didn't deserve it now.

Madison had been throwing tantrums, trying to be in charge. All she really needed to do was sit down with Kelley and tell her how she was truly feeling. She'd done it effortlessly while her parents had been alive. Kelley had always been her champion then. They'd been able to talk, whisper secrets in the dark late at night. Kelley had been not only her sister but her best friend.

Somehow, with their parents' deaths, they'd lost that. But they could get it back. It wasn't too late. If she and Kelley could get as close as they'd once been, they'd go back to Dallas. No problem.

Madison folded the letter up and stuffed it back into the envelope. She grabbed a glue stick out of a desk drawer and quickly sealed it. Kelley would never forgive her for reading this letter. Her sister had obviously forgiven Jack Morgan. Not that Madison could blame her. He was definitely hot. Still, he'd hurt Kelley once before, which meant he could do it again. There was that little matter of trust that Kelley had been telling her about.

She began sorting through the contents of the box again, trying to remember where the letter had been. Not on the bottom but close to it. Would Kelley remember exactly where she'd placed it? Probably not.

She slipped her fingers between random items, lifted them, and froze at the photo of Kelley sitting up in a hospital bed. In a hospital bed . . . holding a baby. She stared at the image. Kelley looked so young. Whose baby was she holding? And why was she holding it while sitting in a hospital bed?

She turned it over. The date—Madison's birthday—and the inscription—*me and my baby*—didn't make any sense.

Every shred of decency she possessed told her to close the lid on the box and put it back on the shelf where she'd found it. To forget everything she'd seen and read inside.

But, just like Pandora, she couldn't ignore what she'd released. Slowly, she began sifting through the box, paying more attention to what was nestled inside.

• • •

Kelley pulled into the driveway, grateful to see Madison's car in the driveway and a police car stationed at the curb. Mike got out and walked toward her.

"Miss Spencer."

"Hello, Mike."

He pointed toward Madison's car. "I know the chief said that I was supposed to bring her here, but she promised to drive herself straight over here, with me following, so I didn't see the harm in letting her do it."

"I'm glad you did. It saves us having to go pick it up."

"That's what I was thinking. You need me to stick around?"

"No, we'll be fine now. Thank you."

"Not a problem. You take care now."

As soon as he drove away, she walked to the front door. She was exhausted after her ordeal in Jack's office, but she needed to face Madison, needed to make her understand that this behavior would not get her any results—if she even knew what results she was trying to get.

Walking into the house, she was surprised that she couldn't hear Madison's music blaring. A quick look in the living room and kitchen assured her that Madison wasn't in either room. She tossed her purse onto the couch in passing. With the carpet muffling her steps, she headed toward the mother-in-law wing, surprised to see that the door to Madison's room was open.

She took a deep breath to calm her nerves before striding into Madison's room. She came to a grinding halt as though she'd slammed into a brick wall. Her heart began hammering with such force that she feared it might erupt through her chest.

Oh, God. Oh, God.

Looking like the stunned survivor of an explosion, Madison sat in the middle of her bed, the fireproof box in front of her, papers, documents, and photos spread haphazardly around her. Her cheeks were damp with tears, her glazed-over eyes seemed barely to register Kelley's presence. She was releasing short little pants, her hands trembling as her fingers moved jerkily from one item on the bed to another, like someone searching for the missing piece of a jigsaw puzzle, the one piece that would bring the image into focus.

Kelley took a gingerly step toward her. "Madison?"

"I was trying to find proof that you and the sheriff . . . before . . . when he was your student. I . . . I found . . . all . . . this."

Oh, God. Oh, God. Oh, God. Normally, she kept everything locked in a safety-deposit box at the bank. But she'd needed the birth certificate to enroll Madison, and she simply hadn't had time to get it locked safely away. She'd thought in her locked box, hidden away in her closet, that it would be protected. Madison never went snooping into Kelley's things. Why now? Why would she look for something involving Jack? And the answer hit her with startling clarity. Madison had been looking for a way to hurt Jack, maybe even to hurt Kelley, so she could get out of painting a damn bathroom. And what she'd ended up doing was hurting herself.

"Madison—"

"There's a picture of you with a baby."

The accusation hit Kelley hard, and she didn't know whether to hope Madison had looked through everything, had sorted everything out, or to hope she hadn't. Kelley's best friend had taken the picture, and Kelley had hoarded it away because her parents had convinced her it was best not to take any pictures of her with the baby. "It'll look strange," her mother had said.

Kelley should have destroyed it, but she'd never been able to bring herself to do that.

"I know," Kelley rasped. "I was fifteen." She took a step nearer.

"No!" Madison scrambled back against the headboard, drawing her legs up against her chest. "I saw the birth certificate. It was a girl. You named her Madison!"

Tears stung Kelley's eyes as she nodded.

"Father unknown!"

"I did know who the father was, but he was a kid, too, and he didn't want the responsibility. Mom told me not to put his name on the birth certificate. She said it would give him no legal rights . . ."

She hadn't known if it was true. She'd simply done what she was told and hoped for the best.

Tears filled Madison's eyes and flowed over, rolling down her face. "It was me," she whispered hoarsely.

Kelley nodded, her throat thick with tears, her chest tightening. "I'm so sorry, baby."

"Don't call me that! I'm not your baby. You gave me away."

Kelley shook her head. "I placed you in more capable hands."

"That's bullshit!" Madison scrambled to her feet, staggering to catch her balance on the bed, standing so Kelley had to lift her gaze to her. "Do you know how screwed up I am? I thought my parents were dead. But they were my grandparents. How could you do this to me?"

"It was the hardest thing I've ever done in my life," Kelley told her as her own tears washed over her cheeks. "I love you so much. I was just trying to do what was best for you. You have to believe that."

Like a puppet whose strings had suddenly been cut, Madison flopped down on the bed, buried her face in her hands, and began to rock. "Everything is so messed up."

Gingerly, Kelley sat on the edge of the bed. "Everyone loved you. Everyone wanted to do what was best for you. You have to believe that."

Madison jerked her head up, her gaze impaling Kelley. "Were you ever going to tell me the truth?"

"I don't know. I didn't want to hurt you, Madison."

"Well, you have. Will you leave me alone?"

She reached out to touch Madison, and Madison drew herself up.

"Wouldn't you like me to explain everything to you?"

"Not right now. I just need to get my head wrapped around everything."

"I can help you."

"Not now. I just want to be alone."

Reluctantly, Kelley nodded. She wasn't certain leaving Madison alone was the best thing to do. Still, she gathered everything up, placed it back in the box, and walked toward the door. Stopping, she glanced over her shoulder. "Madison, I love you."

Madison simply looked away, and Kelley thought her heart might shatter. She closed the door quietly behind her, walked lethargically to the kitchen, placed the box on the table, and grabbed the phone. She dialed Jack's cell phone.

"Morgan."

"She knows." Her voice lacked emotion.

"Kelley, is that you?"

"Yes. I said she knows."

"Who—"

"Madison. She knows I'm her mother. I think she was trying to find something to blackmail us with."

"I'm already in a patrol car. I'll get there as soon as I can."

"All right. I'll—" She heard the roar of an engine, the squeal of tires. "Oh, God!"

She shot out of the kitchen, out of the house, barely aware that she still clutched the phone. She almost missed seeing the brake lights of Madison's car as she careened around a corner. "Jack, she's driving away."

Chapter 22

The advantage to a small town was that it only allowed for one easy escape route out of it—along Main Street. Oh, there were other, circuitous routes out of Hopeful, but a person had to be familiar with back roads to take advantage of them. So, Jack parked at the north end, figuring that Madison was going to head toward Dallas. Just to be on the safe side, he called Mike, and he positioned his cruiser at the south end.

He was surprised that he was able to get Madison to pull off the road. More surprised that she didn't try to take off when he got out of his car and walked back to hers. But hell if his heart didn't go out to her when he leaned down, looked through the open window, and saw the defeated look on her face.

"Did *she* send you after me?" Madison asked.

"Yeah."

She looked as though she wanted to shrivel up. "Do you know everything?"

"I know enough to know that running isn't the answer."

"I don't want to go back there."

"How about spending the night at my place?"

Her surprised look settled into resignation. "As if. So you can make me paint that bathroom in the morning?"

"We'll delay it until you get your head screwed on right. Follow me to my house, and don't get any ideas about heading off in another direction. I'll have the state troopers between here and Dallas alerted in a heartbeat."

"You're such a hard-ass."

Reaching in through the window, he chucked her beneath the chin. "Darlin', you've got no idea."

She gave him the tiniest of grins, and he knew she was remembering the night she'd been introduced to his office.

Striding back to his car, Jack unhooked his cell phone from his belt and punched in the speed dial he'd recently programmed. Kelley picked up on the first ring.

"I've got her," he said.

"Thank God. Is she all right?"

"She seems a little dazed, but she's okay. I'm going to take her to my house."

"Why?"

"I think she's just looking for a little space right now."

"All right. I'll come over."

He glanced back toward where Madison was waiting. "Why don't you hold off on that? Give me a little time with her."

"To do what? Make her dig ditches, collect litter along the side of the road? It was your tough love policy that got us here."

He didn't think she'd appreciate him telling her that she was being a little unfair. "Just give her a little time."

"She's my daughter, Jack." Her voice faltered on *daughter.*

"I know that, Kelley. I'm not trying to take her away from you. I'm hoping to help you keep her."

As darkness descended, Jack sat on his deck and kept an eye on his guest as she lay in a hammock, but she couldn't stay out there indefinitely. The chill of autumn had definitely come to roost. Earlier, he'd offered to let her make a long-distance call if she wanted to connect with Ronda, but she had passed. He'd offered her something to drink. She'd passed. He'd offered her a blanket. She'd passed.

"What's wrong with her, Dad?" Jason asked as he sat with Jack beside the chimenea, absorbing the warmth it emitted.

"She's just a little sad, a little confused."

"How come?"

"It's hard to explain." He glanced over at his son. "And it's not really my place to tell you."

"I guess Riker isn't coming over tonight."

"Nope. I already talked with his mom about it. Maybe tomorrow night."

"I'm getting hungry."

"Me, too. I'm going in to order the pizza. Why don't you let Madison know it's on its way?"

"Okay."

He squeezed his son's shoulder before going into the house. After he ordered the pizza, he changed the sheets on his bed and the towels in his bathroom and put the toilet seat down. He didn't know why women got all bent out of shape when it was up. He just knew they did, so he decided he'd be a perfect host. He gave Kelley a quick call to let her know that Madison was fine—not talking, but at least she was still there. And since he'd confiscated the keys out of her purse when she wasn't looking, he imagined she'd be staying there.

When the pizza arrived, she came inside and sat at his dining table. Her nose was red, but he didn't think it was from the cold as much as it was from crying. Her eyes were red and swollen. She kept blinking as though they felt gritty. She sat with her arms tucked in close against her body as though she wanted to hug herself.

"We rented *Lord of the Rings*," Jason said. "You want to watch it with me?"

She rubbed the heel of her hand over the edge of her nose. "Sure."

She shoved her plate aside with a half-eaten slice of pizza on it. Her one and only slice. She slid her gaze to Jack. "I'm sorry. I'm not very hungry."

Her apology was hard to take. He hadn't expected that. He spent more time angry with her than happy

with her, but he missed her smart-mouthed com-
ments.

"Don't worry about it."

"If we had a dog, he could eat the leftovers," Jason
said.

Jack grinned. "I'm still thinking about it."

"I always wanted a dog," Madison said quietly,
"but my dad . . . I mean . . . anyway, he was allergic to
them."

"Bummer," Jason piped up.

Madison smiled at him before shifting her attention
back to Jack. "Have you talked to *her?*" She looked
guilty. "I don't even know what to call her now."

He decided that was an issue to be determined by
mother and daughter, so he addressed the question
she'd asked. "Yeah, I called her to let her know you
were here and all right."

She nodded. "How'd she sound?"

"A lot like you. Sad. Confused." He tapped Jason's
hand. "Why don't you run next door and see if Mrs.
Hamilton has a bag of popcorn we can pop later to
eat while we're watching the movie?"

"We've got popcorn."

"Just do it."

Jason rolled his eyes, shoved his chair back, and
headed out through the kitchen.

"He doesn't know?" Madison asked.

"No. There will be plenty of time to tell people
what you want them to know when you and Kelley
get all this straightened out."

She shifted in the chair. "I read the letter you wrote her."

Now, *his* appetite deserted him. He leaned back, wondering how many things this kid could do to earn his anger. She was on a hot streak. "I see. So, privacy isn't a concept you fully comprehend."

"I was looking for a way to blackmail you so I wouldn't have to do Gunther's bathrooms." She licked her lips. "So, have you always known the truth about me?"

He didn't want her thinking that Kelley had told him when she hadn't told Madison. "No, I only figured out last weekend that she had a baby."

"How did you figure it out?"

He felt the heat rush to his face. How much did she suspect regarding his relationship with Kelley, how much did she know? "I noticed her C-section scar."

Her red eyes widened slightly. "She had a C-section?"

He nodded.

"Wow. I didn't know that. That's really serious stuff, isn't it?"

"Pretty major, yeah." And he was grateful she didn't ask how he'd come to see the scar.

"I guess she didn't say anything because she was ashamed of me. She didn't want me."

"I think you're wrong on both counts. She's not ashamed of you. And she does want you. But more, she wants what's best for you. In life, you make your decisions based on what you know at that exact moment. When Kelley decided to let her parents raise you, she made the decision with your best interests in mind. Everything she's done, she's done because she loves you."

"Funny. I don't feel loved."

"What do you feel?"

"I feel angry."

"Guess I can't blame you for that."

"By the way, *she* never read it."

He cocked his head to the side. "What?"

"Your letter. *She* never read it. It was sealed before I opened it."

He was torn between anger and relief. He'd poured his heart into that letter—and Kelley had never bothered to read it. So, when they'd begun over again, she'd done so without knowing all she'd meant to him back then. Although he believed in moving beyond the past, it seemed to want to hang around. And Madison seemed to be the one who kept it front and center.

Jack leaned forward and planted his forearms on the table. "In the future, stay out of your mother's things."

Flinching, she cast down her eyes. "I thought I was going through my sister's things," she said quietly.

"And you think that made it all right?"

Shaking her head, she lifted her gaze to his. "It just made it different. Not as wrong." Tears started welling in her eyes. "Your relationship with your mother is different from the one with your sister. I must have told her a hundred times that she wasn't my mother or that she made a lousy mother."

Jack shoved his chair back and moved around to Madison. "Come here, kid."

He pulled her into his arms and held her tightly.

"I don't know what to feel." She released a heart-wrenching sob. "I hate her, but I love her."

Nine years ago, Jack had felt exactly the same way when she'd told him things were over between them. He tucked his fist beneath Madison's jaw and tilted her face up. "Take it from me. Love is stronger. You'll only hate her for a little while, and then you'll miss her like hell."

"Is that how it was for you?"

"Yeah, it was."

"She's part of the reason you got married, isn't she?"

"She's the only reason I got married. She was worried about what Stephanie would go through as an unwed mother."

She furrowed her brow. "I don't understand. Why did you have to marry her? You just have to look at Jason to know he's not your kid."

Before Jack could assure her that Jason was his son, he heard a startled gasp. In the arched doorway leading into the dining area, Jason stood holding an unpopped packet of popcorn, a horrified expression on his face. Jack had been so absorbed in comforting Madison that he hadn't heard Jason come back home.

"Say it's not true," Jason demanded.

It was one thing to avoid revealing the truth, another to lie to Jason's face.

"Jason—"

Jason dropped the popcorn, spun on his heel, and ran out of the house.

"I'm sorry," Madison said, stepping away from him. "I didn't know he was there. I wouldn't have said anything. Honest, I'm sorry."

He didn't think he'd ever heard her voice carry such remorse. Not that he found much consolation in that.

Jack felt as if Wolverine had dug his steel claws into his chest. He imagined Jason felt much the same way.

Jack stood in his backyard surrounded by the shadows of the autumn evening. The beam of a flashlight poured out through the cracks between the boards of the fort. He'd built it when Jason was four, shortly after they'd moved back to Hopeful.

It had become his son's refuge.

He'd always thought that he'd be enough for Jason. Right now, he wasn't even certain that he was enough for himself.

He'd always been torn, wondering if he should be honest with Jason, if he should explain that they didn't carry the same genes. But what did a child care about genes?

Until high school, anyway, when biology teachers would teach students how to compare family traits, and Jason would begin to wonder how he could have brown eyes when his parents both had blue.

Jack had thought if he waited, he'd be better able to explain things. Waited until Jason was as old as Madison. But as Jack was learning with Madison, a teenager wasn't prepared to hear the truth. And if he waited until Jason was older still, ready to get married, would he feel that Jack had deceived him all his life?

There was no easy answer, no right solution. But since Madison had opened the door to the discovery, Jack figured he needed to walk through it with the truth.

Shoring up his resolve, he strode to the fort. Raising his hand, he banged on the door at the second level that was even with his forehead. "Jason?"

"Go away."

"We need to talk."

"No."

Jack climbed up the ladder and made his way along the platform to the door. He pushed on it—and it did nothing more than rattle a bit. He peered through the tiny opening and spotted a bolt. Damn! When had Jason put a lock on the thing?

"Open up," Jack ordered.

"No!"

"Jason, I have a picture of your mom."

He could almost hear the wheels turning in Jason's mind. He heard a scraping along the floor and figured Jason was scooting across. When he was four, he could stand up in the room. No longer. Jack hadn't taken into consideration how much Jason would grow or how long he might want to use the fort when he'd built it. Somehow, he'd always expected Jason to remain little. He knew it was an irrational thought, but still, it had been there.

He heard the slide of metal against metal, and the door sprang back. Jason scooted back as though faced with a nightmarish monster. Jack was totally unprepared for the pain he was feeling as he struggled to reestablish a bond with his son. He squeezed through the doorway, and the tiny room suddenly seemed like a coffin. And yet there was comfort there. Thumbtacks held pictures on the walls. The paper was turning yellow, curling at the edges, but the crayoned drawings all reflected the same thing: a family of four. A mother, a father, and two boys. Where the boys had once both had yellow-crayoned hair, now one had black hair. Straight, bold, black strokes drawn in anger.

Jack looked down and saw Jason clutching a black crayon.

From the stick figures that represented his earliest work when he was younger to the more sophisticated recent drawings, here was the evidence that his son had longed for a family. For the first time in his life, Jack wondered if he should have given Jason up for adoption.

And just as quickly, the answer rebounded through his mind: No way!

He held up the book that reflected the black and gold school colors. "This is my yearbook." In his youth, he'd never been much into keepsakes, but he'd purchased a yearbook his senior year because he'd known it would have a picture of Kelley in it.

Jason simply stared at him.

"You know what a yearbook is?" Jack asked.

Jason nodded jerkily, and it occurred to Jack that his son was afraid.

"Don't you remember? My school has them. I always get one," Jason said.

"Oh, yeah," Jack said quietly. "Guess I'm not thinking too clearly tonight."

Jason pointed toward the book. "Is she in there? My mom?"

"Yeah."

"And my dad?"

Jack nodded, the knot in his throat threatening to suffocate him.

"You know who he is?" Jason asked.

"He's sitting right here with you now."

"I mean my real dad."

His chest tightened, and he thought his heart might actually stop beating. *I'm your real dad.*

He shook his head. "He might be in here. I don't know."

"Can I see?"

"You want to come in the house first where we'll be more comfortable?"

"No. I just wanna see."

"All right." Jack thumbed through the pages until he found the one that showed a very young and very innocent-looking girl. If Jack had a daughter who looked like her and some guy had jumped her bones, Jack wouldn't have threatened him with arrest. He would have beaten him black and blue. Strange how he saw things differently through the eyes of a parent.

He turned the book and watched Jason's reaction. It was slow in coming. A blink and then another and another, until he finally whispered, "She's pretty."

Jason lifted his gaze to Jack's. "She looks kinda like Madison. I mean, not like her twin or nothing, but young like her."

Jack felt as though he'd taken a blow to the midsection. The smart-mouthed hellion probably was the same age—or near to it—as Stephanie had been.

"She was young, Jason. She dropped out of school. She didn't have a job. She didn't know how to take care of a baby. And she sure didn't want to be taking care of a husband."

"Why did she say you were my daddy if you weren't?"

"I think she thought I was. We both thought I was. But as you started to get older, you didn't look anything like me."

"Why'd you keep me?"

Tears rolled over onto Jason's cheeks, while tears stung Jack's eyes. "Because right after you were born, I held you. You were so tiny, so perfect—and you looked at me with those big eyes of yours. At that moment, you were my son, Jason."

"But it's a lie!"

"No, it's not a lie." Jack pressed a balled fist to his chest. "In here, Jason, in my heart, you're my son. I love you, and nothing is going to change that."

Jason sniffed and swiped at his cheeks. "Is there a picture of you in here?"

Jack only allowed himself a small smile of victory. He knew he'd only begun repairs on the bridge to Jason's heart. "Yeah, there is. But I won't show it to you unless you promise not to laugh."

"I won't laugh."

"All right, then." Jack picked up the book and thumbed through the pages until he reached the one he was looking for. He turned the book away from Jason. "I don't know if I should show you."

"Come on, Dad." Jason's eyes widened, and insecurity washed over his face. "Should I still call you that? I mean, if you're not . . . you know? Should I call you that?"

"Always."

Jack tipped his head to the side and patted the flooring beside him. Jason scooted over until they were sitting side by side. Jack opened the book and placed it in his son's lap. He pointed to his photo. "That's me."

"You're dorky-looking!"

"Hey, I was a stud." Although looking at the photo with nine years' experience having passed, he could see where he looked a little goofy.

Jason peered up at him. "Does Riker look like his dad?"

"Yeah, he does."

"I wish I looked like you. I wish you were my real dad."

He slipped his arm around Jason and hugged him close. "I am your real dad, Son."

Chapter 23

It was a little after midnight when Kelley arrived at Jack's house with an overnight bag for Madison. Earlier in the evening, he'd promised to call her as soon as Madison went to bed, and that had happened a little after eleven. Part of Kelley desperately wanted to speak with her, and part of her was hesitant to push.

Talk about violating trust. She'd done it exceptionally well.

She wasn't surprised that Jack opened the door before she was halfway up the walk. She was certain he'd been waiting for her arrival.

As soon as she was near enough, he wrapped his hand around her arm and drew her near, then folded her within his embrace, laying his cheek against her head. Of their own accord, her arms wound around him, awkwardly because of the overnight bag she carried, but still they were around him. He was so solid, so warm. She could almost forget that everything wasn't perfect in her life.

"How are you doing?" he asked.

"Not too well."

He lowered his head, kissing her sweetly and tenderly, and she briefly wondered if he could taste the salt from the thousand tears she'd wiped away on the drive over.

"Come on in." He held the door open and ushered her into the house.

"Is Madison asleep?"

"I think so. I haven't heard a peep out of her since she closeted herself off in my room."

"I want to check on her."

"Be my guest. I'll be in the kitchen fixing us something to drink. Coffee or hot chocolate?"

"Hot chocolate." She was already too wired. She didn't need more caffeine. She walked down the hallway. She was surprised to find the door unlocked. Opening it, she peered inside. The only light came in from the night-light in the bathroom, but it was enough for her to see Madison's form as she lay in bed.

Kelley crept into the room, set the bag at the foot of the bed so Madison would have it in the morning, and eased up until she could see Madison a little more clearly.

Wearing what appeared to be a Texans football jersey—probably Jack's—Madison lay on her back with her hands on the pillows, her fingers curled. She'd slept like that when she was a baby, her hands curled a little more tightly until they formed the tiniest of fists. Kelley had snuck into her room then, too.

Her mother had stressed how important it was not

to confuse the baby, to make sure she realized who her mother would be. In retrospect, Kelley wondered how being shown love by more than one female would have been confusing. She'd been so torn, trying to do what was right for this precious baby she'd brought into the world, trying to please her parents, wanting to be young, feeling so old.

How had her best intentions gone so awry?

All she wanted to do was put her arms around Madison and protect her from all the heartache of the world. She'd certainly never planned to be the cause of her heartache.

Quietly slipping out of the room, she closed the door. She found Jack in the kitchen, one arm crossed over his chest supporting the other as he sipped from his mug, his gaze focused more inward than outward.

He shifted his attention to her and nodded toward the mug on the counter. Melting marshmallows bobbed on top of the chocolate. For some reason, she found comfort in them.

Facing him, she pressed her own hips against the counter, assuming a stance similar to his.

"How was she?" he asked.

"Asleep. She actually looked peaceful, which is more than I can say for myself." She studied him a little more closely. "Or for you. You look as bad as I feel."

Nodding, he sipped his coffee, his gaze moving away from her.

Not at all the reaction she'd expected. Something

was drastically wrong, and alarm bells began pealing through her mind. "Jack, what's wrong?" She groaned. "What a stupid question. Everything is *wrong*." She took a tentative step toward him. "But there's something you're holding back."

"Madison and I were talking earlier. She mentioned that she didn't think Jason was my son. Neither of us realized he was standing there listening."

"Oh, no." Her heart ached for him, for Jason. For everything she and Madison were putting this family through. "What did you do?"

He swung his gaze back to her, and she could see the depth of his pain. "What could I do? When he asked if it was true, I had to tell him the truth."

"Oh, Jack, I'm so sorry."

He shook his head. "I've been wrestling with telling him for some time. I thought about waiting to tell him when he was older"—he moved his hand toward the doorway, indicating where Madison was—"but that approach doesn't seem to work real well."

"Still, he's so young. He must have been devastated."

"Yeah, he was pretty upset. I would have preferred handling his learning the truth very differently. But the odd thing is, once I explained things, convinced him that I was still his dad and got him to come back into the house, he and Madison were inseparable until bedtime. He was curled on her lap while she sat in my recliner. They watched TV, talked. Two wounded kids trying to heal, I guess."

She released a sigh that made the few remaining unmelted marshmallows in her chocolate bob. "I never meant for all this to happen."

"Madison admitted that she was trying to uncover something she could blackmail us with," he said quietly.

"And the shoplifting?"

"I think she was hoping it would wedge us apart. How could you care for someone who keeps arresting her?"

She wanted to scream. "So, you think she was trying to put me in a position to choose?"

He nodded. "Me or her."

The entire situation seemed hopeless.

"Do you know what's really awful, Jack?" She didn't wait for him to attempt an answer. "Sometimes, in the beginning, after she was born, I wished that I'd given her to strangers. It was so incredibly hard watching her grow up and not being able to tell her that I was her mother."

"With your parents' support, why couldn't you have raised her and acknowledged her as your daughter?"

A question she'd asked herself a hundred times in the passing years. "When my parents and I discussed possible solutions to my 'problem,' as they referred to it, it was always an absolute giving up claim or nothing. They were so convincing. They wanted total control, convinced me it was in the baby's best interest. I still had to finish high school and college and find a job. Where was I going to find a young man willing to take on the responsibility of a child?"

She smiled softly with remembrance. "She was such a sweet baby, Jack. She had such a sweet disposition. Seldom cried. I'd go into her room late at night, when everyone was asleep, and simply look at her. This little marvel that I'd created. I'd start to doubt my decision to let my parents raise her." She tightened her hold on the mug. "And yet, realistically, I knew I had no choice. Because if I didn't do it their way, they'd withdraw their support."

Tears stung her eyes as she held his gaze. "I know I should have been grateful that they gave me any sort of support at all, but after a while, I despised them for taking her from me. I don't think they intentionally kept me from her. Sometimes I'd wish for a way to have her back, as my daughter. But I never meant for them to get killed."

"Don't start adding more guilt to what which you already feel. A drunk took them out."

"That sounds so military."

"Military or not, you had no control over what happened, regardless of what you might think."

"My parents and I had a falling out just before they were killed," she said quietly. "I thought they were letting Madison get away with too much. They were moving into their golden years and not paying much attention to some aspects of her life. I thought I could do a better job of raising her. And here I am doing everything wrong."

"Not everything. She's basically a good kid. She's just lost sight of that."

"As long as I don't lose sight of it."

"You won't."

"You have so much faith in me."

"Because I know you."

She and Madison had been so close before her parents died. Sisterly close. She'd often had Madison over to her town house. When Madison wanted to host a sleepover with her friends, she'd had the event at Kelley's because Kelley wasn't always telling her to keep things quiet. Kelley had loved being there for Madison, but it had been hard as well.

Being a sister to her daughter, when what she'd really wanted was to be a mother. The passing years had shifted her priorities. Once she'd been afraid of taking on the responsibility of raising a child. Now, she'd give anything to be a mommy.

"Maybe I'm the one who should paint Gunther's bathrooms."

"It's not much fun."

"You've painted them?" she asked.

"When I was fourteen. He caught me walking off with a Coke."

She smiled at that, imagining that he'd probably walked off with a lot more.

"I want to take her home, Jack."

"Tonight?"

She shook her head. "I mean, I want to take her back to Dallas."

"I don't see that your reasons for leaving Dallas have changed."

"They haven't, but being here isn't working, either. I ruin everything I touch. You don't need me in your life."

He took a step toward her. "That's not true."

Setting the mug aside, she wrapped her arms around herself. "Prom night, you told me that you loved me, and I didn't want to hear it, not while I was your teacher. So you turned to Stephanie."

"Kelley, that's the past. You've got to let it go."

"I understand that, Jack, but I encouraged you to marry her. You wouldn't have if I hadn't."

"But I got a terrific kid out of that marriage. I don't regret it."

She shook her head. "But because of the way I handled Madison when she was born and for the past eighteen months, we've hurt you and your son. I am so tired of hurting people. I don't deserve you, Jack. And you sure as hell deserve better than me."

"I love you, Kelley. We can work things out. Between us. With Madison. With Jason."

She moved away from him, needing the distance. "Jason, who wants you to marry Serena? Madison, who wants to keep us apart so she's breaking the law? Madison, who hates us so much that she's searching for ways to blackmail us?"

"The first step, Kelley, is you and me. If what we have is strong enough, we'll make the rest of it work."

"I think you've been reading too many romance novels, Jack."

She turned for the doorway.

"If you walk out on me, Kelley, I'm not going to come after you."

She looked back over her shoulder. "I always knew you were smart, Jack."

Walking out through his front door was one of the hardest things she'd ever done, but she'd caused him enough anguish. She wasn't willing to cause him any more.

Chapter 24

Jack dumped the oats into the boiling water, then turned toward the sink. He was not in the best of moods, having slept off and on, mostly off. Around dawn, he'd finally crawled off the couch, where he'd bedded down after Kelley left.

Left. Walked out. Thinking she was doing him some sort of favor. Damn it! He didn't want her damn favors. He wanted her, her heart, her love. He wanted her in his bed when he went to sleep at night, and he wanted her curled against him when he woke up in the morning.

He turned on the water and placed the plant she'd given him under it.

"I think you're probably drowning it," a soft, feminine voice said.

Turning off the water, he glanced over his shoulder. Madison stood in the doorway, one foot on top of the other. Her hair was its natural golden brown, her face had no makeup on it. She looked young, vulnerable. And sad.

Did everyone and everything in this house have to be sad?

"I don't think it's going to survive," Jack said.

She gave him a winsome smile. "Too much water can be as bad as too little."

"So, you think I was so worried about it dying that I killed it?"

She crossed over to him and took the plant. "I think if you leave it alone for a while, it'll recover."

"So, it's a little like people?"

"A little."

Smelling the burning oats, he cursed beneath his breath, rushed to the stove, jerked the pan off the flame, and cursed again. The water had boiled away.

"I'm pretty good at making omelets," Madison said.

The little criminal offering to do something shocked him so much that for a minute he didn't know what to say. Finally, he grinned. "Oh, yeah?"

She nodded. "I could make us some. Figure I ought to eat something before I go paint Gunther's bathroom."

He walked to the sink and began filling the pot with water, hoping the burned oats would soak away. He'd probably have more luck if he just trashed it. "Don't worry about Gunther's today. You can do it another time."

"I'd rather do it today. It beats hanging around here with nothing to do but think."

"All right." Bowing slightly, he swept his hand toward the refrigerator. "Have at the omelets."

She began to make herself at home around his kitchen.

"Are you a coffee drinker?" he asked.

"Tea."

"No tea. How about hot chocolate?"

"With marshmallows?"

"Is there any other way?"

She smiled. "I could go for that."

While he worked on making the hot chocolate, she was whipping up the omelets, using whatever odds and ends she found in his refrigerator. Leaning against the counter, he watched her.

"Kelley came by last night," he said.

"I know. When I heard her come into the room, I pretended to be asleep."

He reached for his mug of coffee and took a sip.

"Actually, I did worse than that," she said. "I snuck out of your bedroom, stood outside the kitchen, and listened while y'all talked."

"Madison, I swear—"

"I know I shouldn't have done it, Jack."

Everything within Jack stilled as he recognized the shifting in their relationship. She wasn't the kid any longer. And he wasn't the sheriff.

Tears filled Madison's eyes. "I thought she might tell you something that she wouldn't tell me. And I know it was wrong to listen, but I'm trying to get my head wrapped around all this. Do you know how much it hurts to lose a parent?"

"Yeah, I do," he said quietly.

"Only I didn't. I just thought I did. It's like nothing is what I thought it was. No one is who I thought they were. I'm totally messed up."

"I understand that you're confused, but you have to realize that one thing hasn't changed. Kelley still loves you."

"But now it's a mother's love, not a sister's love."

"Madison, Kelley's love for you was always a mother's love."

Madison released a heart-wrenching sob. Jack crossed the kitchen and took her into his arms. "Shh, it's all right."

"Do you know anything about my father?"

Her shoulders were shaking, and he could feel her tears dampening his shirt. "From what I hear, he was a good man."

She lifted her tear-filled gaze to him.

"And he was killed by a drunk driver," Jack said solemnly.

"You mean Marcus Gardner?"

Jack nodded. "Fatherhood isn't determined by genes, Madison. I might not have been the one who gave Jason life, but I'd die before I let anyone hurt him. You had three people willing to do the same for you. You're trying to label them, and love can't be labeled."

"So, how come you know so much about love?"

"I had a good teacher."

"Kelley?"

He nodded. She worked herself free of him and went back to stirring her omelet mix, then poured it into the pan.

"I'm sorry I screwed things up for you," she said. She darted a glance at him before turning her attention back to the omelets. "I was only thinking about what I wanted, what was best for me. I wasn't thinking about what Kelley might want."

"It's not too late to start thinking about someone other than yourself."

"What are your intentions toward her?"

He stared at her. "I beg your pardon?"

"Your intentions. You hurt her once. Are you going to hurt her again?"

"I wasn't planning on it."

"She deserves someone who loves her a lot."

"I agree."

Blushing, she placed the omelets on the plates and headed for the table. He joined her there, took a bite, and moaned his approval. "Pretty good."

She shrugged.

"Do you think Jason's mom abandoned him?" she asked.

"Before she ever walked away."

"He's a neat kid. I'm really sorry he heard me say what I did about him not being your son."

"He and I will work it out."

"He's lucky to have you."

A compliment from Madison. Maybe she'd grown up a little in the past twenty-four hours.

"I'm lucky to have him," Jack said.

Madison sighed, moved her plate aside, propped her elbow on the table, and placed her chin on her palm. "I'm so confused. I don't even know who I am anymore."

"You know who you are, Madison. All you have to do is look in the mirror."

Kelley pulled into Gunther's parking lot and parked her car next to Jack's truck. He'd called to tell her that Madison was in a little better frame of mind and had decided to go ahead and paint Gunther's bathrooms. Kelley had deliberated her best course of action for half an hour. She didn't want to hurt Madison, but neither could she let things go on as they were.

She got out of the car and cautiously walked around to the side of the building where the rest rooms were. Jack was leaning against the brick wall. He was in uniform, gun at his hip.

"Figured you'd show," he said as he shoved himself away from the wall.

"Do you really think you need to guard her as though she's a serial killer?"

A corner of his mouth hitched up. "Don't get your panties in a knot. I'm on my way to the station. I just brought her the paint and equipment and decided to hang around for a few minutes in case she needed anything."

"Oh," she said, contrite. "I'm sorry. I tend—"

"To be a little overprotective?"

She nodded. "So, how is she?"

"She's doing all right. She was a regular chatterbox at breakfast."

She stared at him, not certain she'd understood. "Madison?"

"Yep. She doesn't think much of my plant-raising skills."

She couldn't help but smile. "I'm not surprised."

Silence eased around them, as though neither knew what to say next, yet both knew there was a good deal that needed to be said.

"Well, I'll leave you to her," Jack finally said, and started to walk off.

"Jack?"

He stopped and looked at her.

"Thank you for giving her a place to go last night."

He slowly nodded. "She's a good kid."

Before she could respond, he'd disappeared around the corner.

She walked to the rest room doorway, and her heart constricted at the sight of Madison rolling cream-colored paint over the wall. She was wearing a large T-shirt that she'd knotted at one side, a shirt that Kelley was fairly certain belonged to Jack. She had some sort of bandanna over her hair. She was humming, actually humming, a sad sort of song. Kelley resisted the urge to pop her knuckles and instead swallowed hard before asking, "Would you like some help?"

Madison spun around, a dollop of paint decorating the side of her nose. Kelley knew it wasn't the paint fumes that had made Madison's eyes turn red. She held her breath, waiting for Madison's response. Her stomach quivered, the blood rushed between her temples, and she finally broke down and popped her knuckles. *Answer me, baby, answer me,* she silently pleaded.

Madison shrugged her body. "If you want."

Kelley stepped over the threshold, from the cement walk to the tiled floor. "It's kind of a gloomy place, isn't it?"

"Yeah." Madison lowered her gaze and began to fiddle with the handle of the paint roller. "I'm going to paint over that sign that says to flush feminine hygiene equipment." She shook her head. "Equipment."

"The sign was probably written by a guy."

"You *think?*" Madison asked with her usual sarcasm.

Tears stung Kelley's eyes as she fought to smile through them. "Madison, I always only wanted what was best for you."

Madison lifted her gaze, and Kelley could see the tears welling in her daughter's eyes. Her daughter. She'd never wanted her ever to experience any pain.

"I love you so much, Madison. I just want you to be happy."

Tears rolled over onto Madison's cheeks. "I feel lost," she rasped.

"I know. So do I." And without thought, without planning, with nothing more than instinct and love, she stepped forward, took Madison in her arms, and hugged her tightly.

She didn't know how long they held each other and wept, wept for the secrets, the years gone by, all the while trying to reweave the broken threads of their relationship.

Madison was the first to pull back, wiping at her eyes. "I got paint on you."

Kelley glanced down at her hip, where the paint roller had made contact with her jeans. "Doesn't matter. These are old clothes."

Madison sniffed. "I don't suppose Jack is my dad."

Jack? She'd never heard Madison call him that. Kelley released a little nervous bubble of laughter and shook her head. "No, he's not. He was only about twelve when I got pregnant."

"That's too bad."

Kelley stared at Madison. "Excuse me?"

"He's a good dad. He wouldn't have left you to go through it by yourself."

"No, I don't think he would have."

Madison lifted her shoulders and dropped them back down. "I don't know what to call you."

"Whatever you're comfortable with."

"That's just it. I'm not comfortable with anything. So, like, the guy who *did* get you pregnant—"

"His name was Randy. I didn't love him, Madison. I'm sorry for that. He didn't love me. I have no idea where he is, but Jack could probably help us find him."

Madison shook her head. "No, I'm not ready for that. But will you tell me everything else?"

Kelley nodded. "Yeah, I will."

The dingy old rest room was probably the most

unlikely place for healing to begin, but as they worked to repaint it, Kelley bared her heart and soul, telling Madison everything she'd shared with Jack, feeling a cleansing that gave her hope that maybe she could rebuild the bridge to Madison's heart.

Chapter 25

Jack couldn't recall a single time in his life when he'd wallowed in self-pity. Not even when his mom had left town. No pity party then. But he was certainly on the brink of having one now. As soon as he'd made sure the town was secure, he'd headed home to a dying plant, grabbed a brew out of the fridge, come outside, and settled into his hammock. The night was almost as dark as his thoughts.

Jason was spending the night with Riker, and that worked perfectly. Jack didn't have to worry about him. He didn't have to worry about anything except going inside for another bottle of beer when he finished drinking the first one. If he'd been thinking clearly, he would have loaded up a cooler and brought it out there. Then he wouldn't have to get up at all. Just find oblivion right there. Considering the state of inebriation he was shooting for, he'd even turned off his cell phone. He'd never had a single night of irresponsibility since he'd gone to work for the police department. He figured he was long over-due. One night where the only person he had to think about was himself. Then, tomorrow morning, he'd hoist all his responsibilities back onto his shoulders and carry on.

He thought he'd had something special with Kelley. Obviously, he'd been mistaken. It wasn't as though he expected or needed to come first in her life—he understood that Madison was extremely special to her and that the two of them had a lot of feelings to sort through and family dynamics to shift around. But he would like to warrant at least a *consideration* before she made plans to leave town.

He caught a movement in the shadows and turned his attention toward the side of the house. He watched as a familiar figure moved through the shadows toward the hammock. He'd been fantasizing about her for close to ten years now, and he figured he'd be fantasizing about her for the next fifty. She turned him inside out and upside down. She always had. She always would.

"Hi, Jack," she said quietly. "I tried to call, but I only got your voice mail."

"I turned off my cell." He held up his beer. "In about an hour, I don't plan to be in any condition to drive."

"That's not the responsible Jack Morgan I've come to know."

"Yeah, well, after nine years, I figure I deserve a night off without any responsibilities."

She leaned against the tree, placed her hand on the end of the hammock, and made it gently swing.

"Madison and I finished painting Gunther's rest rooms."

"I know. I stopped off and checked them on my way home."

"Did they meet with your approval?"

"Almost. She painted over a sign that I told her to leave alone."

"The one about the *equipment?*"

"That's the one."

"We decided that we'll make one that's a little less crass."

"So, you and Madison got things worked out?"

"A little. I don't think there's a quick fix. She had a moment of dismay when she thought perhaps you were her father."

"She should be so lucky."

"That's what she and I both thought. How's Jason doing today?"

"He's young enough that he heals quickly. He thinks he needs a dog, though. So, in a few weeks, I'm going to take him to see Serena's dad, so he can pick out one of the old man's pups."

"Madison wants a dog."

After all that had happened in the past forty-eight hours and the past week, he couldn't believe that they were talking about dogs. "What are you doing here, Kelley?"

"I read your letter, Jack."

"Yeah, well, the kid who wrote it doesn't exist any-more."

"Neither does the girl to whom he wrote it."

"Okay. So, we're not who we were. Where does that leave us?"

"Depends."

"On what?"

"On whether or not there's room on that hammock for me."

His first thought was to ease over and make room for her, but he was tired of having women who walked into his life only to walk out of it. "I thought you were taking Madison back to Dallas."

"We talked it over and decided that's not where we needed to be."

"After all the hell she put you through, she doesn't want to move back to Dallas?" he asked. He found that difficult to believe.

Kelley gave the hammock a gentle push. "Rick came by and helped us finish painting the bathrooms. I think his hanging around might have influenced her decision."

"And if he's hanging around with someone else next week?"

"I don't think that will be a problem. On the way home from Gunther's, she stopped by the police station and apologized to Mike for her behavior that night at the Broken Wagon."

"Well, good for her."

"He's taking her to the Broken Wagon the next time there's a teen night."

"Well, good for Mike."

"I thought maybe you might talk to him—talk to Rick, too—just to make sure that they understand"—in the moonlight, he saw her lift a shoulder—"I don't want my baby to get pregnant, Jack."

"For what it's worth, Kelley, I'd already put the fear of God into those guys before I let them help you move. Mike understands she's underage. She's safe with either of those guys."

"But sometimes things get out of hand—"

"Nothing you can do about that, babe. You give her a good foundation and hope for the best."

She moved up until she was standing near his waist. "I thought I should follow Madison's example and do my own apologizing. I am so sorry, Jack. You were right. When I heard that Stephanie was pregnant and you were the father, all I could think was that I didn't want her to have to go through what I did. I wouldn't even entertain the notion that it wasn't your baby. I did everything you accused me of doing. I projected my feelings for Randy onto you. As insane as it sounds, I thought I was being given an opportunity to do right what I'd done wrong before. I thought—"

He grabbed her arm, pulled her near, and pressed his finger against her lips. "I forgive you for nine years ago."

"And for last night?"

"Forgiveness could probably be arranged."

"I love you, Jack."

He tossed his beer bottle onto the ground and

pulled her down until she was straddling him. The hammock was swinging wildly, almost as wildly as his heart. Cupping the back of her head, he brought her mouth to his, kissing her deeply and thoroughly, not holding anything back.

It was now or never. If they were going to move forward, it needed to be at a faster clip than they had been traveling. He wanted an openness to their relationship in private and in public that they'd never had.

He lifted her head. "Any other secrets?"

She was breathing harshly. "No. You?"

"No."

He brought her mouth back down to his, his tongue sweeping with an urgency hers met. Darting, thrusting, as though neither could get enough.

She drew back. "I want to be the only one, Jack."

"Hell, Kelley, that's what I've been trying to get you to be for as long as I've known you."

Hungrily, he returned his mouth to hers. He couldn't get enough of her. He didn't know if he'd ever get enough of her, but it was a goal he didn't mind striving to meet.

"You wearing panties beneath that skirt?" he asked.

"Wouldn't you like to know?"

"Damned right."

Her head came up, the hammock swayed, and he shifted slightly, capturing her mouth with his own. With one arm around her, he drew her more closely against him—even though she was almost as close as she could get. He cradled her face with his other hand and swept his tongue through the silkiness of her mouth.

Kelley welcomed his ravishing kiss, welcomed his impatient touch. It was as though all the barriers had been knocked down.

His mouth finally left hers, his lips trailing along her throat, his teeth nipping, his tongue soothing while her shoulders curled inward, and desire unfurled.

"Jack, people will see."

"No, they won't." His voice was as breathless as hers.

She knew she'd offered up a lame excuse, one he wouldn't buy. She'd been modest for too long. With Jack, she'd have to give it up. For him, she'd do it willingly.

It was dark beneath the canopy of leaves. A cedar fence enclosed them, separating them from the nearest neighbors.

The hammock began to sway with more force as they twisted and squirmed against each other, searching for a comfortable fit. His mouth came back to hers in a soul-searing kiss that made her stop caring that she was outside, beneath the stars, in the backyard of a little neighborhood on the outskirts of a small town. She felt his hand slip beneath the hem of her skirt. He squeezed the back of her knee, rubbed her thigh, and skimmed his hand up, up, up over her hips.

"Dear God." He splayed his fingers over her bare bottom, and she could have sworn she saw his grin sparkling in the moonlight. "You're wearing a thong."

She scraped her fingers up into his hair. "What you gonna do about that?" she whispered.

"Something I've always wanted to do but didn't have anyone to do it with."

His hand traveled over her hip and slipped beneath the flimsy silk. She moaned his name. "We really shouldn't be doing this."

"That's what makes it so much fun."

And it was fun. But old habits of modesty were hard to break.

"Jack, the neighbors."

"Can get their own hammock."

He blanketed her mouth, capturing her groans, stifling her cries. Shivering within his arms, no longer from the cold but from the heat, she dug her fingers into his shoulders.

She was aware of so much—her skirt bunched around her waist, the roughness of his jeans against her bare thighs, the coolness of the breeze against her bare bottom, his long fingers tenderly stroking, exploring, working their magic—and she was aware of nothing except the pleasurable sensations, ebbing and flowing, spiraling, and threatening to burst forth like fireworks lighting a midnight sky.

All she could do was feel; her nerve endings were raw with the need to be granted release, her body undulating against his palm where he cradled her intimately, his fingers never ceasing their constant caressing. She released a tiny cry, a resounding plea.

He deepened the kiss as his fingers increased their pressure. She writhed against him, seeking escape, desperate to remain, as he carried her over the edge . . . and beyond.

The hammock swayed to the side, and she held him tightly, tearing her mouth from his, pressing her face into the curve of his neck. Her quick pants filled the night air.

"I can't believe we did that," she rasped, her breath slowing as her body went limp.

"And we're not even finished yet," he said.

Resting her forearms on his chest, she lowered her mouth to his for a kiss. Leisurely, warm. Once. Twice. Three times.

He slid his hand beneath her shirt. "So, what are you wearing under here? Something equally skimpy?"

He unhooked her bra, eased his hands around, and filled his heavenly rough palms with her breasts.

"Not fair," she whispered as she shifted her weight to one side so her hand was free to give her access to what she wanted.

She wasn't in any great hurry as she freed his buttons, one after another. She felt the increase in warmth as though she'd opened the door to a furnace. Slipping her hand beneath the parted cloth, she traced the indentations of his chest, every hardened muscle, every shallow dip, every flattened plane. She lowered her mouth, kissing the hollow in the center of his chest, stroking her tongue over his heated skin, taking satisfaction in his low, feral growl.

She sensed his possessiveness as his hands kneaded her breasts, his fingers and thumbs teased her nipples. She trailed her mouth over his chest until she could taunt his nipple with her tongue, lathing, circling, tightening her lips around the turgid nub. He purred, not like a pet kitten but like a lion in the wild, waiting to pounce, patience barely tethered.

With his large hands, he bracketed either side of her rib cage and hauled her up until her knees were planted on either side of his chest. With his nose, he nudged her shirt up until he was able to reach her breast and give back to her what she'd been giving to him. Only she couldn't imagine her mouth being this hot, this determined. Pleasure danced along her spine as she lowered herself, placing her arms in a cocoon around his head, relishing the feel of his mouth greedily enjoying what she had to offer.

With his breath growing harsher, he glided his hands down her sides, around her hips to her bottom. He eased her up slightly, and then his hands were gone. But she could feel his movements, heard the metal rasping as the teeth of his zipper separated. Then he was moving aside the scrap of cloth that served as her underwear.

She eased up slightly, and his mouth released its hold. There wasn't enough light to see him clearly, and yet she still felt his gaze was hot enough to scald her.

"I need you, Kelley," he rasped, and she knew that

he was referring to more than the need for physical release her body could provide.

"I need you, too, Jack."

He dug his fingers into her hips, lifted her slightly, and eased her down the length of his throbbing shaft, inch by incredible inch. A slow shuddering rippled through him as she sank down completely, enveloping all of him, absorbing his fullness.

Bracing herself with her hands planted on either side of his shoulders, she slid her hips up slightly and plunged down. Groaning, he dug his fingers into her bottom, holding her as though he never intended to let go, each breath he took sounding more labored than the one before it.

With his hands guiding her, she rocked against him, increasing the tempo until her movements became fast and furious, the sensation of pleasure spiraling beyond her control, upward, outward, throughout her body until there was no way to contain it.

With a moan for deliverance, she dropped her head back, her spine arching, her body shuddering violently with the force of her release. It was as though a thousand fireworks burst forth behind her eyes, a glittering panorama of diamond-studded lights in every color imaginable. She was barely aware of him pumping deeply into her one final time, his guttural groan echoing around her.

Her body, limp and sated, sprawled over his. She nestled her head within the curve of his shoulder and listened to the hard, steady pounding of his heart as it kept rhythm with hers. She wanted to laugh for the joy of what she'd just experienced, but she wasn't certain she'd ever move again. She would simply spend the rest of her life lying in the hammock with Jack beneath her, to shelter and keep her warm.

The cool evening breeze was in direct contrast to the heated bodies stretched out in the hammock. Jack imagined that if he had the strength to open his eyes, he'd see white, willowy wisps of steam rising off their skin. But he had neither the strength nor the willpower to do anything but let his sated limbs continue to enjoy the weight of Kelley's body sprawled on top of his.

Jack thought he could spend the rest of his life there and never want for anything else.

The silence stretched out between them, calming and comfortable. Their harsh breathing, which had only moments ago punctuated their lovemaking, was now easing into a shallow quietness. A chill had yet to settle in, but because of the dew covering his body, he knew it was coming, would arrive soon to both him and Kelley. Maybe he ought to carry her to the hot tub. No chill there, and he'd always fantasized about having sex in the swirling waters.

But he wasn't even certain that he could carry himself to the deck, much less carry her. She'd turned his muscles to mush and his bones to sawdust. He couldn't have moved if he had to.

"What are you thinking about?" he finally forced himself to ask.

"How my moving here didn't turn out to be the simple solution I thought it would be. They say the grass is always greener on the other side, but you know what I've learned? It doesn't matter which side of the fence you're on. The grass still has to be mowed."

"Marry me, and I'll keep it mowed for you."

The hammock swayed with her movements as her head came up, and she braced her forearms on his chest. "Do you mean that, Jack?"

"I love you, Kelley. I always have."

Then she kissed him, slowly, sweetly, tightening her embrace, combing her hands through his hair.

Jack drew back. "If you marry me, you marry my son."

"Marry me, and you marry my daughter."

He almost told her he was getting the bad end of that deal, but he had a soft spot for the little criminal. Besides, she cooked a hell of an omelet.

"I can't see our getting married sitting well with Madison."

"I think you'd be surprised. I don't know what you said while she was over here, but I spent half my time with her hearing about how wonderful you are and how I should have read your letter. But what about Jason's reaction? I'm not exactly Martha Stewart next door."

"Will you let him call you Mommy?"

"Oh, yeah," she whispered. "I'd love that."

"Then I don't think he'll have a problem with it."

"There might be one little problem," she said.

"What's that?"

"I want to be your teacher."

"What the—"

She kissed him, stopping him from completing his outburst, but if she thought for one second that she was going to continue to view him as her student . . .

"You told me that I had to admire a man who couldn't hold on to a woman. Your mother may have left you. Stephanie may have left you. I want to teach you that you're a man who can hold on to a woman. You can hold on to me. I fell in love with you nine years ago, and I never stopped loving you, Jack."

"Prove it," he said as he brought her mouth back to his, kissing her thoroughly.

"I will," she promised. "I'll be here when you're old and gray."

He grinned. "I like the sound of that. Want to fool around in the hot tub?"

Her laughter echoed through his backyard, and Jack thought he'd never heard a sweeter sound.

Epilogue

Kelley was drifting . . . so tired. And yet she wanted to wake up. Madison was crying. She knew she was supposed to let her mother take care of Madison, but she wanted to do it. Wanted to feed her, and rock her, and read to her. And then the years spun out of control, and Madison didn't need her anymore.

And she was alone, so alone. And then he was there. Jack. Bad boy Jack. Smiling at her, taking her hand, forgiving her. Forgiving her for her secrets, forgiving her for asking of him what she'd failed to ask of herself.

Then she heard Jack's soothing voice and the snuffling sobs turn into tiny whimpers.

"Shh, little one. Mommy's had a rough morning."

Mommy. Mommy.

Smiling softly, Kelley opened her eyes to see Jack holding their daughter. Their daughter. Kelley felt the tears sting her eyes, the ache increase in her chest. An ache brought on by so much love that she thought her heart might burst.

"Jack?"

He lifted his gaze from the tiny bundle in his arms to her, and she knew she'd forever remember the look of pure joy, unadulterated pride, and absolute love in his eyes when the doctor placed the baby in Jack's arms for the first time only a few hours ago. Now he looked as tired as she felt, his face unshaven. But he also looked as though he had the power to move mountains.

She held out her arms. "I want to hold her."

Grinning, he laid the baby within her arms. Then he kissed her and trailed his fingers around her face. "I love you."

Tears stung her eyes. "I love you, too."

She gazed down on her precious baby daughter. "I think she has your eyes, Jack." Gently, she touched the fine black hair. "She definitely has your hair."

He sat on the edge of the hospital bed. "She's beautiful, Kelley, beautiful just like her mother."

"Have Madison and Jason seen her yet?"

"Yeah, they got here just a little while ago, but I wanted to let you sleep a little longer since this little one was stubborn and took most of the night to get here."

She patted his hand. "Bring them in."

Jack walked to the door and opened it. Madison and Jason burst through as though they'd been catapulted. Jason, wearing an "I am a big brother" T-shirt, was carrying a bouquet of flowers.

"Here, Mom, these are for you."

After a year and a half, Kelley still felt a tightening

in her chest whenever he called her Mom. "Thanks, sweetie."

Jack sat on the edge of the bed and lifted Jason onto his lap so Kelley could reach him for a quick kiss on the cheek.

Then Kelley turned to Madison. Another couple of months, and she'd be graduating. She'd already been accepted to the University of Texas. It seemed to Kelley that she'd had her for such a short time. She knew she'd always worry about her, but when she let her go this time, it would be to give her wings.

"What do you think, Madison?"

"I can't believe I have a sister. A real sister this time." Her voice held no censure, just a measure of acceptance. Her gaze darted between Kelley and the baby. "What are you going to name her?"

"Caitlyn."

"I like that. When will you come home?"

Home. She so liked the sound of that. Jack's house had become theirs, a place where plants thrived and laughter abounded and curtains hung in the window. "Probably tomorrow."

"Cool." She glanced at her watch. "I've gotta go. Rick and I are going to take Jason out to eat before drama practice. Jack, are you staying here tonight?"

"Yeah, I thought I would. You can drop Jason off at Serena's."

"Okay. Come on, sport, let's go."

" 'Bye, Mom," Jason said as he gave her a hug.

" 'Bye, sweetie. Keep Madison out of trouble."

"Right."

Madison moved up to the head of the bed and hugged Kelley. "She's one lucky little girl, Mom."

Tears flooded Kelley's eyes. "Oh, Madison."

Jack reached in and took Caitlyn from her, freeing her up to embrace Madison with all the love she felt for her firstborn. "You have no idea how much I've wanted to hear you call me that."

"The moment just seemed right."

Leaning back, Kelley brushed her hands over Madison's hair. "I'm glad."

Madison straightened. "Come on, Jason."

She watched her two children walk out of the room before turning to her husband. "I finally feel as though everything is going to be all right."

He placed Caitlyn back in Kelley's arms. "Are you happy, Jack?"

"Incredibly. And I can prove it right now." He started unbuttoning his shirt.

She laughed. "We can't make love for six weeks."

"Why do you always think I'm talking about sex?"

"Because you usually are."

"Not this time."

"You're taking off your shirt because . . ."

"To show you what I had done while you were napping." He peeled back his shirt to reveal his bare shoulder, the one with the tattoo. But the ragged edges of a broken heart were gone. Instead, her name now resided within a whole heart.

More tears stung her eyes. "Oh, Jack."

He shrugged his shirt back on, sat on the edge of the bed, and cupped her face. "You make me whole, Kelley. You always have."

He kissed her tenderly until their daughter started fussing. Kelley began nursing the little one who had already stolen her heart.

"I'm going to be greedy, Jack. I'm going to want another one."

Leaning near, Jack kissed Kelley once again and whispered, "I think I can arrange that."